MAX TAKES THE MALL

S. A. FANNING

Immortal Works LLC
1505 Glenrose Drive
Salt Lake City, Utah 84104
Tel: (385) 202-0116

Cover Art by Pete Fanning

ISBN 978-1-953491-90-9 (Paperback)
ASIN B0DN4SC2JW (Kindle)

To Mom, for the bus fare. To Dad, for the castles.

1

I pressed the doorbell and took a step back, working to peel off the clearance sticker from the wilting flower arrangement I'd picked up on the way to Tara's house. Looking through the wrinkled cellophane, it was hard to tell if the little splotches on the pink flowers were by design or symptoms of disease, but there was no time to dwell on that as there was some banging around inside the house followed by approaching footsteps. I wiped my hands on my pants and smoothed the wrinkles from my shirt.

Deep breaths. I forced myself to stop bouncing on my feet. Everything was going to be fine between Tara and me. I'd been on this porch maybe a hundred times before, just not since she'd left for college a few weeks ago.

The door opened and there stood her little brother, Adam, with the cordless phone shouldered to his cheek. His gaze fell to my sad little flower collection, and a smirk parted his lips before Tara's voice called me back to the kitchen. I brushed past the little hoodlum with a quick glance over my shoulder to see if I could figure out what he was giggling about. Probably planning which house he was going to egg that night.

Back to Tara. Wow. Her hair was shorter, and she looked different—a great kind of different—which only made it worse when I presented her the flowers then went to slide my arm around her waist, and she side-stepped me like a dancer. Or a boxer. Or a girl who'd gotten a taste of college and didn't want to be hugged by a loser townie. Yeah, that last one.

"Aww, thanks so much, Max."

Safely out of arm's reach, she smiled politely, as though I were a family member or a teacher, when I was neither. I was her boyfriend, still, maybe, at least I hoped. She regarded the clearance-rack flowers—which looked even worse in her well-manicured hands, blinking her eyes rapidly, probably afraid to sniff or even breath near the blossoms for fear of a bacterial infection—before she set them aside on the counter. "Hey, so how's work going?"

Work? Since when had my job at the car wash been of interest to her? "Oh, you know." I shrugged, still stinging from the hug dodge, the polite smile, this weird small talk. It was all starting to add up, and I wasn't liking the math.

Tara had been home from school since Thursday. She hadn't called me back until Friday, yesterday, only to let me know she had a family thing and then Tina wanted to hang. I took it in stride, mostly, and eventually she agreed to let me come over today. Now, here we were, talking about my job at the car wash.

She seemed preoccupied, or worse, uninterested. Bored. I needed to make an impact, to grab her attention and snap her out of...all this. Staring at my scuffed-up Vans, my head popped up.

"Oh, I'm going to enroll at LVCC," I blurted out. "Next semester," I added, referring to Linwood Virginia Community College. I drummed my fingers on my leg, wondering what I was saying. Sure, I'd thought about it on and off, mostly off, in a

Yeah, I could do that, kind of way. The kind of way you *could* clean up the kitchen if you were really trying to get after it.

Adam snorted loudly from his place near the dinner table, the twerp. Whatever, my little college confession got the intended reaction from Tara. She blew her hair back and leaned in with newfound interest. "Really? Max, that's great."

"Yeah," I said, inspired by the sparkle in her eyes.

Tara's eyes always shined with ambition. She lit up whenever she talked about someone who'd traveled or when she returned home from touring a college campus. You could hear it in her voice when she counted down the days until she could blow town and set off on her adventure. And when the day came—a few weeks ago—when her parents had slammed the trunk shut with such finality it made me flinch, she'd been so giddy she could pop.

And her ambition worked on me now, as I straightened my posture and smiled. While LVCC wasn't Harvard or anything, it was a start. I could do it, bang out a few classes in the morning before work, get off and still have time to hang with Dre or Jason. Piece of cake. I had to do something. Tara's world was busting wide open with new possibilities and new people. She'd left town to study philosophy and cultures, to meet all sorts of interesting characters—girls and guys alike. In other words, it wouldn't take long for her to see she could do better than me.

Truth was, I had nothing to offer besides a robust mixtape collection, some free car wash coupons, and a 1982 Volkswagen Rabbit I parked on hills so I could pop the clutch to get it started. Oh, and I was about to be homeless, as Mom had just recently kicked me out of her house. But I was trying to take it one problem at a time.

I realized I might have overplayed things on the college front as Tara quizzed me about when I'd changed my mind and what classes I would take. I shrugged, told her I was keeping things broad, general studies and all. She nodded, eyeing me closer and talking about majors and fields. I fumbled a bit in an attempt to keep things vague, telling her I wanted to keep my options open.

It was all good for a few minutes, as she worked on the flowers, got them in a vase, fluffed them up so they looked not so shabby. She had the touch, that was for sure. Then her face changed like she'd remembered something terrible. Adam had moved to the living room and crashed on the couch, the TV so loud it distracted me from coming up with more brilliance for Tara.

"Where are the parents?" I said, trying to get away from any more college talk.

She rolled her eyes and went for the fridge. "Oh, some lunch thing for Dad's work. You know how that goes."

"Yeah." I nodded with a smile. I liked how she was talking. Familiarity. I *did* know how that went. I'd been here plenty of times, her father rushing out the door, fixing his jacket, bickering with Mrs. Walker about being late. We shared those experiences, Tara and me. It felt like we were getting back on track.

I managed a smile. The sun was out and streaming into the kitchen. Maybe I'd overreacted. I took a chance and slid in again, closer, but she ducked into the fridge, grabbed a Diet Coke, and slid deftly out of my reach.

Adam perked up again, murmuring into the phone. Was he in on this? He kept tabs on Tara's social life, gathered info he could use as a ploy or blackmail. But the look on his face was sheer joy. Was he waiting for the ax to drop?

More drumming on my leg, still playing it casual. "So, what do you want to do? We could rent a movie?" My voice cracked with desperation. Never mind that I needed a small loan to cover my late fees at Blockbuster.

Tara simply frowned, took a sip of her Diet Coke. Even the way she drank soda had changed. She used to slug it down, three or four gulps before she'd take a deep breath and unleash a burp you could feel in your shoes. Now, she held the can like it was a wine glass and we were at some posh dinner party.

She set the drink down with flourish. "I'm not feeling a movie. I need to get outside. I might go to the park and read."

I took a step back, wincing as though I'd walked through a cluster of gnats. What was happening here? I felt like a pilot fighting to keep his battered plane in the air even as he was plummeting to the ground. *Mayday... Mayday...*

I recovered and nodded along. Mr. Go-With-the-Flow. "Oh, okay. Cool."

She sighed, cut a glance toward the living room. "Max, can we go out back?"

Adam's face was buried in a pillow, the cordless phone antenna like a snorkel as his shoulders convulsed.

Even I knew I was sunk. I couldn't get over the change. Her hair, her mannerisms, and she was thinner now too. She did not need to lose weight. Her collar bones jutted out from the loose-fitting Tori Amos shirt. *Go to the park, and read?* What gives?

It was nice outside, though, mid-seventies and sunny. Rare for August, as Tara perched herself on the lounge chair like some new adult version of herself. "I'm not sure how to say this."

My heart hitched. This was not how you expressed your unwavering love to a person. This was bad. Bad. Bad. Bad. Time to look for a parachute bad.

She gazed out to the yard before she looked at me again. "Well, it's just that, I feel like we need some time off to do our own things. I'm a hundred miles away now, and, well..." Her lips tight, she looked up into my eyes. And it was a little bit of the old Tara again.

That killed me.

Her gaze went soft to match her voice. "I have a new life, you know?"

I managed a quick nod, determined to stay strong. The deck had recently been stained. I'd told her dad I'd help with that.

Tara plunged ahead. "Max, I'm sorry. I really like you, you know that. And I hope we can stay friends. I'm not just saying that."

I should have reached out to her dad over the summer. Maybe if I'd stained the deck, her dad would have said something to Tara. How much he liked me or whatever.

"I would still like to hang out sometimes. I just can't be in a relationship right now. You understand that, right?"

You know, that Max came over and stained the deck. Never asked for a dime. What a guy!

"Max?"

"Huh?" I forced my gaze away from the deck. "Yeah, no, I understand. I mean, you're in school. I'm in, well, I'm going to be in school. It's...yeah." Whose voice was this? And why was I nodding? I didn't understand any of this. And school? Who was I kidding?

She nudged my shoe with hers. A small tap that filled my entire body with warmth and hope. She followed it up with a shy smile, as though relieved this was going so well. "Yeah?"

What choice did I have? I did have *some* pride, enough that I wasn't going to beg. I had standards. Rules. I would wait until I got down the road in the car, and then I'd allow myself to bawl out. But for now? I nodded again. "No, totally. I'm busy too." I couldn't stop my runaway mouth.

Tara perked up some. "Wow, I thought, I don't know. I thought this was going to be much harder than it was. And it was, I mean, is," she said, recovering. "We've been together what, six months?"

"A year. Well, ten months. It was Halloween, so..."

Tara frowned in thought. "Oh, yeah. That's right."

She glanced away for a moment, taking this in. Was she second guessing her decision? Did she think maybe we should try to make this work? The foot tap, the smile, that far-off look in her eyes, the hopeful expression. It was all too much. My head bowed, and I broke down like a baby.

Forget about pride. I threw myself at her feet and begged. I cried. I said some things I'm not proud of.

And none of it did me any good.

2

A blur of tears fell from my eyes as I sat in my car, mumbling to myself. I wiped my nose and lowered the rearview to search my face. I needed a haircut. My ears were off balance and there was a new zit on my nose that couldn't have helped my we-should-stay-together pitch.

And those stupid discount flowers. Smooth. Before I could dwell on it, the mirror fell off, bounced off the console, and landed in my lap as though it was tired of holding my sorry reflection. Fine. It was probably best to go somewhere else and get myself together.

I tried to start the car, but of course nothing happened. I set my forehead on the steering wheel and pounded the dashboard. I'd been so hopeful, parking in the driveway even though the battery liked to play dead sometimes. Only this was *not* the time.

And here I'd managed to avoid Adam by escaping off the deck and trudging out the side yard, but now, sitting on Tara's perfectly flat driveway, I needed some help to push the car out so I could get a running start.

It took everything I had left to carry myself back up the

stairs to knock on the door again. Adam answered, again, still clutching the phone, glancing off like he couldn't bear to look me in the eyes after what he'd seen.

I cleared my throat and spat it out. "Hey, I need help with my car."

"Huh?"

"My car." I sighed. "Think you can give me a hand? Help me push?"

Tara shuffled down the stairs. Her voice happy as sunshine. "Hey, is that... Oh."

Wow. She was fully composed, excited even. She'd changed clothes and done something with her hair that didn't exactly scream *reading at the park*. All this mere seconds after ripping my heart out. Awkward didn't begin to cover the situation, what I felt as I stood on her doorstep, begging her little brother for help after she'd refused all my groveling. I'd even told her I loved her. And still, she'd told me it was best if I went home.

I swallowed down the lump of shame, looked at Adam. "Can you help?"

He sighed, the little twerp, before glancing back to Tara, who so graciously nodded. "Go help him, Adam."

"Hey, man, I gotta do something for Tara. I'll call you back," he said into the phone before he tossed it to the couch. He slid off the doorjamb. "Yeah, okay."

We pushed the car out to the street. I turned the wheel and advised him to push from the back so I could pop the clutch. He closed his eyes. "You need a new car, dude."

"Yeah well..."

And then it hit me, what he meant. Being with Tara for so long, there had been no need to worry about what kind of car I drove. In fact, she usually drove Mrs. Walker's Saturn whenever we went out for dinner or a movie. But now, having been set free, I'd have to get back out there, go out on dates. My Volkswagen was not a first-date car.

Its paint was some sort of Band-Aid beige, with rust creeping up on both the front and back fenders. The front bumper hung at a slant. The interior seats were split and ripped, and everything reeked of diesel fuel. There was a leak somewhere in the floor so the mats were always wet after it rained. The kid had a point.

After we'd pushed and popped, the car bucked, and with a whiff of diesel, the engine caught. I called back to him over my shoulder. "Well, thanks."

Adam shook his head, and something about the way he simply turned and started back to the house without a second thought made me feel insignificant. I wanted to call out to him, tell him a girl would do this to him one day, when the beep of a horn stole my attention.

A shiny Audi rolled to a stop. The window lowered and wispy guitar strums leaked from the car. Tara's best friend, Tina, yelled over the driver—some tool with white wraparound sunglasses that were only marginally smaller than the smirk on his face. "Hey, Max, you okay?"

Okay? I'd just gotten dumped, then had to slump back to the door and ask my newly ex-girlfriend's brother to help me push my bucket car out of the driveway so I could pop the clutch. Now I was pumping the gas pedal to keep the car from stalling as I sat in the middle of the street. I probably looked like I'd been crying, because I *had* been crying. So nah, not okay.

That's when it occurred to me that Tina knew Tara was going to dump me, same as she knew all about my problematic car. She'd been with us many times, laughing in the backseat as I hopped out to nudge the car down a hill to pop the clutch. I used to tell myself Tara liked me for me, not for my car, so it killed me to think Tina and Tara were giggling as though it were merely some footnote in the wild adventures of their youth. Something they'd shake their heads and laugh about while their kids swam in the pool together or waited in line for ice cream at the country club.

"Uh, yeah, I'm good," I managed. When I went to pull the door shut the pesky mirror fell out. White glasses laughed. Someone else too. And it's while I was scrambling to get the mirror that I realized there was a third person in the car—a dude.

Maybe they were all going to the park to read together.

Dre shook his head as I pulled into the car wash. It wasn't weird for employees to show up on their day off to wash their rides, unless you were me, with a ride not worth washing.

I parked near the vacuums and collected myself as I approached the cashier booth, where Dre was busy ringing up customers. Carol didn't trust anyone but Dre on the register, and for good reason. The last guy skimmed something like fifty bucks a day for himself. It wasn't hard to do, sell some Armor All, then "forget" to ring it up. Just that easy, three bucks in the pocket.

I waited off to the side while Dre finished up the last transaction. A lady with spikey short hair fussing about something she deemed "unacceptable" as she crossed and uncrossed her arms. There was always somebody complaining over streaky windows, dirty whitewall tires, brake dust on the rims, or even a few drops of water on the hood.

The lady curled a finger and summoned Dre out to her Toyota, where her middle school daughter did her best to sink into the seat.

Dre took it in stride in a way I never could. It didn't hurt that people always said he looked like Tyson—the model, not the boxer—with his square jaw and sculpted features. The guy could smile his way into or out of anything. It was no wonder he was not only the register clerk but our leading salesperson too. One time, a lady offered him a hundred bucks on the spot to hand wash her car without his shirt on. When I asked why he shot her down, he'd shot me a look. "What would I look like doing that?"

I had no answer for him, because a hundred bucks? I would have used my shirt as a Shammy.

Now, after Dre nodded through angry-lady's complaints, he offered to send the car through the wash again. When the lady said she didn't have time, he looked around coyly, like he was doing something he wasn't supposed to do. I'd seen him do this before, and it was working for him once again as he slipped her a coupon for a free clear coat on her next wash. Her frown loosened. Dre smiled. She left happy.

As she pulled off, Dre winked at me. He kept those worthless coupons for that exact occasion. Sometimes people just wanted free stuff.

Soon as they were out, he turned back to me. "What's up with you?"

I sighed. "I just left Tara's."

Dre knew all about my troubles with Tara. Not on a personal level, as I don't think he'd ever been dumped or in a relationship that lasted longer than a week or two, but he'd listen to me groan and complain about it for the past month.

"Man," he said. "That bad, huh? But I mean, you knew this was coming, right?"

"Yeah, but I thought maybe..." I trailed off. He was right. Of course I knew it was coming, but I'd almost convinced myself it wouldn't happen.

I was about to give him the rundown on Tina and the Audi

when another wave of cars rolled into the lot. Saturdays were always slammed, and I'd asked off. Now, here I was standing around as Carol, our angry little manager, stormed outside. I backed off before she could catch me, leaving Dre to do his thing as I started for the Rabbit. Carol lit a smoke and shot me a glare as I left.

I drove home in a daze, TLC's *Waterfalls* on *Flash 102* as I made my way to Mom's townhouse, where I was supposed to be packed and moved out by the time she and Rob got back from their cruise. I'd sort of let the days slip away on the packing, and the moving, as my every thought had been on Tara's return.

The bumper scraped as I pulled up the steep entrance, where Mom's townhouse sat in a row with the others behind a strip of fast-food spots, a Pizza Hut, the pharmacy, and a hair salon place. I parked the Rabbit on the hill near what used to be tennis courts as the radio cut to commercial. "Want to be King of the Mall?"

Nope. I killed the engine.

I hiked down the walkway. Only the crooked, peeling yellow shutters of Mom's townhouse set it apart from the rest. It was almost like a movie set, the little walkways and tiny eight by eight patches of grass. Mom's plastic pink flamingos assisted the shutters to make it stand out.

Moving out. I wasn't even close. Mom had ambushed me a few days before she'd taken off with Rob for a cruise in the Bahamas. She'd thrown her hands up in that way of hers and said it was *well past time*. When I'd asked how I was supposed to up and get my own place on a week's notice, she didn't blink. Her mouth went tight, and she said I'd been there a year longer than I was supposed to be and so that gave me a year and a week's notice. Obviously, she'd been waiting to use that line.

I sorted through the mail. A couple of bills for Mom. Wait, one for me from the bank. No point there, I must have overdrawn. My relationship with the bank went like this: Give them money. Try to spend my money. Owe them money.

Lots of owing money. Because at five bucks an hour and around eighteen hours a week, I was always broke.

On that note, I took inventory of my life. My girlfriend had dumped me. I had no money. No place to live. And, looking around, no options. I dragged myself to the tiny kitchen, more like a narrow hallway in the small townhouse, where I searched the cabinets for something to eat.

Add "no food" to my growing list.

I found some Triscuits behind the canned vegetables and flopped down on the couch, watching reruns and trying to put the day's events in order. It went to commercial, and I zoned out, staring at the ceiling, a heavy dread taking hold in my chest. My stomach sank and twisted with loneliness, or that could've been the stale Triscuits. I was searching for answers when a familiar voice filled the room. The screen flashed to RiverView Mall. Old English lettering, some corny royal music.

Want to be the King of the Mall? Dost thou have what it takes?

Enter today to join up with Pepsi and local sponsors and set off...

I dug around for the remote, about to turn off the amateurish commercial screaming at me. *Flash 102* was always doing over-the-top stunts. Jason's dad was a disc jockey there, and he'd done it all—broadcasting from billboards, hot air balloons, while playing donkey basketball. The more outrageous the better. Anything to get people to tune in.

This stunt seemed especially stupid. I found the remote control when Terrible Accent Guy continued...

"Win five-thousand dollars and a brand-new Ford Ranger pickup truck. Enter today and listen to Flash 102.9 for details.

And remember, 102.9, the only source for Virginia's hottest hits. Call now!"

I clutched the remote, staring at the TV as today's date—August 10, 1996—splashed across the screen. Registration was at the mall, today, right now. I wiped my face, trying to follow all the fine print scrolling with rules and stipulations. Something about living in the mall until the soda was sold. But forget all that. Five grand? I jumped up, Triscuit crumbs flying as I went for the phone.

A brand-new truck. No more searching for hills. And that kind of cash, I'd tell Carol at the wash to shove it. And there was a third appeal here that drove me to call. A free spot to crash until I figured out my next move.

This would take some planning if I really wanted to make it happen. It would also take Jason's dad, at the station. With that in mind, I paged Jason and punched in the 911 code to speed things along. Five minutes later the phone rang.

"Yo, Max, where's the party at?"

"Your house, right?" I tried to muster up some enthusiasm. I did, after all, need a favor.

"Word."

The deep bellow of Method Man's smooth delivery filled the background. Jason was the world's biggest Wu-Tang fan. He had posters all over his apartment—most of them curling from all the weed smoke—the apartment that might become my last resort if nothing else came along. There were a million reasons I didn't want my life to come to that, and near the top were his two roommates and the never-ending flow of potheads coming and going at all hours.

I waited for Jason to turn the music down. When he didn't, I plowed ahead. "So, I saw the commercial for the mall contest thing. Have you seen it? Is that for real?"

"Man, it's the bomb. I'd enter if it was a castle of Natty Lite instead of Pepsi."

"So, this is for real? It's a castle, built out of Pepsi cans?"

"Hell yeah. Dad said they've had engineers in there working on it all week."

Weird, but, whatever. I paced the room, my knee bumping into the bamboo side table. "So um, I think I'm going to enter. You think your pops could hook me up?"

"You trying to be King of the Mall? Ha, dude that's awesome." More giggling. People talking over the music. Coughing. Giggling again.

"I'm trying." I needed to drill the message into his head before he got too stoned to remember. I had to keep things moving. "So, umm?"

"Yeah, I'll say something. I bet he could hook that up. Although I owe him a hundred bones, so he may or may not take my calls."

"Hook what up?" I heard through the phone.

I banged my head against the wall. Great, Sauce and Tony were there. They were going to want in on this. Although Sauce wasn't exactly one to follow through with things—even things like showers, getting dressed, or getting off the couch—so I was safe there. Tony, however, might like the idea of crashing at the mall.

Movement on the other end, the phone brushing against Jason's dreads. "That castle thing at the mall. Max is trying to get in."

Scattered laughter in the room. "He could get me in with Tara."

I gripped the phone. Tony was always talking about Tara. But after today it hit a little harder.

"Boo yaa." Jason laughed.

I rolled my eyes. Time to appeal to our friendship. Call in a favor. "Jason, I need this, anything you can do. Mom is kicking me out this week." I lowered my voice. Time to seal this thing. "Come on, man. Remember that time in eleventh grade? When you, you know, with the pants?"

Silence. Ghostface Killah took over in the background. Jason coughed. "That's just wrong, man. I can't believe you'd bring that up."

Our junior year, Jason shat himself something epic. I'm talking drop the Jincos and leave them in the nearest dumpster, epic. I gave him my jeans and wore my gym shorts the rest of the day. I'd never said a word about it, until now. But I was desperate.

I waited him out, hoping that favor would get me somewhere. It did.

"Okay, I'll call him soon."

I breathed a sigh of relief. "Awesome. Thanks, man. Get back to me, okay?"

Wu-Tang went silent. All I had was a dial tone.

Next, I called *Flash 102* to get more details. Yes, contestants would actually live at the mall day and night until the castle was sold off. But I'd better hurry, registration was being held today, as in *right now*, until four.

My quick rush of hope was swallowed up in panic. I bolted upstairs, coming to a stop at the doorway where I found the wasteland that was my bedroom. Or what used to be my bedroom. Mom had brought home several boxes from work and piled them in the middle of the room so I wouldn't get confused about what she wanted me to do while she was gone—which was pack my things and leave so she could get more alone time with Rob.

No time to worry about that now, I found something to wear and got moving.

3

In a town full of hills, I usually had no problems finding a place to park the Rabbit for an easy clutch-popping getaway. But the mall parking lot was a vast, flat desert of asphalt, so I ended up across the main drag at the Radisson where the back curled up an incline for overflow parking. I crossed the five-lane road, Frogger style, doing my best not to get creamed by a UPS truck that looked to be running late.

Our mall wasn't like the big city malls with two or three floors and different wings in different zip codes. It was all one level, a low-slung star-like sprawl with five department stores anchoring the ends. It had recently been remodeled as part of the town's bid to keep businesses from fleeing to the outskirts or moving back downtown. Now, with skylights and gleaming floors, everything had been brightened up with colorful tiles over the old dull bricks. There was a fourplex movie theater, food court, and all the little stores in between.

I was feeling hopeful for the first time that day as I shuffled down the hill to the parking lot. Lots of cars, a few buses, and who could miss the bright purple and yellow *Flash 102.9* van parked at the curb. Yes, Tara had dumped me, but this could happen. Everything was set. There was a reason I'd seen that commercial. This was fate.

The jam-packed parking lot should've been my first clue. Walking in, that sudden gust of good feelings and fate was sucked out of my lungs. Clearly, I wasn't the only one looking to become King of the Mall.

The line snaked around kiosks and fountains, between posts and tables where it frayed out to a messy end at the food courts. I found a spot in the back where it was all I could do to make out the banners. My steps slowed seeing all the hopefuls waiting to sign up. But what had I expected, that no one else saw the commercials?

Snagging a flyer, I fell in place at the back of the line, scanning over the details—which seemed too good to be true once you read through all the small print on the back. The contest was sponsored by Ford, Radio Shack, Kwikie Mart, and of course, Pepsi.

The gist of it was simple: Four lucky contestants would be posted at separate ends of the mall, where they would occupy castles built almost entirely out of six-packs of Pepsi products. The "castles" came fully equipped with porta potties, cots, and mini fridges. The first contestant who sold all the sodas comprising their castle would be declared the winner.

And the perks were sweet. Meals were catered. Free pizza and all the free Pepsi one could consume. I looked around. Lots of middle-aged dudes. Lots of dudes my age. Lots of dudes, period.

The line moved slowly. Another straggler fell in behind me, and he might've been the world's last grunger. He cast a cynical gaze, shaking his head. His stringy hair fell to his shoulders. A flannel was tied to the waist of his cut-off cargo shorts. He seemed simultaneously too good to be here yet here all the same.

With time to kill, my mind roamed. I tried not to think

about Tara, but it was no use. She consumed my thoughts. How she'd changed. The Audi, the other dude in the backseat. Was she going on a double date minutes after dumping me? All of it sent an imaginary ice pick into my chest. That was cold.

Tara and I met at a Halloween party. I'd seen her around at school, but she was a grade behind me and ran with a different crowd. She was hard to miss that night, decked out as Cher from Clueless in a plaid miniskirt and matching top with a headband in her blonde hair. She was pulling it off—spectacularly, I might add—as I and every other guy in the room couldn't stop staring at her. Being how I hadn't dressed up at all, I knew I needed something to stand out if I was going to make a move.

I'd come with Dre, as we'd recently started working at Clean Car and gotten tight over our love of music and movies. Dre's girl-of-the-week that night was Kendra, and when I mentioned a costume, she'd pulled me into the nearest bathroom and whipped out her make-up kit. Before I could protest, she'd sat me down and gone to work.

Looking back, it's crazy that it worked. I returned to the party wearing mascara, eyeliner, and some blush, I think. Dre said I looked like a deranged glam rocker, but Kendra thought it was great, so I went with it, even as some guys started snickering, pointing and laughing—right up until Tara approached with a smile and told me I needed to fix my lipstick.

The next thing I knew she sat me down, flipped her hair back, and with a lick of her lips she leaned in close. I held my breath, as she was only a few inches from my face finishing what Kendra had started. When she ever so casually blew something from my eye, I nearly melted into the floor.

We talked most of the night. By the time Tara left, we had a date set up. The next weekend we doubled with Dre and Kendra, or by then I think it was a new girl. Either way, Tara and I hit it off. Those first days were the best. Late night kisses, getting to know each other, holding hands, and the way I'd forget my own name when she smiled at me. I taught her hip-hop, and she taught me poetry. She said I was the only guy who'd ever danced with her, who'd driven to the parkway in the middle of the night to watch the sunset. Those first few weeks were the best.

Even when she started narrowing down her schools, I didn't worry too much because she was right there with me. And when she talked about staying in state, I saw myself driving out every weekend. Things would work out, they just would.

"Hey, dude. Go."

A tap on the back as the grunge kid nudged me from my memories. I shuffled ahead, realizing I'd spent the better part of an hour wallowing in the past. This was really all I had, rigging some mall contest.

Some commotion started up front. A guy with his gut hanging out of his Batman t-shirt was badgering the registration people with a million questions. Apparently, you had to have a quick physical evaluation before you could participate. No existing health conditions. Gut Guy wasn't having it.

"All right, people! Who's ready to be king?"

The crowd's attention shifted as Scott Snyder—Jason's dad—entered the building. He was all smiles as he breezed in and set up near the registration desk, working the crowd like a pro in his blazer and jeans, chatting up the hopefuls, asking who wanted to be the king, and borderline flirting with a few of the more attractive girls in the line.

When he saw me, he winked. I sort of nodded and gave him a half wave, unsure if Jason had talked to him and whether or not to keep it on the hush or make it a big deal. We'd hung out a few times when Jason was little. Scottie—Mr. Snyder—took us to a few school dances he'd worked. My heart sped up. Was this really going to happen?

Grunge guy nudged me again. "Dude. They're calling you."

The girl at the desk pushed a clipboard my way and zipped through the instructions. I glanced left, where Jason's dad was untangling a microphone cord.

He nodded. "Slide that one to me, okay, Annette?"

My breath caught. I sneaked a look around, waiting for someone to call foul, when the girl simply looked over to him and smiled. "You got it, Scottie."

A flash of heat warmed my face, and I scribbled my name on the form, then Mr. Snyder motioned me over. Grunge guy sauntered ahead.

Still working the cords, Mr. Snyder—Scottie—began setting up what I knew to be the remote broadcast equipment. He smiled at someone, nodded, he was constantly waving at people. With all his stunts, he was sort of a local celebrity. He clicked something on, fiddled with a switch, and turned to me. "Jason said you were in a jam."

"Yeah," I said, filling out my address—Mom's address. I had no idea how this worked. Did I play it cool? Beg? Pretend I didn't know him? He looked up again, another nod, rolling the cords, waving, nodding, smiling, talking to me like a ventriloquist.

"Okay, look. Fill out that bottom part. That's what they tear off. I'm drawing the names at four-thirty. Look surprised, okay?"

"Really?"

He gave me the side-eye, talking out of the side of his mouth. "Yeah. Now stop cheesing and get that filled out. Got it?"

It was that easy. I filled the bottom portion out and glanced over to the line, where it must have been a few hundred people vying for five spots, plus alternates. "Yeah, thanks. Thanks... uh...Sco..."

I always had trouble calling him Scottie. He was Mr. Snyder

to me. Plus, *Scottie?* The guy was like fifty or something. He nodded again.

I handed the clipboard in and turned to walk off but snuck a glance over my shoulder just in time to see Mr. Snyder walk over and whisper something to Annette.

Holy crap. I was in.

4

I still had a few hours to kill before the winners were announced. And after the rollercoaster of a day I was having, I needed to get out and clear my head. I was quaking with nervous energy as I hustled back to my car, figuring I'd wait things out at Jason's place. My string of good luck continued as the Rabbit cranked up, Bone Thugs and Harmony crooning on the radio as only a few puffy cotton clouds made their way across the vivid blue sky.

Okay, so RiverView Mall was going to be my home for, what? Days? Weeks? How big were the castles? I'd wanted to go peek, but they'd been curtained off as construction took place, building up to the big reveal on Sunday. Could I really be living in the mall for weeks? For months?

Whatever it took, because as soon as Tara caught wind of what I was doing, well, things would change. And if I actually won this thing, I'd collect five grand and get a place of my own. Then Tara would come around. I'd no longer be some loser townie but a local *celebrity*. I'd be the guy with a new truck and his own place at nineteen. Not bad at all.

The honk of a truck brought me back to reality. Green light.

Okay, I was getting ahead of myself. One, I couldn't be one hundred percent sure Jason's dad would come through. Sure, he was a big name around town, but it seemed like with stakes this high, some sort of failsafe would be in order.

Hmm. I also had to prepare myself for the worst—which was Jason's couch. Jason had said from the beginning that I could crash for a few weeks if I ever needed. As much as I appreciated it, I was trying my best to avoid that rockiest of bottoms. Stay positive. This would happen.

At Jason's, I knocked a few times on the side door before opening it and coming face to face with Tony in the kitchen.

"Yo, Maxi pad." Tony was elbow deep in a bag of cheese puffs. He came out of the bag with a fist full of orange and crammed it into his mouth, then used the cheese hand to slap me on the back. "What's up, homie?" he said as he turned for the living room.

The guy was the worst. But I couldn't let it get to me. Not today. I dusted myself off and followed him in, where six or seven bodies lay sprawled out on the sectional and floor in a fog of weed smoke. I thought I spotted a girl in there, somewhere, cuddled up with Sauce, who was mashing buttons on the controller in his hand.

I'd been hoping to speak with Jason a bit more privately. At the same time, I should've known better. Since they'd gone in on a Sony PlayStation, Jason's place was *the* spot to get high and game. Funny how they had to scrounge to pay the electric bill each month, but three hundred bones for a PlayStation? No problem.

Not for the first time, I told myself this mall thing had to work out, because sprawled out before me, quite literally, through a pungent haze of smoke, was my alternative. I took a quick inventory of my surroundings.

First and foremost was the aforementioned weed smoke.

Even when they weren't smoking, which, someone was *always* smoking at Jason's place, the dank smell clung to the tapestries hanging on the walls, the rug, the clothes on the floor. Whenever you left Jason's place, the funk stayed with you. Tara always made me change my clothes if I was coming from Jason's house. The force was strong, to say the least.

Also, everything was sticky. Your shoes always stuck to the floor, *tick tack tick tacking* as you walked around, like a human roach motel. Trust me, I'm not the neatest dude in the world, but the counters, the cabinets, and the walls were coated with stick. You could slap a picture on the walls without tape or tacks. Between the flies—the sink was constantly full and bags of fast-food trash piled up in the kitchen until someone, usually a girlfriend, took it out to the dumpster—and the smell, did I mention the smell? The best you could do was open a window and bury your nose in a hoodie.

I hung back, standing awkwardly against the wall, waiting for an opening. Tony licked his fingers and readied himself for his turn on the brand-new console. Where these guys wouldn't clean, they treated the PlayStation like a newborn baby.

Jason threw his head up and nodded at me with a smile. "I talked to Pops."

"Yeah," I said, as heads turned my way. "I just saw him. Thanks, man. Really. I owe you one."

"Yeah, well, as long as you put that story to rest, we good."

Sauce passed the controller to his left. "Max, you for real entering that King of the Mall contest?"

More staring. Tony was smirking like the Joker. He balled up the cheese puffs and turned to Jason. "Hey, man, why didn't you hook *me* up?"

Jason swung his head around, his dreads taking flight. They were getting long and thick, to where it was hard to see where one dread ended and the other began. "Yo, my man Max and I go way back. Besides, it's not like you would do it anyway. You hate the mall."

A lot of people thought I smoked since I hung out with Jason and his crowd, but I wasn't a fan, didn't like the smell or the way it made me feel. Still, Jason and I went back to second grade, when we'd ridden the bus together, played GI Joes. I don't know, we had history. I don't think either one of us was ready to give that up, even if we had grown apart.

Tony sat back, adjusted his Yankees hat. Tony and I had a history as well, one not worth remembering. He was from upstate New York but liked to act like he was from NYC, even after he'd been in Virginia half his life. And now, as he sat back, set his Jordans on the coffee table, I tried and failed to remember ever liking him.

He laughed to himself. "Yeah, so what, you stay in the mall, like crap in a bucket or something? Sounds like prison."

"No, I don't think so. I don't know the rules." What could I say? *Need a place to crash? Need five grand and a truck?* My face warmed. I didn't want any more attention from him than I already had.

Too late, Tony did that giggle/laugh he did when he was tripping on someone. He ribbed everyone, he was pretty much an all-around douchebag, but he had it out for me especially. "Yeah, Maxi pad is going to be in there with a bucket, security pig watching him. Don't drop the soap, homie."

The couch came alive with sniggering. Even Jason chuckled. Tony got his turn on the PlayStation, and eventually I was forgotten. I left without saying goodbye.

So much for that.

SINCE THE FUNK had attached itself to my clothes, I made a quick stop at the townhouse to get changed. The whole time I was overflowing with witty comebacks I should've said to Tony, muttering them to myself as I found a clean Bugle Boy tee and a pair of jeans that looked presentable.

I turned around and knocked into the stack of boxes. It was hard to believe I was really getting the boot. Probably so she could have more alone time with Rob.

Rob was okay. He was quiet, mostly, sort of nerdy, but to his credit, he never tried to sit down and have man-to-man talks—only the occasional corny joke. He and Mom had been together for a bit now, and he was perfect for her because he was sort of spineless and let her rule the house.

I kicked a box across the room. This new ultimatum, I wanted to blame Rob, but I knew it was Mom all the way. Ever since I graduated, she'd been after me to go to school or get full time work. Since I did neither, she'd become unbearable.

It started subtly. A few weeks after graduation, the classified section of the paper (complete with entry-level jobs circled) showed up on the kitchen table in the mornings, along with a few quarters for bus fare. When I got a job at Clean Car she was over the moon. Then I started seeing Tara and cut my hours. Now I had a car and part-time work, which meant I barely had enough money to pay insurance, gas, and fix whatever broke each month. I kicked another box on my way out. Told myself things were about to change.

It was four-thirty when I got to the parking lot at RiverView after parking across the street and playing Frogger with the traffic again. Inside, there was no line, but all the food court chairs were taken as a crowd of people moved in around the makeshift stage where Jason's dad was handling business.

"Okay, people," he announced, pacing around, a fake smile beaming across his orange face. It was no secret Scottie Snyder loved all the freebies. Being a DJ, he was privy to free tanning sessions, free haircuts, free movie tickets, free Putt-Putt, free anything so long as the station was promoting it.

I fought for position in the crowd, trying to get a decent view as Scottie Snyder unveiled a clear barrel tumbler holding the torn off pieces of paper with our names and info. I chewed on my fingernails as he worked the crowd like a magician. Grunge Guy leaned against the wall, trying his best to appear uninterested, but his eyes darted to the stage as he anxiously waited with the rest of us.

Scott Snyder said something to the sound guy and then got back to the action. "Okay, so who's ready for the King of the Mall?"

A few girls screamed, but again, this contest was designed for the desperate. Lots of dudes, ranging in age from eighteen to fifty, not counting the couple of geezers in attendance. To Scottie's left was a table of official-looking people, along with a bunch of corporate types wearing suits on a Saturday, at the mall. I figured they must be the sponsors. Scottie Snyder was nearly giddy with all the attention.

He turned left, then wheeled right. "Alllllll right, let's do this. Marissa, if you would please?"

His deep baritone rumbled through the mall. Shoppers lingered to witness the drama unfolding. An attractive but no-nonsense looking lady stood from the tables and strode over to the barrel. Scottie raised his eyebrows conspiratorially. Marissa's mouth tightened. She spun the barrel around a few times then took a step back.

With a huge smile, Scottie Snyder reached in. "Here we go. Our first winner." He came out with a sheet of paper, unfolded it, then rolled his eyes. His shoulders sagged as he tossed the piece of paper to the floor. "Okay, very funny. I've been in this business long enough to know when I'm being taken for a ride."

Some scattered laughter. Scottie Snyder reached back in the barrel when a voice in the crowd spoke out. "Hey, that's not fair, what's the name?"

Scottie Snyder shook his head at Marissa, who urged him with a tight smile as she nodded at the piece of paper. Scottie picked it up, then shrugged. "Okay, I'll play along. Our first contestant is Mark Faartz."

A boom of laughter. I was too distracted by the disappointment of not hearing my name that it took me a second to catch on. Scottie Snyder's face flashed red before he tucked it away with a smile. "Ha, very funny. Good one. Okay, let's move on."

"Hey wait, that's me."

The crowd parted. Some commotion rippled through the crowd before Gut Guy—the same guy who'd been haggling over the forms earlier—came forward. Whatever his fashion, he had no problems with confidence, as he emerged from the crowd and walked right up and glared at Scottie Snyder.

Scottie, in a rare show of unprofessionalism, only gawked as Mark Faartz stood before him. A quick glance to the tables and he nodded. "Okay, okay, this one's legit. Mark Fa...uh Mark, you are our first winner." He went for a handshake, but Mark wasn't having it. "Right. Congratulations. You will be given first choice of location."

With the matter settled, Mark followed Marissa to a table where he produced an ID and was handed a certificate. The suits whispered amongst themselves, clearly unhappy with the unflattering start to their competition.

Still flummoxed, Scottie Snyder fixed his collar and tried to reset. "Okay, who's next?"

My stomach twisted. I stood helplessly as three more names were selected and called to the stage. First came a geezer who had to be in his mid-seventies, followed by a bouncy redheaded girl with freckles, and, to my complete surprise, my grunge buddy, whose name was actually Timothy Dillinger.

So much for my streak of good luck, I stood elbow to elbow amongst the other also-rans in the crowd, all of us seething in disappointment. But I should've known, because wouldn't that have been too easy? It was all I could do to watch Timothy and the others accept their certificates, all smiles and nods. I tossed my flyer in the trash and started for the exit, ready to wallow in this black hole of a day as it seemed the show was over.

As the crowd was breaking up, Scottie Snyder called us back. "Okay people don't leave just yet. We still have to call the two alternates, who, in case one of our fine contestants cannot take part, will be called in their place."

With one hand on the door, I spun around as Scottie went back to the barrel. "Let's see." He dug in, picked one right off the top.

"We have, Jerome Cardwell. And," he reached back in, found a piece of paper and smiled, "Max Miller."

My surprise was genuine as my name echoed in the mall. My brain clicked gears, from gloom to boom as I had no idea about this alternate thing, but I quickly made my way up to the front, reaching for my wallet before it sunk in. *Alternate.*

Hmm, okay. My elation took a hit as I got to the stage. Yeah, alternate was better than nothing but not exactly the path I'd been hoping for. Still, I whipped out my ID for the officials, and the Marissa lady smiled as she handed me a certificate and pointed the way to the stage, where Scottie shot me a quick look and a shrug that I took to mean, *Best I could do, kid.*

The military guy beside me introduced himself as Sergeant Jerome Cardwell in a manner much too serious for a mall castle competition.

Meanwhile Scottie Snyder worked the crowd. "And there

we have it, folks. How about a round of applause for our four winners and two alternates."

A few claps and murmurs as the crowd of hopefuls deflated in earnest. And they were still shuffling for the exit when Sergeant Jerome looked around and asked what hadn't even crossed my mind. "Who's next in line?"

Marissa blinked. "I'm sorry?"

"The alternate." He nodded at me without looking at me. "I was called first. Does that make me first alternate?"

She consulted her notes. "Well, let me... Yes, I assume since your name was called first, it's you, then..." She looked at me, her face going soft with pity. "Then you."

The sergeant turned to me and grinned. I'd just been demoted to second alternate.

5

Obviously, the second alternate spot was not what I had in mind, but I did get a shoutout on the radio when Scottie Snyder wrapped up his broadcast. Maybe someone would tell Tara about it. That would be cool.

Meanwhile, Sergeant Cardwell and I joined the contestants at a sectioned-off table where Marissa waited with a stack of forms for us to sign. Consent forms so we couldn't sue the station, the mall, or the sponsors. Forms about our health and well-being. Forms to be sure we were who we said we were. And Mark Faartz had something to say through it all.

When he wasn't badgering Marissa about the health stuff, he was asking about freebies—meals and soda and all that. He had questions about discounts, promotional items, even if there would be cable TV provided in our castles. All the time I kept an eye out for Scottie Snyder, but he never came around, so I couldn't get anything out of him about the alternate situation.

I'd all but come to the conclusion I'd be living at Jason's come week's end, when we got to a questionnaire about allergies and Timothy Dillinger threw back his hair and ever so casually pointed to an item on the list. "So, I've got peanut allergies. Does that mean I'm out?"

Sarge's eyes flashed as we turned to Marissa, who shot Timothy a frown. "Oh dear. I think umm…" She rifled through some papers then flipped over a form. "I'll have to call, but yeah, it says here no preexisting conditions."

Everyone jumped as Timothy rocketed out of his seat. Everyone except Sarge, who remained seated with a wolfish grin.

Timothy slapped his palm on the table. "That's ridiculous. I have my EpiPen right here. The soft drinks don't have peanuts."

Sarge crossed his massive forearms. "Yeah, but no telling what's in this mall," he said helpfully.

Timothy glared at him. "Shut up, you're only trying to take my spot."

Sarge quit smiling and cocked his head in a way that told me bad things were coming for the kid, but he collected himself with a few deep, nasally breaths. "Correct," he said evenly.

Timothy shook his head, pacing and muttering. His chain wallet flopped with his movements as he did everything but stomp his boots. Marissa promised to make a call and left us to argue amongst ourselves.

Soon as the door shut, Mark Faartz glanced up from the little map diagram we'd been given. "I think I'm taking the Sears location. Gets the most foot traffic, I would guess."

Timothy flung himself against the wall and glowered at Mark. Sarge shrugged, although the gleam in his eyes wasn't nearly as casual. Percy, the old man, only chewed on his lip and said it was an excellent choice.

At this point, the girl spoke up. "I'm allergic to poison ivy. Like, seriously. I break out in hives." She looked around the room. "I think I'm safe here, though."

Percy turned his twinkly smile to the girl, prompting her to continue. "Had a bad case of it when I was younger. Took weeks to heal."

Timothy rolled his eyes and let out a wet hiss of a sigh. While it sucked for him, his departure would make me Alternate *Numero Uno*. I took inventory of the contestants in the room, eyeing which one I'd need to bow out next, when Marissa rushed back in.

"Timothy, I'm deeply sorry, but you won't be able to participate in the challenge." She tapped the page on the section which was now highlighted. "Again, our apologies, but it's in the fine print. We are willing to offer you a year's supply of Pepsi and a free oil change at Franklin Ford."

Timothy kicked a chair, and it went skidding across the floor. "Fine print. What a joke. Yeah, thanks for that." He clicked his teeth and glared at us as though it was our fault. Sarge kept a level stare on him until he turned and stormed off.

The door shut, and Sarge looked around the room. "And then there were five," he said with a deep chuckle.

We filled out more forms as Marissa went over the details. As an alternate, I remained on the outside looking in, and I wasn't sure what was going to happen as Marissa instructed the four real contestants to arrive at the mall no later than six pm next Sunday. Mark Faartz declared he would like the Sears spot, Percy grabbed JCPenney. Julie got the Cineplex, and Sarge was left with Montgomery Ward. I was basically ignored through the process but took in the details.

The "castles" were constructed using six packs of Mountain Dew, Pepsi, and Diet Pepsi. Each contestant was bound to his castle until one contestant successfully sold every can in the castle. There were limits though. No bulk sales. The maximum amounts were listed.

Mark Faartz sighed. "Shoot. I really like Coke."

Marissa regarded him with a mix of disbelief and confusion. She opened her mouth to respond then decided against it before she turned to the other contestants. "You will be allowed fifteen minutes of exercise in the mornings and evenings. An hour for lunch where you are free to leave, however you must stay within the mall at all times. Outbound calls are allowed from the nearby payphones. Otherwise, you will stay in your castle until we have a winner. If you choose to do so, you are free to drop out at any point. If three contestants drop out, the remaining contestant will be deemed the winner. Questions?"

Mark wanted specifics about morning and evening exercise times, prompting a snicker from Sarge. Marissa calmly answered his questions—about lunch tickets, incoming calls, even conjugal visits—with a straight face and patience. Then she continued. "Also, the winner will agree to be in spots and promos for sponsors—"

Mark interrupted. "I have some questions about that."

Marissa blinked. She was patient, I'd give her that much. But this guy was the worst.

I continued to gauge the contestants. While I wished nothing ill on these people, I needed one more to drop out so I would get a chance. I couldn't help rooting against Mark, he made it too easy.

As we were leaving, the girl came up to me and introduced herself as Julie.

"Hey, I'm Max."

"Ma-ma-ma Max Headroom."

I laughed out of politeness. I'd heard that roughly eight thousand times in my life. Julie fell in stride with me as we passed the food court. "So, first alternate." She cocked her eyebrows at me. "Who are you going to bump off?"

"Definitely Mark."

"Yeah, Mark is gross. Did you see him picking his nose? He totally ate it too."

For the first time, I really looked at Julie. She was a tad older than I initially thought, early twenties maybe, with a spray of freckles on her nose and cool green eyes.

She'd do well in the contest as the only female, and her energy was contagious. She walked along in little hops, at least until we stepped outside and her entire demeanor dropped. Her smile fell, then her shoulders. She nodded a quick goodbye and started for a low-rider Mazda truck parked at the curb. The bass was pounding so hard I could feel it in my chest. I started to cross the lot when she turned quickly, almost as an afterthought. "Well, good luck with, you know, getting in. Do whatcha gotta do, you know?"

I laughed. "You too, I mean, you're already in but...well, thanks."

A small smile before she ducked into the Mazda, and as the door shut and it took off, I was thinking how she didn't seem like a bass truck kind of girl.

By the time I made it back to the Rabbit, I was feeling a mix of excitement and disappointment. Yeah, I was almost there, thanks to Timothy's allergies, but what were the chances someone else would drop out? Julie seemed healthy enough, although what was up with the way she changed when we got outside? Sarge wasn't going anywhere. Obviously, my chances were with the geezer and Mark Faartz. Neither of them looked as though they could go more than a few days on a cot.

At home there were no new messages on the machine. I fell back into the couch and took full advantage of having the place to myself as I turned on the TV and sort of zoned out. Still, I thought about Tara, hoping maybe she'd caught my name on the radio. When I tried to force myself to think of something else, she found ways to haunt me. I fell asleep and had a dream I was locked in the mall, only there was no soda, just Tara, running away from me.

And I couldn't catch her.

6

The phone started chirping way too early the next morning. I was still on the couch, where I rolled over and dug the cordless out from beneath the cushion. I hardly got a hello in when Mom began gushing about the trip, all chipper and giddy as she gave me the rundown. The weather was great, they were in the Bahamas and Rob was nursing a sunburn. Oh, and had I found a place to live?

I wiped my eyes, still adjusting to the daylight streaming in through the sliding glass doors to the patio. Only my mom would call home from vacation to check up on my apartment hunt. I told her I might have found a place but was still waiting to hear back about it. Kind of a lie but kind of not. Either way, Mom and Rob must've been going hard on the margaritas already because the news sent her on a tizzy. "Oh, sweetie" and all of that, she was proud of me. This is exactly what I needed. She sounded happier about giving me the boot than the dinner buffet.

Mom prattled on for a while about the islands and how she'd somehow already lost three rolls of film. I was only half-listening as I glossed over all my info from the King of the Mall contest. I almost wanted to tell her about it, but first I had to get in. I let her talk about customs for five or ten minutes before she ran out of steam and announced she needed to put more aloe on Rob's back. Poor Rob.

I lounged around the house for a few hours, brainstorming. And I'll admit, I was thinking bad thoughts about Percy the Geezer by the time I got ready for work.

Sunday mornings at Clear Car meant cleaning the pit— basically a sewage system for the automatic car wash. In the tunnel, lurking beneath the fifty-pound metal slats, was all the dirt and grit and sludge from a week's worth of washing cars. It didn't help that Chris had opened last Sunday, an older guy with a penchant for day drinking and a hatred of physical labor, which meant there was basically two weeks of guck to scoop up and haul out by the bucket. Lucky me.

That said, the work gave me something to do. I fell into a groove, scooping and dumping and getting lost in my head. It's what I loved most about manual labor, how my body became a robot while my mind was free to roam and wander. I finished up with ten minutes to spare and tried to stay out of the way, but it was no use. Carol called me in, and I was rewarded with bathroom duty. I took the mop, filled the bucket, and just as soon as Carol was back in her office, I used the pay phone and called Tara.

It was part habit and part desperation. For almost a year now, it was second nature to call Tara in my spare time, in my busy time, all my time. And now she was gone, about to head back to college and forget about me altogether. I had to do something.

Of course Adam answered, as the kid seemed to always be clutching the phone. I could practically hear his smirk as he told me Tara was still asleep because she'd been out so late.

I was about to hang up on his face when there was a scuffle, and Tara wrangled the phone away and answered with a breathy "Hello?"

"Hey, Tara."

The way she sighed wasn't exactly welcoming. While things had not gone well yesterday, to put it mildly, she'd been the one who said we could still be friends. Now, as I glanced around the car wash lobby, it was all too clear she'd only been saying that to let me down easy.

"Hey, Max. Umm..."

There was no denying the hint of irritation in her voice. I squeezed the phone. Only four minutes until we opened, and cars were already forming a line outside. I had to fix this. Make a splash. "Look, I wanted to—"

Carol's office door juddered open. I covered the phone with my hand as my five-foot two-inch boss roared at me as she stepped outside. "Maaaxxx! We got cars out here."

Meanwhile, Tara continued. "I really don't want to hurt you, Max. But again, I think it's best if we took some time apart and..."

Hurt? Had I been gunned down in my kneecaps and left to grovel in the streets as people took turns kicking me in the jaw it would hurt less than this. More cars squeezed into the lot out front. I turned toward the wall, blinking through the agony. I had to get her back. I had to do something big.

Down the hall the outside door opened, followed by a spine-raking shriek. "Max! Now!"

No time. I took a breath and went for it. "Hey, I got picked for the King of the Mall. That big promotion at RiverView?"

"The what?"

"Yeah, the King of the Mall contest, it's like a live-in deal, the winner gets a new truck and five Gs. Not bad, right?"

Silence. I'd stunned her into silence. I allowed myself a

smile. Sure, I'd been hoping to wait until I actually got picked, but this was it. I was losing Tara fast.

Some rustling on Tara's end. In the background, Adam whined about the phone to Mrs. Walker.

Tara sighed again. "Oh wow, Max."

The *beep-beep* of a horn outside. Twelve on the dot and we were open for business. Still, I smiled, my heart spiking with dangerous levels of hope and anticipation because I was thinking Tara meant *Oh wow, Max* in a good way. Like, *wow you've really done it, made something of yourself and I want you back.* It was worth being late, risking Carol's wrath. Even possible pit duty next week for punishment.

Customers were getting out of their cars, looking around for assistance. I closed my eyes to be in this moment with Tara, about to say something like, *You can stay at my castle whenever you want,* when she spoke up. "I can't believe you're going to fall down that corporate trap. Do you know what they put in Pepsi? They market that poison to kids like it's healthy. It's why we have an obesity problem."

"Well, I..." Hang on. She'd been drinking Diet Coke yesterday. *Yesterday!*

"Yeah, Max," she continued. "I've seen the commercials: King of the Mall. It's just another stupid way to promote this stuff. Make fools of people. It's like I tell Adam, they package this poison with bright shiny labels and they're like drug pushers. What they should be doing is going into the communities and..."

A man tapped on the front entrance, cupping his hands around his face to peer inside. He wore a suit with leather shoes, probably on his way from church. He shot me a look, obviously wondering why I wasn't vacuuming his car as it was 12:01. But I was too stunned to do much of anything. What had happened to Tara? Talking about corporations and poison? I only wanted to win a contest and get her back. Somehow, I'd made everything worse.

"Tara, I gotta open the store."

She sighed. "Okay, well. Max, I really think you should reconsider this. They're only going to make a fool of you."

I wiped my face. The back door opened, followed by the *whoosh* of the humming vacuums outside, followed by the violent slap of Carol's shoes as she stormed down the hall and into the lobby. The guy at the door was still tapping away. He saw us and threw his hands out. Carol smiled tightly, then cut a look at me that could slice steel. "What the hell are you doing? Get out there now!"

"Tara, come on. It's a stupid contest. I could get my own place and—"

"They lock you in the mall, right? And people come by and gawk at you like a carnival attraction. It's..."

"Max." Carol's eyes held a maniacal gleam. She fiddled with the keys, cursing through gritted teeth as she went for the door.

"Tara, the store. I have to go."

"Okay, Max. But remember, cars are nothing more than shiny trophies to capitalism. Okay? Bye."

The line went dead, and I stared at the phone, wondering what in the hell I'd just heard. Not only was I crushed, heartbroken, I was confused. And now people were filing into the lobby. I was about to get fired. With a breath, I set the phone on the receiver and trudged down the hall to wash cars, Carol badgering me the entire way about how she should fire me on the spot.

The first car I touched was a wreck. Nothing but gunk in the console and french fries in the seat. And the owner, a Mark Faartz lookalike, was a grumbling guy pointing to his watch, talking about twelve means twelve. I offered him a free spray wax, like Dre would have done, and he told me I'd better do more than that. Carpet Shampoo. Air freshener. The works.

Corporate slave. Mockery. Shiny trophies. Tara's words banged around my head for the rest of the morning. I hiked down to the gas station for lunch and grabbed two hotdogs. When I got back, Dre was pulling in. I told him I'd been selected as an alternate.

He ducked in his car, grabbed his blue Clean Car shirt, pulled it on, and shot me a pearly-white smile. Meanwhile, I had two mustard spots and pit-sludge stains to go with the wrinkles on my own shirt.

"For real," he said. "Max, that's..." He popped his collar, then his smile fell. "Hold on. If this plays out, what are you going to do about work?"

I hadn't thought much on that. "Well, I'm not in yet. But if I do get in maybe Carol would let me have the time off." As soon as it left my mouth, I knew how crazy it sounded.

"Pshh, yeah okay. You know how she is. She already said she almost fired you three times the other day."

And this morning, I thought. We started for the vacuums. "Yeah, well. Tara said it's corporate slavery. That they were going to make a fool of me."

"Well, you're doing just fine with that second part on your own."

"Thanks."

"I'm playing. Corporate slavery, huh? So, Tara's still on that philosophy trip?"

"Yeah. But it's worse than I thought. It's like I don't even know who she is anymore. I was hoping, I mean, this whole King of the Mall thing, I was only doing it because I thought maybe if I got some cash for my own place and a new truck, she'd... Why are you shaking your head?"

We arrived at the register booth and Dre entered. I hung at

the window while he reached under the register, grabbed the key, and unlocked the drawer. I felt like Charlie Brown waiting on advice from Lucy. Sure enough, Dre wiped off the counter and looked me over. "Man, Tara's cool and all, but there's so many girls out there." He cocked his head and looked me over. "Don't be King of the Mall for Tara. Be King of the Mall for you."

The growl of an engine as a huge truck drove in. I rolled my eyes. "Easy for you to say."

Dre was fiddling with some coupons. He stopped. "What does that mean?"

Before I could respond, a man wearing overalls approached the counter. "Excuse me," he said in such a drawl we exchanged glances.

Dre smiled. "Yes?"

"I need a warsh for my truck." He spat a dark stream of tobacco juice on the lot.

Dre's eyes widened. He shot me a sideways glance as he stepped out from the booth. I was struggling to hold in the laughter. The truck was roughly the size of a small apartment building and entirely caked with hardened mud down the sides. It wore mud like a coat of armor, all the way up to the roll bars. The tires, which looked like they belonged on a farm tractor, had shed bits and pieces of dirt clumps all the way down the lot.

Dre rubbed his chin. "Oh, well, we could handwash it, I suppose."

The man snorted and spat again, a wad of brown on the sidewalk. "How much for that?"

Dre regarded the spit stain on the sidewalk, balling up his nose. While he was a people person and got along with most anyone, this guy was testing his patience. "Hundred bucks."

"A hundred bucks for a *warsh*?"

This time I had to cover my mouth. Dre shrugged. The guy

spat again as he stormed off, muttering about getting ripped off the whole way. He cranked up the truck, and I was waiting for him to monster-truck his way over the Rabbit and off the lot, when Carol came out and saw the mess he'd left behind. "What's this? What did he want?"

Dre laughed. "A warsh."

I threw an arm around Dre as we doubled over. Even Carol smiled as the dude roared out of the lot, shedding dirt in his wake. It was one of those rare moments where we all banded together, the dregs of the service industry, before Carol rushed off, cursing about idiots and everything else. "Max, get this dirt off the lot."

I grabbed the broom and dustpan, getting back to Dre. "Anyway, this contest, if I can get in, it could change things. Tara might look at me differently. That's all I'm saying."

Dre yawned, stretched, then picked up a vacuum hose as a car pulled in. "Okay, man. This Tara thing has gone far enough. I think it's time you let me school you on how to play the game."

7

Life as an alternate was a drag. The week slowed to a crawl, and I spent my day off on Friday sinking into Mom's flowery couch, watching talk shows and reliving my favorite moments with Tara. Every time I considered doing something or going anywhere, I'd remember how her lips felt on my ear when I kissed her neck. I could hear her husky whisper as we sat under a sunrise, as though if she spoke too loudly, she'd scare it away. I thought about how she'd take my face in her hands when she was excited about something.

She'd returned to school without saying goodbye—not counting that train wreck of a phone call we'd had in the car wash lobby—leaving me here in Loserville to fend for myself while she immersed herself in culture. I wasn't buying all that corporate stuff she was talking though. Thinking back to the Audi, with Tina and white sunglasses guy, it sure didn't look like they were eschewing all things retail.

And still, I needed to figure out my living situation, and fast. Somewhere that wasn't Jason's place. It wasn't looking like I'd get into the contest, as I was still the odd man out as an alternate, which left me without much hope for anything to change. So in a rare moment of inspiration, or desperation, I drove out to the community college to make good on my promise to enroll.

Fall classes were in session, even as the August heat and humidity had returned to normal. It was nearly ninety degrees outside as I made my way to the admin offices to talk student aid and tuition and enrollment cut offs. With each form, my inspiration faded. While sometimes college seemed almost possible, whenever I considered all the paperwork and phone calls, the financial aid and scheduling evening classes around my job, I found it easier to back away. A couple of classes a semester? That would take forever.

Instead, I crossed the terrace for the cool confines of the library, the only building on campus with which I was familiar.

I liked the LVCC library. It was less crowded and cleaner than the public library, and while I wasn't a student, no one ever said a word about me being there. Sure, I couldn't check out books, but the magazine selection was top notch, with anything you could imagine. *Rolling Stone, The Source, Sports Illustrated, Sport.* I skimmed through a few of them before I picked up a *Business Weekly.*

Maybe I could find some interview tips. Sometimes I fell into these daydream fantasies where I won the lottery or snagged a great job and made a ton of money. I could drift off for hours, thinking about all the things I'd buy and all the exotic places I'd visit. And now, as I settled in a comfy seat by the large, arching windows, I suppose I was looking for inspiration.

Warmed by streams of sunshine, I flipped through the pages with a yawn, settling in for a nap when I found an article about selling yourself versus selling your product.

Typical dribble, written by some video rental chain guru. It touched on the usual pillars of preparation, knowledge, and confidence—all things I did not possess. But as I skimmed along,

I realized these were things I could possibly fake, at least for the span of an interview. *Confidence.* I glanced around, thinking how maybe I could do three classes a semester. *Drive.* Then I could get a job in packaging or sales or programing computers. *Knowledge.* I could work my way to the top the old-fashioned way. It could happen, I just had to go after it.

Then I fell asleep.

The phone was ringing when I got home. I figured it was a bill collector or one of Mom's appointments. Or even worse, Mom herself, asking where I'd moved. But what if it was Tara?

With that in mind, I snatched up the cordless. "Hello?"

"Is this Max Miller?" asked a female voice that sounded both professional and vaguely familiar.

"Yeah, uh, speaking," I managed with a wince. I couldn't tell if the humming was on her end or all the blood my heart was flushing to my eardrums. I thought I caught the echo of broadcasting, a commercial playing in the background, something clicking then beeping. Wait. Was this someone from the radio station?

"This is Maxwell Miller?"

The room took a spin. I sat down. Then I stood. I cut through the kitchen and out toward the front door before I swung back to the living room where I bumped into the stupid bamboo table and knocked a basket off the wall. Why did my mom put baskets on the wall?

I cleared my throat. "Yeah, yeah. Speaking."

"Mr. Miller, this is Marissa Kenzora. I'm the assistant program director with 102.9. There's been some shuffling, and it seems another contestant in the King of the Mall contest had to drop out. We have you listed as an alternate. Are you still interested?"

"Yes!" I blurted out, my heart still thumping in my ears. Was this real? Did she really ask if I was still interested? Was I on the air? I ran a hand through my hair. "I mean, yes." I cleared my throat. "Sure. I am available."

"Great. We'll need you to drop by the station today to make it official. Congratulations, Mr. Miller."

I fumbled through a goodbye, tossed the phone on the table, and did a flip onto the couch. I was in. This was real. I had a shot. Five grand. A truck. Me.

I got to my feet and ran up the stairs, laughing as I set out to find something to wear. I'd have to call Carol and get the time off approved, which might prove tricky, but whatever, *whattheheckever*, I was in the King of the Mall contest!

Yes, I nodded to myself, ideas flashing in my head like the sun on a glittering ocean of thoughts. Promotions. Carol would go for it; she loved promotions. And Dre would help talk her into it. Maybe we could do some promos at the store, have people come in and buy some sodas. Okay, enough about work. If Carol had a problem with it, so what?

Back down the stairs. Then up again. Tara. Carol. Mom. I wondered who got bumped. Percy, Julie, Mark Faartz, Sarge? I hoped it was Mark, but the smart money was on Percy.

The phone. I needed to call Tara and tell her everything. How many minutes were left on my calling card? Wait, no, "corporate slave." I stopped, dropped my head, then I caught my breath. There was no Tara.

No, no, nope. Enough about Tara too. This was my time, and I was determined to be happy. My luck had changed. Even when all I wanted to do was hop in the car and drive to her school and beg her to take me back all over again. I had to pull myself out of it. This was my big chance. Fate. Destiny. Peanut allergies. How else could you explain it?

I had to play this right. Had to think ahead. Down the road. I'd win, and Tara would see that I wasn't some loser. I was doing things. Big things. It took time, that's all.

By the time I got to the radio station I was riding a wave of happiness. I filled out more paperwork, hardly able to sign my own name I was so hyped. Marissa smiled and wished me luck. She reminded me to be at the mall no later than five minutes before six on Sunday evening. Got it. I could be there now if she wanted. I was about to leave when it got the best of me.

"So, can I ask who dropped out?"

Marissa shot me a smirk and waited a beat. "Well, you're going to find out anyway, so...Mr. Faartz ran into some legal issues. He won't be able to compete."

"Really?"

Hearing this woman say "Faartz" was funny enough. Watching her try to contain her professionalism was something else. Obviously, she was thrilled he was gone.

"So, I get his spot? Like, his location?" I asked, remembering the prime Sears location.

"You do." She nodded.

"Sweet."

"Good luck to you, Max."

"Thanks. See you Sunday!"

I GOT to work a half hour early on Saturday. I'd wanted to be an hour early, but my car wasn't having it. Anyway, I even smoothed down my hair and tucked my shirt in like a nerd.

Carol was her regular old bubbly self, grumbling about how someone had left the gas tanks on all night. I nodded through her grievances, unfazed by her miserableness. Nothing could stop me. I followed her around the lot, to the back, and into the equipment room as she muttered about firing Gary or Chris or whatever dunce had closed last night.

Clearly, there was never going to be a "right time" to ask for a favor, so with a deep breath I plowed in and went for it.

"Oh, so have you heard about the King of the Mall contest?"

With her free hand, she patted her pockets for a smoke, which was odd because she was clutching the wooden dipstick we used to measure the tanks and gauge the fuel levels. "No," she said without looking up.

"No? Okay. Hey, did you do something with your hair? It looks extra, you know, bouncy today."

Carol stopped and looked at me like I'd offered her a fist full of cockroaches to eat.

"Yeah so, anyways, the contest, it's over at the mall." I glossed over the details. "And guess what? I've been selected."

She hardly blinked as she shook out a smoke and stuffed it in her mouth. Then she turned and started for the lot, heading for the tanks.

I kept jabbering away about how the contest worked, hoping to get her to agree to two weeks. I figured if I couldn't sell seven thousand six-packs in two weeks, I was sunk anyway. But Carol didn't hear me; she was still worked up about the fuel. People were always stealing gas, and she was obsessed with checking the tank levels. So yeah, she wasn't paying much attention, but I wasn't expecting her to actually light the cigarette in her mouth.

I fell back a step, stumbling some in panic. Carol, puffing away, lowered the stick into the gas tanks beneath us. She glanced at me. "Max. I can't fill the schedule that fast. And you're supposed to clean the pit tomorrow."

Another step back, as though that would help when the entire block ignited. Sure, I'd expected her to say no, but *the pit?* Who was thinking about the pit? It killed me the way she treated the car wash as though it were some Wall Street conglomerate. We sent cars through a tunnel. This wasn't difficult.

She retrieved the dipstick and laid it on the asphalt, ashes drifting off the glowing red coals of her cigarette as she mumbled the numbers she jotted down on her clipboard.

"Carol," I dodged a plume of smoke, "this contest, I could spread the word about Clean Car. Think about it. I'll be interviewed by the local news. The paper. It would be all kinds of free publicity."

She glanced up, and as worried as I was about our impending explosion, I summoned the courage and went for the kill. "Think about that. How much free promo I could do, talking about Clean Car."

Carol looked me over, and I almost had her when someone honked, and she snapped out of it. With a huff, she checked her watch and told me to grab the dipstick. I did as I was told and followed her to the booth, where she stubbed the cigarette out on the sidewalk, then stuck the butt in her pocket. "Go put that around back. I gotta get back to the register." Then she added. "I'll think about it, okay?"

It was the best I could hope for. I smiled. "Yeah."

She started off, but then stopped and spun around. "Two weeks. That's it. And you'll need to fill your shifts. Oh, and take this hose and give it to Frank. He's up front. Go!"

"Right. On it."

"And get these cars vacuumed."

"You got it."

Carol stormed off, and I got after it. I delivered hoses, vacuumed, waxed a station wagon while whistling to the beat of opportunity drumming in my head. I was buzzing with nervous energy and euphoria. This King of the Mall thing was enough to keep my mind busy, away from Tara, mostly, to where I wasn't obsessing over her every three minutes; I didn't hear a love song and wallow in the depths of my misery. Nope, not today, the sun was out, and I was on my way to five grand and a truck. I was so inspired I even washed the Rabbit, shredding a towel on a flake of rust as I wiped her down.

After work, I stopped by Jason's place where he and his merry band of stoners took turns clowning me about living in the mall, Tony doing most of the work.

"Yo, Max. You ready for prison?"

"Ha ha." I refused to let Tony ruin this for me. I took it with a smile because I would be the one laughing when I rolled up in my new truck.

Eventually, after most of the crew left with Tony to pick up some girl who had been "sweating him" for weeks, I got the chance to ask Jason about that alternate spot.

Jason, who hadn't changed out of his pajama pants or left the couch all week, sat back, holding in a huge hit from the bong, and pondered this question like a Buddhist Monk mulling over his principals. Stifling a cough, he exhaled. "Probably the best he could do. Yeah, he's got some pull, but he can't do whatever he wants, you know?"

Fair enough. What did it matter, anyway? I was in. "Yeah, that's what I was thinking. Either way, I owe you one, big time."

He laughed, packed another hit. I told him all about the other contestants, Mark Faartz and good old Timothy Dillinger. I was rambling and didn't think he was listening, which, actually was one of Jason's biggest assets as a friend. Sometimes it was nice to be able to sputter and spill all your worries and fears knowing the person you were speaking to would forget it all in a dank cloud of weed smoke. But after several deep hits of the bong, he set his stringy hair into a bun and picked up the game controller.

"Okay, you're in. There's a hot chick, an old dude, and a sergeant. So, what's your plan?"

"Plan?"

Jason stared at the ceiling as GZA preached through the

thump of the speakers. "Yeah, like, the military dude probably has a bunch of buddies and vets and stuff lined up to buy him out. The chick will probably show some skin or something. Old dude might have the Moose Lodge backing him. What about you? You need a plan, son."

"Well…" He stumped me there. All I'd thought about was making the cut, but Jason was right, I had no plan. I shrugged. "I don't know. Maybe the car wash? But everyone at work is broke. I don't know."

He scooted to the edge of his seat, reached for the baggy on the coffee table. He dug in, sorting the buds from the stems and seeds. "Well, you've got your shot. Now you need to come up with something."

Still in his pajama bottoms, like a wise old stoner Yoda, Jason had me thinking. Together, we flipped through the rule book, combed the fine print, and tried to come up with a master plan. Jason thought I should play up my talents, until we realized I had no real talents to speak of. With that, he snatched up the controller again and fired up the PlayStation.

Apparently, I'd exhausted all of his mental energy, I got to my feet and said I'd give him a call later. He nodded, his face transfixed by Crash Bandicoot on the screen. Realizing I had no gimmicks or special talents to offer, I gathered my things and drove home.

8

"**E**xplain it one more time. You live at the mall? Like, *live* live?"

Try as he might, Dre couldn't grasp the appeal of living at the mall in a castle made of Pepsi. He shook his head and said he'd need a lot more than five grand. I guess for a guy used to sneaking girls into his grandmother's basement and eating home cooked meals every night, it was a hard sell. He kept going on about where I was supposed to go to the bathroom and wash my butt. But in the end, he had my back.

Carol had me come in and clean the pit on Sunday morning before she let me go pack and get ready. She'd cleared my schedule and made it clear she wasn't happy about it, even as I promised to mention Clean Car all the time, especially when the local news showed up that night to do a big story on the contest at the mall.

I spent most of Sunday afternoon packing up my room. I stuffed a duffle bag full of clothes I was taking with me, then finally put those boxes to use, stuffing in old button-downs and sweaters, along with tapes and CDs and baseball cards and whatever else, and lined them against the wall. That left the top drawer to the dresser, where I found all the pictures of Tara and me. In a moment of weakness, I put those in the duffle bag too. I wasn't quite ready to throw them away.

Being that I wouldn't be around when Mom returned home sunburned and miserable, I wrote her a note explaining the contest, adding that she should tell all her work buddies to come by and grab some sodas. Rob too. I had no shame. I needed all the help I could get.

Lastly, I did some light cleaning, wiping down the counters and firing up the vacuum before I took a long, hot shower, thinking how it could be the last one I'd enjoy in the townhouse.

That evening, Dre met up with me in the mall parking lot. Sure, it was risky parking the Rabbit on flat ground, but that would be a problem for future me. Besides, I was too nervous to care at that point.

Watching me get out, he looked me over. "Well, at least you don't have to vacuum any cars, right?"

"This is true." I laughed.

We hit up Sal's for pizza. Dre told me about some girl he'd met at work. He was going out with her tonight.

I shook my head. "Does it ever get old for you?"

"What?" he deadpanned.

"You know." I shook my head. "Like, a new girl all the time. Umm..."

I blew it off because it sounded lame. But that's what was cool about Dre. Where Tony would have been sprawled out on the couch, laughing, making jokes about my sexuality, Dre was genuinely trying to understand what I meant.

He sipped his drink, sat back. "I mean, if you're asking do I want a long-term relationship, commitment, something other than hookups with random hotties, well..." He made a face, puzzled by the bizarre notion that one could grow tired of such circumstances.

I threw my hands up, laughing. "Okay, okay, sorry I asked. I meant—"

"Tara. You meant Tara," he said, leaning forward. "Look, in all seriousness, yeah. I get it. Would I like a relationship with an intelligent, good-looking girl who worked all the time and wanted to take care of me? I suppose that wouldn't be too awful, you know?"

"Okay, again, not what I meant." I shook out some red pepper onto my pizza. "I think you forget, not all of us look like a Polo model, you know?"

He lowered his brow. "Here we go."

I laughed. "Chill, man. What I mean is I can't just walk up to girls, wink at them, and they throw themselves at me. And even if they would, I like, I don't know. I like knowing someone."

Again, I waited for him to laugh or chuckle, but he didn't. He pursed his lips in thought. "I can respect that."

I stopped short from taking a bite of pizza. "Really?"

"Yeah, it's cool. You're a man who likes commitment. It's a good quality."

"But?"

He grinned. "That's just it," he said, grinning as two girls strolled into the restaurant. "Butts."

Dre agreed to spread the word around and said he'd have me out in a week. For the first time since the talent talk with Jason, I felt something close to hopeful. Sure, I needed more than Dre's help, but here was a guy who could sweet talk a girl into going out with him while vacuuming her boyfriend's car. Not a bad weapon to have on my side.

We tossed around some ideas. Dre was thinking he could print off some flyers and hand them out at the wash, maybe toss in a free wax for anyone who showed proof of purchase. It was a good idea, if Carol would ever go for it—not likely, though.

When we were leaving, I got to see Dre's plan in action. He casually approached the girls we'd seen coming in. They smiled as he strode up to them and introduced me. He asked if they would consider buying some drinks to set me free, and they agreed, giggling and blushing, looking over their shoulders as they walked off.

"There you go," he said, holding up two fingers. "That's two six packs down."

WE HUNG out in the parking lot. It was still muggy out, but I wanted to savor all the outside time I could get before I went in. The mall shut down at five on Sundays, and at quarter of six, Dre wished me luck as mall security arrived to let me inside. It was all fun and games until the click of the deadbolt echoed in the eerily quiet mall. A chill ran down my back.

And so it began.

Marissa was all set up and waiting for us at the food court. Sarge was already there, of course, standing stock still at attention, his green canvas duffle bag at his feet. He looked like he was boarding a train to go to war.

I'd packed light. My duffle with a few pairs of boxers, shorts, three t-shirts, those stupid pictures of Tara and me. Hopefully, this thing wouldn't last more than a few days. Where would we do laundry, shower, things like that? Hopefully Marissa would explain.

"Welcome, Mr. Miller," Marissa said before she checked her watch, glancing at the guard. "No sign of the other two?"

The guard shook his head. Marissa eyed her notes. "They have five minutes."

"Six o'clock is six o'clock. If they aren't here, they should be eliminated," Sarge declared, saying *eliminated* in a way that made it sound like certain death.

"Five minutes, Sergeant Cardwell."

I smiled at Sarge. "Hey, have you seen the movie *Major Payne?* You sort of look like Damon Wayans."

Sarge's round shoulders locked in place as his head turned robotically. Under his stare, it felt like his intense brown eyes were boring into my soul.

I backed off. "Never mind."

With a click of the doors, we turned to find Percy, the old man, flanked by security, jabbering about the locks and asking about the keys.

The guards looked happy to drop him off. Marissa perked up. "Mr. Goodwin. I'm surprised you needed someone to let you in."

The old man's eyes twinkled. "Who's to say I did?"

Marissa smiled.

The old man yowled.

Marissa filled us in. "Percy, here, was a locksmith."

"Still am, young lady."

Marissa smiled. "How are you doing this evening, Mr. Goodwin?"

"Ah, well, I'm still kicking. Just not as high."

I stifled a groan. Sarge regarded the old man without interest, more concerned about his watch, grumbling about the time.

The windows shined with bright, evening sun. The distant traffic seemed at odds with the stillness of the mall. The floor sweepers and vacuums hummed. Another click, then footsteps. With one minute to spare, security arrived with Julie.

"Ah, Miss Childress. Glad you could join us."

Sarge harrumphed. I was smiling until I got a closer look.

Her shoulders were slumped, her gaze glued to the floor. Her face was puffy, and it was clear she'd been crying.

Marissa cocked her head with concern. "Everything all right?"

Julie sniffled as she gave a quick nod.

"Okay then," Marissa said, still watching Julie, her smile fading as she launched into her spiel. "Welcome to the King of the Mall contest. One of you four lucky contestants will walk out of this mall with five grand and a brand-new Ford Ranger truck. For your participation, each of you will receive prizes from Radio Shack, Montgomery Ward, and plenty of other sponsors.

"Now, as we've been over the basics, and you have chosen your locations–"

"Question." Sarge cleared his throat and Marissa lowered her notes. Sarge gestured to me. "Why does he get the top spot?"

"Well, Mr. Cardwell—"

"*Sergeant* Cardwell."

"Right, *Sergeant* Cardwell," Marissa laughed. "Of course, there are no top spots. We've conducted tests, and each castle gets the same amount of foot traffic."

"I'd like to see the data on that."

Marissa blinked a few times, and I got the feeling she was slinging around some choice words in her head.

I smiled. With a shrug, I threw my hands out. "I'll switch with him. It doesn't matter to me."

Sarge swung his glare to me. Obviously, I didn't want to give up such a sweet location, regardless of the data. The Sears castle had everything going for it. It was near the main entrance, Radio Shack, and the arcade. But I'd learned a few things hanging at Jason's place with Sauce and Tony—being so quick to give something up kills its value. It plants a seed of suspicion in the other person's mind. If I was itching and ready to hand over Castle One, it must not be so great after all.

It worked. Sarge shook his head. "I didn't say that."

Marissa gave him a minute before asking if she could proceed. I did my best to hold back a smirk. Sarge continued huffing and puffing about data.

Finally, Marissa, sort of smiling herself, looked from Sarge to me. "Well, guys, are we good where we are? Or is a trade happening? Now or never."

Sarge hesitated. His eyes flicked to me, to Marissa, now irritated with all this potential switch talk. He'd stepped right into my trap, and I nearly lost it, although it was a bit scary how easily this hardened military veteran fell victim to my mind tricks. Not sure what that said about our national security.

After a few half-hearted complaints about data and analytics, Sarge waved it off in an attempt to save face. "I'm good where I am. I wanted to bring it to attention, that's all," he grumbled.

Marissa exhaled. "Okay. Noted. Now, let's go over break times."

Each castle had a "yard" roped off where contestants would be allowed to interact with customers. Otherwise, we were not allowed to leave our castles with the exception of the allotted break times. We had an hour a day to leave for lunch, where we were, under no circumstances, to exit the mall. If we were caught outside the mall's premises, we'd be disqualified immediately. If we didn't return to our castles at the allotted time, we'd be given a warning. Two warnings, and after that we'd be disqualified. Nearly every rule ended with: *will be disqualified.*

We were *allotted* two fifteen minute breaks. Once a week we'd be given time to wash our clothes and shower (at the mall, where they'd set up a station. Anyone failing to return from laundry on time...you know, *disqualified*).

I was yawning by the time we wrapped with instructions and rules. Marissa announced it was time to meet our big-time sponsors. She sent a guard, and after an awkward four or five minutes, they returned with a stampede of swishing suits and tapping shoes as the sponsors rolled in, looking awfully formal for a Sunday night.

The Pepsi guys were first. One was tall and lean with a grayish beard and a tan. The other was short and squat. Neither seemed the least bit impressed with us, as the taller one made no secret of checking his watch while the shorter guy took a call on his fancy cellular phone midway through the spiel, as though he might miss his flight and have to stay in our little dump of a town for the night.

Between time checks, the taller one announced this was the first in what they hoped to be a major promotional campaign. Pepsi was a proud company with a storied history, *blah de bloop de blah*. They wished us luck, shot us a smile, and then they were gone.

Ford Motors swooped in next, claiming how they were happy to be a part of things. Then it was Montgomery Ward, some guy from mall security, before finally, a nerdy Radio Shack guy—Wilbert or Wilford or something. Either way, he was the only one who looked like he wanted to be there at all.

He obviously didn't have a speech planned and spent the next ten minutes geeking out about technology. From computers to internet to email to online usage, he spewed numbers and gibberish, and even broke out a handheld video camera.

Sarge muttered some choice words, looking ready to attack as Wilford glanced up from the camcorder and motioned for us to move this way then the other as he explained how excited Radio Shack was about all this. Marissa stood to the side, bemused as the guy fiddled with things, jabbering about the battery percentage.

Bathroom breaks were next, and everyone was more than ready to bolt. I hung back, and it was out of sheer boredom that I approached old Willie when the others were gone.

"Hey, how about you let us have a camcorder? That way we could record our experiences."

I was half kidding, but I had nothing to lose. Marissa watched closely, and I shrugged, figuring we could do some *America's Funniest Home Videos* or something. At least it would give me something to do to pass the time. To my complete surprise, Wilford looked up and gave it some thought. He glanced over to the other sponsors, not wanting to be outdone. "Well, uh..." He looked to Marissa for help.

She consulted her massive book of notes. "Nothing against it here."

Back from his break, Sarge bristled, seeing me talking to a sponsor.

Finally, Marissa tapped her book with her pen. "It could be fun, have them *record their experiences*." She raised an eyebrow at me as she said it.

Wilford gave it some thought, then nodded. "Okay, let me make a call."

With the pressure on Radio Shack, the suits exchanged a nervous smile while the remaining sponsors crossed their arms, studying me with interest.

Two minutes later, Wilford was back. "Yeah, okay. This could be interesting. I think we can make it work." Again, the sponsors eyed one another. Wilford looked over the small group of contestants. "Is that what everyone would like, a camcorder to record their experiences?"

I nearly lost it, hearing everyone use my line.

Percy shook his head. "Oh boy. Not me. I wouldn't know the first thing on using that gizmo."

Sarge grunted, still at ease but looking stiff over there. "I'm not here to record anything."

Julie's eyes had cleared up, but she was in no mood for smiling. She declined with the shake of her head. Once again I wanted to know more about her story, but for now, I pounced on my chance to snag a camcorder. I went in for the kill, using my car wash salesman skills to the fullest.

"I guess I'll do it for everyone. I could film the contest and maybe even give you guys a shout out. It would be great pub, you know?"

Sarge grunted, his eyebrows pinched as he worked to figure out my angle. I shot him a smile as Wilford chatted with Marissa. Percy was talking to absolutely no one about the old circus and drive-in that used to be in this very spot where the mall now sat.

Marissa and Wilford broke from their little huddle. Wilford held up the camera. "Okay, so yeah. We'll have one ready tomorrow." He turned to me. "What's your name, again? Mick?"

"Max," I said, taking his hand.

"Ma-ma-ma Max Headroom..."

I bit my tongue, glancing over to Julie who never looked up. "Yeah, that's it. Ha ha."

With my little deal done, Marissa got things back on track. The next sponsor gave a little speech, but I wasn't listening.

I sat back and smiled, because maybe I didn't have any talent to speak of, or even a plan, but now I had a camera.

It was a start.

9

Knowing I was going to be living in a castle built out of soda cans had not adequately prepared me for what awaited us at the Montgomery Ward end of the mall.

Castle Number Four was a sight to behold. A glittering spectacle of seven thousand six-packs orchestrated in greens and blues and reds with dashes of yellow, white, and silver. There were windows and turrets, as the walls spanned up fifteen feet high and about twenty feet deep.

Marissa spouted out details, how for the sake of fairness, every castle was comprised of the exact same number of Mountain Dew, Pepsi, and Diet Pepsi. I caught Sarge moving his lips as he tried to count every can.

At six feet tall, I had to duck to get through the rounded doorway, where things opened up to reveal the wooden framework that held it all together. It was wild how the inside was about the size of my living room and kitchen. There was a cot, a porta-potty, an outlet strip, and even a small television set and mini fridge. Mark Faartz would have never left.

"Home sweet home, huh guy?" Percy said to Sarge, who glanced at Percy's hand resting on his massive shoulder.

We swiveled our heads to take it in. Wilford recorded our reaction as Marissa explained how engineers in New Jersey had designed the structures and flown down to inspect the construction over the course of the past few weeks.

I rolled my eyes as Marissa stated for the millionth time how we were not—under any circumstance—to consume our own drinks. If we did, "We will 'be disqualified'," Julie and I mumbled at the same time.

We exchanged glances, and she smiled for the first time that evening. It was good to see she was getting over whatever had happened before she arrived.

"Right," Marissa said to us. "Glad you understand." She turned to Sarge. "Sergeant Cardwell, if you don't have any questions, we'll leave you to it."

Sarge mumbled something about being in a hurry to get this thing won. He set his military issued bag to the floor as he lowered himself on the bed, his back straight and his face a stone —his version of relaxing. I took one last glance around as we filed out, when Sarge called to Marissa, "Oh, what time does the mall open tomorrow? I have a platoon coming in to buy some drinks."

Wilford's laughter echoed through the empty mall. Marissa's eyes widened with her smile as she turned around. "The mall opens every day at eight. The stores between ten and twelve. Big day tomorrow, WLET will be here first thing."

The makings of a grin washed over the sergeant's face. "Okay then. I'm all set."

A *platoon*? How many was that in military math? Ten, twenty—gulp—a hundred guys? My stomach dropped.

Marissa turned to us, brow raised, as though we were all competing for second place. "Well, shall we?"

Wilford begged off, and that was it for the sponsors. I was next on the drop-off list. Marissa explained in detail how my castle was like Sarge's, but the six packs were arranged differently, giving each structure its own unique design.

Percy and Julie hung back. The old man was a bit winded after all the walking, and Julie was back to moping. Marissa went over a few things as I got settled, and I thought it was going to be more rules and regulations when she turned and shot me a quizzical smirk. "So, what was that all about, with Wilford? The camera?"

It was the first time she'd broken character. I smiled, looking off. I had no real reason at all. "I don't know. Just thought it was cool, that's all." Then, rubbing my hands together, I added. "You know, seeing how much power we have."

She narrowed her eyes at me. "What's next, going to ask for a helicopter on the roof?"

I set my bag down, sat on the cot. "That's not a bad idea. I'll keep it in mind."

Marissa laughed. "Okay, well, good luck to you, Max Miller."

"Thanks."

Once she was gone, things got quiet. I was alone in this section of the mall. Only the faint gurgling of the fountain to accompany my thoughts. I poked around, taking things in before laying back on my cot. It was springy, not exactly cut out for the long haul, but for now I was in the contest and determined to make the best of things.

Inside my tomb of six-packs, I gazed up through the open roof of the castle to the shiny, vast darkness framed in the skylight above my head. Up until now it had all seemed like pretend. But here I was, locked in for the night. This was my chance.

The compressor of the mini fridge turned on with a click. Restless and bored, I opened it up and found it stocked with sodas. What else?

Thirty minutes, then an hour. I hadn't brought a book or a Walkman or magazines or much of anything to occupy my time. I had fourteen bucks in my wallet. Maybe tomorrow I could hit up Borders about a sponsorship, see if I could land any free reading material. But for now, left alone without distraction, my thoughts quickly went to Tara.

What was she doing at this moment? Was she at a party? Studying? Reading poetry with some guy with a ponytail? In the silence of the empty mall, her parting words of "corporate greed" and "slavery" came back to haunt me. I looked around at my walls of cans. It seemed impossible that I could sell all of this.

If I could find a way, though, I would show up at Tara's dorm in my new Ford Ranger with money to burn. Maybe that would change her tune. I'd make good on my claim and enroll at LVCC, do more than sit in the library next time. I'd become a college guy—sort of—and she'd have no reason not to take me back.

Sleep wasn't happening. I got up and paced, ran my finger along the cans. It was dark but not, quiet but noisy. It was weird, lonely, and the night promised to be endless.

I checked out the Porta John. It was clean, with a sharp, minty chemical smell. Another look around my new home. Hmm, nearly nine o'clock, nothing on TV anyway but that stupid *Lois and Clark* show. I sat back, forcing my thoughts away from Tara. It was time to plan, plot, strategize.

I had to come up with something. Carol wanted me to plug the wash. I brainstormed on that for maybe three and a half minutes. Then I woke up disoriented. Sitting up, it dawned on me. I was on a cot, in the mall.

The continuous flush of water in the distance. I turned one way, then rolled over. I was a rotisserie chicken on that cot. At some point I finally gave in and fell asleep again.

10

My eyes flew open against powerful shafts of morning sunlight. A shuffle of footsteps, some jingling of keys accompanied by the sharp, precise whistling of someone with ample time to practice. I sat up and wiped my face as a guard I faintly recognized from last night set his enormous head in the doorway. "Good morning. How'd you sleep?"

"Okay," I said with a squint.

He was a big guy, looked to be in his forties, with brownish hair going gray at the sides. Same for his beard that didn't do too much to hide his double chin. He was breathing heavy. It could've been all the whistling.

I yawned, rubbed my eyes. "What time is it?"

He chuckled. "Eight-thirty, bub. You only got a few minutes to put yourself together. The news station is coming in today."

"Huh?"

Had Marissa mentioned anything about this? I was still processing that when a portly woman wheeled a cash register to the desk parked outside my castle. She glanced at me without interest, then began wiping down the chair.

The guard turned and helped her with the register,

chuckling as he hefted it onto the desk. "Hey, looks like you lucked out. Paul's got Sergeant Caldwell's castle. Place is jumping already. Looks like a military parade over there."

The cashier lady paused mid hum and cast a reluctant glance my way. "Hmm, well, I forgot my book."

My stomach grumbled as I got to my feet. My hair was spikey from sleep, and I was still in my clothes from yesterday. I wasn't off to a great start, not with this whistling guard guffawing and slapping his meaty thigh. And I didn't think Cashier Lady was joking about the book. Seeing me watching, the guard straightened, still smirking, he tipped his hat to the cashier lady. "Welp, good luck."

With another chuckle he was back to whistling. Cashier Lady got to work. She managed to get the register plugged in. She set a calculator and a notepad on the desk and looked over things. She wasn't exactly eager to make conversation, so I went and got myself cleaned up the best I could, wondering if this would be my only night in the castle. Wouldn't that be my luck, for the military to swoop in and buy Sarge out on the very first day.

Great. I'd have to crawl back to Mom's house and beg her and Rob to let me stay all over again. I pushed that out of my mind, ran my hand through my hair, and paced around the castle. We didn't get out until ten for our first break, but with the news team on the way, maybe we'd get some extra time.

I brushed my teeth, spitting in a bowl as there was some commotion outside. I closed my eyes and took a couple deep breaths. Big smile. Time to make a sale.

Outside, I found some early bird mall walkers swishing by in twos, threes, and even a group of ten. I was struck by the brisk movements of these elderly athletes, most of whom were wearing windbreakers in blinding shades of neon pink or orange.

A few of them waved, and it dawned on me that I should be working. I zeroed in on a few of the older guys eyeing my castle closely and put on my best smile. "Bet you could use a cold drink, am I right?"

Cashier Lady actually snickered. I shot her a glare, but all that was quickly forgotten as an old man with sloped shoulders nodded, then began tottering over to me. He was almost there, too, this hobbit-like creature, wheezing and reaching for a piece of my castle, when a hyper lady reined him in. "Walter, I told you, I don't want you drinking that stuff."

I watched in horror as she led him away. A few pity stares as the old brigade swung their way around my castle and started swishing off the way they came. I was so close, and now they were getting away. I thought how Dre would have them eating out of his hand. Desperate, I tried again as the next Golden Girl smiled at me in passing. I shot her my best grin. "Hey uh, what do you say? Buy some Diet Pepsi?"

Her cherry red smile dropped like an anchor. "Oh dear, I'm sorry young man, but I don't drink Pepsi Colas."

"Well, uh... How about some drinks for the grandkids, right?"

Another grimace, and her wrinkles webbed together like a shattered windshield as she pleaded with the other permed and curled old lady for advice. But her friend had a flight to catch, judging by the way she pumped her arms as she continued marching. "I'm sorry, sonny."

They shuffled off, leaving me alone with my smirking cashier. "You're going to have to do better than that," she said without looking up.

As the mall came alive—employees arrived for work, rolling up the gates—my cashier was content to file away at her nails before she settled in for a nap. I couldn't help thinking about Sarge over at the other end of the mall, directing the large-scale military operation. I pictured soldiers with walkie-talkies directing helicopters and vehicles arriving to haul out caseloads of soda from RiverView Mall. Although, there was the "No Bulk Sale" rule in place, so maybe things weren't as bad as I feared.

But Percy was going to kill it with the Golden Girls. And who knew what Julie had in store, but anything was better than I could manage—which was zero. I should've known I was in over my head. All I could bank on were a few stoner friends who wouldn't wake up for hours, and when they did, it would be to hit the couch and pass around the bong and PlayStation controllers. My other hope was a coworker who was too easily distracted by a sundress.

Eventually, I landed my first sale when a man leaving Sears grabbed some Mountain Dew. Then a lady and her daughter bought some Pepsi. I was thankful, if for nothing else than to keep my cashier awake, but I had to do better. I needed more, needed something big to happen if I was going to keep up with Sarge over there.

Then Mom showed up.

From a distance, she looked tan and relaxed from her cruise. But as she neared, I saw the lines around her eyes, the stress and exhaustion from everyday life returning to form.

"Hey, Mom."

She regarded the castle the way one might come across an awful car accident. "Max, what in the world? I got your note. What's going on? Is this what you call moving out?"

"Yes, I moved out. I mean..." I gestured around the mall.

Cashier Lady made no effort to hide her interest. I decided I'd win this contest for no other reason than to put this woman to work. But for now, I had to contend with Mom, who was anything but convinced.

She shook her head and sighed. "This isn't what I had in

mind. Max, you can't *live* here," she said, glancing around like it was too shameful to say in public.

A man and woman approached, pulling a six-pack of Diet Pepsi from my front wall.

I smiled. "How about one more?" I asked desperately. The man shook his head. "Okay, thanks!"

Mom ducked her head. "I mean, what is this, exactly?"

"It's a contest," I said, my voice breaking. My mom had a way of bringing out the worst in me. But at least Cashier Lady had to set down her nail file to ring up the purchase. I tried to make one last pitch to my customers. "You sure? I mean, you never know, right?"

The couple declined again. Cashier Lady gave them an apologetic glance, and they paid for the measly six-pack and got on their way. I turned to Mom, lowering my voice. "I have to sell all these sodas to win."

Cashier Lady raised an eyebrow. "He needs to sell a *lot* more sodas to win. And soon." She picked up the nail file.

I sighed. "Could you...*not* do that?"

Cashier Lady merely shrugged and got back to it.

I rolled my eyes and waved Mom to the entrance. "Here, come in."

Mom followed me inside, clutching her pocketbook as though I'd invited her into a dark alley. I offered her a seat on the cot. She declined, brushing back her feathered bangs. Her dye job was wearing thin, revealing her dark roots. "What about work?"

"It's taken care of. If I can win this thing, I can get my own place."

"If? And when you don't?"

Wow, the confidence. I turned away. "I'll, uh, move into Jason's."

Mom frowned.

I picked up clothes, folding up my hoody. Anything not to look at her. "Can we worry about it later?"

"I suppose." Mom looked around. "Well, this is something."

I smiled, happy for the change of subject. "It is. How was the cruise?"

She nodded. "It was fun, really fun. Rob got sun poisoning, then food poisoning. He had to spend the last few days in the cabin." A guilty smile spread across her face. "I played at the casino."

"You win?"

"Actually, yes. I did. A few hundred dollars." Her smile grew. "Can you believe that?"

My mom had been gambling and still made more cash than me. "Yeah."

Some commotion outside. For a moment I thought it was someone buying some cans. It wasn't. It was the suit from Radio Shack. And he had the camera.

"Sweet. It's here." I stepped out, glad Mom was there to witness this.

The suit hurried over. "Hey, Max, got your camcorder here."

Mom stood behind me as the suit brought it to the window. "You'll want to plug it in, charge the battery all the way, two to four hours, at least. Here are some blank tapes. I can bring more." He caught Mom peeking out and smiled. "Hello."

I took the camera and looked it over. "This is awesome. Thanks! Oh, this is my mom. Mom, this is..."

"Wilford Milders. It's a pleasure." He looked past me, taking in my castle. "Yes, on behalf of Radio Shack, we wish you all the luck." He nodded to Mom, then back to me. "This is a loaner, however," he added, all wink, wink, nudge, nudge. "So be careful. Here's the instruction manual."

"Got it. I will. Be careful and all." I turned over the box, looking at the picture. "Thanks again."

Wilford left, and I was itching to charge up the camera. Thankfully, Mom begged off as she was running late, although she hung around for a few minutes, with this sort of stunned look fixed on her face as she kept asking what I was planning to do with a video camera. Whatever her doubts, seeing old Wilford come by put a stop to all her questions.

On her way out she offered me some money, but I turned it down. She said she'd be back soon, with Rob, and I nodded along as I fiddled with the camera. "Cool. I've got to get ready for the news team, anyway."

She stopped in her tracks and brightened. "Oh, is it WLET?" She'd plucked a case of Diet Pepsi. The cashier lady rang it up with a smirk.

"Oh, I'm not sure," I said, realizing my mistake. There was no way I was telling her Chip Banner was coming. She'd been not so secretly crushing on the dude for as long as I could remember. The last thing I needed was my own mother looking like a groupie on TV.

Cashier Lady opened her mouth. "Yes, it's—"

"Okay, Mom, I'll talk to you later," I said, sending a death stare to my cashier.

Mom looked around for any sign of Chip. "Well, I'm late," she said, hefting the sodas. "So I guess I'll scoot."

Ten minutes after Mom "scooted," local weather-man-turned-reporter-turned-tool, Chip Banner, stormed the scene. A tornado of teeth-whitening and self-tanner, Chip and his crew gushed about Sarge and the scene over at Castle Four. "Now there is a story for ya," he said with a laugh.

Apparently, Sarge had already sold nearly an entire wall of his castle to the military. Chip's pearly white smile took a hit as he glanced up and took in my quarters. "Oh, well at least this one is still intact."

My shoulders fell. I'd sold maybe—*maybe*—twelve six-packs so far, and I sure as hell didn't need Chippy or anyone else laughing about how lousy I was doing right before I went on TV. I caught myself. Deep breaths. It was *Business Weekly* time. This was an opportunity. It could be my turning point.

Time to make an impact.

11

With a smile bolted onto my face, I strolled out to greet Chip Banner. He saw me coming and brightened. "There he is," he said, hustling over to me with a quick glance at his little cards. "Max Miller."

He wrestled my hand like a fish he'd yanked out of a river. Before I could blink, they were positioning me at the door to my castle.

Chip's charms weren't limited to my mom; Cashier Lady went all moony as she got to her feet. "Would you like something to drink, Mr. Banner?" she said softly.

"No, thanks," he said with a wink. "Don't touch the stuff. Only Sunny D for me."

I never knew there were so many anti-soda people until it became my life's mission to sell them. Chip did some teeth clicking and neck rolling as they set up the camera—which reminded me of *my* camera, still charging on the fridge. What in the world was I going to do with it? How could I use it to sell more cans? That was a question for later as Chip, through with his warmup routine, went laser focused with intensity.

The camera guys gestured for me to stop slouching. I finger

combed my hair in place as Chip's eyes darted left to right. With a comically fake smile plastered on his face, he beamed his dazzling white chops at the camera as the cameraman began a countdown.

Three...two...one...

"Hi, Chip Banner here, back atcha' from RiverView Mall. I'm here with contestant number four, Max Miller. Max, how do you feel about your chances of being crowned King of the Mall?"

My face went hot and rashy. It felt like a bug was crawling around in my hair. I blanked as my mouth hung open. I had no idea what to do or say as they'd been at my castle for maybe ninety seconds. And the question, what had he asked me?

"What?"

Without missing a beat, Chip asked me again. Something about the way I felt. I was hot, the lights were bright and assaulting my face. How did I feel? Terrible. I was getting crushed.

I managed to nod my head, I think. My brain spun like a tire in the mud as the lights worked to suck the life out of me. I could hardly catch my breath, much less think of a single word to say.

"Max?"

Max. Me. Everyone would see this. How I was bombing royally on television. I forced myself to say something. "Well, I'm happy to be here, you know?"

Chip's smile tightened. He blinked twice. "Ha, yeah, but it looks like you've got your work cut out for you." He nodded toward my castle, then leaned in and gave me a nudge. "So tell me, what's your plan to become King of the Mall?"

"My plan? Um, to sell Pepsi. And..." And *what?*

"Ah, right. Good one," Chip said with an uneasy chuckle.

I was blowing it, big time. Any chance I had to convince

people to come out and buy some soda was going up in flames as I tried to reset and put something together on the spot. In a panic, I reached for the mike, but Chip yanked it away. And that's when things started clicking.

A nervous laugh before I remembered what I'd promised Carol. The promotion, my friends, everything. The word vomit came tumbling out all at once. "I'd like to give a shoutout to Clean Car on Mason Ave. What's up, Dre? Come down and buy some drinks, get me out of here."

"And there you have it." He took a step to put some distance between us "Max Miller at Castle Number One. This is Chip Banner with WLET Linwood. Good evening."

I squeezed in a few shoutouts before the light zapped off. "Jason, Sauce. You suck, Tony!"

Chip tossed the mike to the camera guy, glaring at me as he fixed his cufflinks. "You know, I'm here to do a community story. The least you could do is show some respect."

I laughed. "I was only saying hi to my friends."

The fake smile vanished, packed away with the bright lights and the rest of the equipment. Chip tugged at his collar. "You know, you should take a trip down to Castle One, see how it's done."

The camera guy shrugged. And with that, Chip Banner raced away, his little news team giving chase.

I called out to him. "Thanks, *Chip!*"

"Whatever," I mumbled, turning for my castle. My favorite cashier stared at me with dead eyes.

"What?" I said, done with her and Chip and all of it.

She closed her eyes. "You gotta do better than that."

I threw my hands out. "I'm trying."

"Mmm-hmm." She got back to her nails.

On my first break, I basically sprinted down to Sarge's castle to see things for myself, replaying the awkward interview in my head, hoping maybe it wasn't as bad as I'd thought it was. Rounding the corner at the jewelry store, I nearly ran into the crowd.

I jostled my way forward, the thump of patriotic music finding my chest as I made it to the front of the line. Sure enough, an entire wall of Castle Four was gone. You could see straight in where Sarge had hung a giant American flag. Huge speakers sat up front, obviously hauled in and mounted at taxpayer expense. And it was working. I almost felt morally obliged to buy sodas.

His register guy worked feverishly to keep up with demand. Everyone was smiling and chatting, some kids holding balloons like it was the county fair. I was cursing under my breath when I caught Sarge watching me. He set his shoulders back, chest out, swelling with pride as he chuckled. I couldn't even hide my disgust.

When he gave me a salute, it was all I could do not to roll my eyes. Dread rushed over me as I turned and set off for the bank of pay phones. I needed help, and fast.

"Clean Car Carwash, this is Dre."

"Hey, man."

"Max. Hey, I saw your interview. You okay?"

I closed my eyes. "That bad, huh?"

"Carol and I watched it in the lobby. It was..."

"Bad."

"It wasn't great," he laughed. "But check it out, we're going to put up a poster in the lobby. I'll get a picture of you in front of the castle, and we'll display it everywhere."

A poster. Sarge had a regular Fourth of July parade going on. But Dre was trying. And it was something. I gripped the phone, watching the shoppers drift by. "Nice. But we got to hurry, man. This military dude, he's moving cans fast."

"I got you, homie. I'll be there at lunch."

I only had four minutes left to get back, but I wanted to see how Julie was making out, so I took off in the direction of the movie theater. I was already sweating, not just from the running but because it felt like I'd just got here and now everything was slipping away. I didn't know what else to do, promotion-wise. A few posters and Dre's word of mouth was all I had going for me.

Julie had a crowd as well, probably because she was wearing next to nothing. Short cutoffs and a bikini top. I stopped and gawked as precious seconds ticked off the clock. This was crazy. Yeah, Jason had mentioned it, but I never thought she'd actually go that route. And it was working.

Even as far away as I was, her ridiculously fake laugh bounded off the bricks as she flirted with a couple of guys lugging two armloads of six packs. Wow, she'd gotten half the side wall down near one of the turrets. I took one last, long glance, but there was no time. I shook it off with two minutes to spare, hurrying across the mall, weaving and sprinting as I told myself I had to be doing better than Percy.

I was in a panic by the time I got there, but relief swept over me. He wasn't anywhere near Sarge, or Julie, although he was still faring better than me, making way with a nice dent in the front of his castle.

Reality hit hard. We were only hours in, and I was easily in last place. And my spluttering interview wasn't going to help things. I turned around and got myself together. No time to dwell on it, I bolted for my castle, where I made it back with ten seconds to spare.

Cashier Lady noticed. "Cutting it close, Max."

She was seriously enjoying my every failure. I started to say something about it, but before I thought of anything to say, she got back to her nails.

Safely tucked away in my very intact castle, I picked up the video camera and powered it to life. Not a full charge, but I had no time to waste. For some reason, I thought back to the *Business Weekly* article about selling yourself as I tested out the zoom and checked out the buttons. I popped in a tape and worked the focus.

Getting the feel for the buttons, I panned the walls, the hundreds of soda cans. Outside, Cashier Lady still looked bored to death until she saw me with the camera. I laughed as she shielded her face.

I shot her a smile. "What's wrong? Don't want to be on Max TV?"

"Shouldn't you be selling drinks?"

"Don't you worry about that," I laughed, ducking back in my castle where I flipped the camera around to my face and got the feel of it. I crossed my eyes, stuck my tongue out. Bits and pieces of the article flashed through my head. *Know Your Audience. Be Confident.*

I tried out a few terrible accents, then settled on something closer to my own voice, but louder.

Have a Story. I paused the tape. "Okay," I said to myself. "Let's give this a shot. Here goes nothing." I cleared my throat and pressed the record button. "Well, this is Max Miller, contestant Four," I started. "I'm, um, I'm not off to a great start. In fact, I bombed my news interview, big time. We're talking worst interview of all interviews known to man, right? So then, check this out, I went and scoped out the competition. Sarge is down there killing it. You'd think it's like Independence Day or something. He should be out by dinner at this rate."

Cashier Lady peeked in. "Who are you—" Her gaze fell to the camera, and she made a hasty retreat.

Be Relatable. I pounced, training the lens on her. "And here's the lady who loves to give me grief. Hey, I don't even know your name, Cashier Lady."

Happy to have something to do, I followed her out to the

cashier desk. She held her well-manicured hands over her face. "Get it away."

A few potential customers took notice, mainly a guy and girl standing a few feet away. The guy nudged the girl with a smile. He picked up a six-pack of Pepsi and made his way over.

"What are you guys filming?"

"Huh?" I asked. "Oh, I'm making a documentary for...Radio Shack." I widened my eyes at Cashier Lady. "My assistant is being difficult."

The guy's face brightened. "Oh, cool. Can I be in it?"

"Yeah, sure." I turned the camera around, trying to fit both of us in the picture. "Here's my good friend, uh..."

I turned to the guy, and he laughed. "Eric. I work at Sears," he said, nodding toward the store.

"Yeah, Eric from Sears. Hey, thanks for helping me out. Tell your friends, okay?"

"Will do. Peace."

A few more came in behind Eric. Cashier Lady could only frown at me while I worked the line. For a while it was fun, doing interviews and chatting them up, until the line died down and it was just us again.

Cashier Lady declared she was going on break.

I threw my hands out. "What about the customers?"

She made a show of looking around. No one was in line. "I'll take my chances."

Some help she was. I plopped down on my cot and placed the camera on the fridge. I was worked up from the brief spike in sales, so I left it rolling and tried out some skits. A new character had come to mind as I'd filmed the shoppers, and I was having a bit too much fun with that when Dre showed up with a bookbag slung over his shoulder. He had a rolled up poster in his hand.

"Max, what's up, though?"

I stopped recording and got to my feet. "Welcome to *mi casa.*"

He ducked his head coming in, hooked a thumb over his shoulder. "I almost didn't make it. You know there's a chick in a bikini at the other castle, right?"

I shook my head. "Yes. I am acutely aware of the chick in the bikini." I gestured to the camcorder. "But hey, I think I got something going here."

"Yeah?" He smiled. "Cool. Well, I hope this helps." He unzipped the bookbag and pulled out a Clean Car hat. He tossed it to me, then rolled out a poster.

Support Clean Car's Finest. Max Miller, Castle One, Ear the Sears.

"*Ear the Sears?* What's up with that?"

Dre scratched his chin. "Yeah, they made a mistake." He smiled. "But they were free. I got six of them."

The mistake wasn't the worst of it. Beneath the heading was a picture of me leaning on a Corvette I'd waxed. My shirt was tucked in, and my shorts were jacked up to my arm pits. I looked like a world class dork. "Was this the only photo you had of me?"

"It was in the office." Dre held it out for a better look. He cocked his head, then cut his eyes to me. "Look, it would have cost forty bucks to have all these redone. Carol wouldn't come off a penny. She really has it out for you, man."

I threw the hat down. My stomach growled. It had been a long morning, and I was itching to get out of my castle. "Well, thanks, for these." I gestured to the poster. "Really, it's cool you did that for me."

"Hell yeah. We can take a Sharpie and fix the lettering. Not much we can do for your pic, though."

"Funny."

Cashier Lady, back from her sabbatical, snorted or sneezed. She was turned all the way around and watching us with a smile. I shook my head. "Well, I got a long way to go. Want to hit up Sal's? I've got coupons."

"Cool."

I punched my card, and we started off.

Cashier Lady called out in a sweet voice. "Bye." She shot Dre a beaming smile.

I stopped and glared at her. Barely a word all day and now she's the welcoming committee.

Dre waved, and she fluttered her eyes like a schoolgirl. I stopped, about to call her out on it but gave up. Unbelievable.

SAL'S WAS PACKED, and it didn't take long to figure out why. Julie was there, still in the bikini top. She saw us and skipped over, all smiles and giggles. I had to admit, she wore little-to-nothing extremely well.

"Hi, Max." She looked at Dre. "Hi."

Dre smiled. "You must be Julie."

"I am," she said, then turned to me. "So. How's castle life?"

"Not great," I said before Dre nudged me in the ribs. "How about you?"

Julie's eyes widened with her smile. "It's great. I've sold two hundred six-packs already, which, would be good, but I hear Sarge is moving soda by the pallet."

The mere mention of Sarge set me off. "Yeah, he's already through a wall. He's playing up the military thing, kind of like you're playing up the—"

With a nudge, Dre stepped between us. "Two hundred six-packs, huh?"

Julie nodded, there was no sign of the sad, sullen girl from the other night. She leaned in, lowering her voice. "Yeah, and I think I just sold ten more. That guy over there wants my autograph." She rocked back on her heels. "How cool is that? We're like celebrities, right, Max?" She came around Dre and hip checked me back into the convo.

"Yeah."

"So, what have you been able to sell, a thousand?"

No way was I going to tell her I'd sold fifteen six-packs, and that was rounding up. "I, uh, lost count."

"Heck, yeah," Julie said, holding up her hand for a high five. Dre shot me a look. I slapped her hand. When she smiled, she scrunched up her nose. Again, those freckles were distracting.

I nodded toward the line at the counter. "Well, uh, I'm gonna grab something."

Julie clapped her hands. "Right. And I have to get back to my fans. Fans, ha, it sounds ridiculous. Hey, see you next break, maybe?"

"Sure."

She skipped back to her adoring crowd.

"Yo, just what are you doing?" Dre asked, glancing back at Julie.

Some guys were outside the store, pointing in her direction. I ordered a couple slices and a couple of drinks. Pepsi for Dre. Water for me. I was already over soda.

"What do you mean?" I asked.

Dre leaned closer. "She's asking you to hang out and you're all like, whatever. This is exactly what you need."

"What? How?"

"Not to win. To get over Tara."

"What, Julie? She's like twenty-something."

"And?"

"She's playing a game. You of all people should understand that."

He filled his cup with ice. "That's cold."

"I didn't mean it like that, but I mean, she's already got fans."

I turned for a seat, but the tables were full and people lined the walls, watching Julie. Maybe watching me. I was about to suggest we take our lunch out to the mall when Julie called my name and waved us over. Dre smiled and started for her when I stopped him "Dude. No."

"What do you mean, *no?* Look, fine, don't get over Tara. But you should be building some buzz too."

"That's what we're doing, right? The posters. *Ear* the Sears? The news this morning. I'm on break man."

"No breaks, Max. You need to get back in this thing."

I gripped my tray and followed Dre over to Julie's table, where she actually *was* signing autographs. At first, no one seemed to notice me, which was fine, but also wasn't. Dre was right, I was going to have to step up my game if I wanted to catch up. I just didn't know how to go about doing it.

Julie introduced me to her fanbase, setting her arm around me as we took some pictures. She was bubbly and flirty, nothing like the girl I'd met walking out of the mall the other day.

"Isn't this fun?" she said, shaking my arm.

"Yeah, a blast."

"What's with you?" she asked, accepting some guy's filthy baseball cap.

"I don't know, just...Sarge and all. We might as well be competing for second place."

"Ah, come on, Max. Think positive." She signed the brim, then looked over to Dre, who sat back with a smirk. A smirk that could've meant two things. I told you so about this contest, and I told you so about Tara.

Julie wiggled her eyebrows, and I laughed. *Sell Yourself*, I thought. It's what she was doing, and it was working for her. And in the packed restaurant, with people clamoring to get close, it wasn't too hard to believe that I could make something happen. Maybe I wasn't going to parade around in a bikini top, or blast the National Anthem all day, but this morning, I'd noticed one thing—people liked being on TV. So that's what I was going to do.

"Okay, I'm thinking positive," I said to both Julie and Dre. "And I'm thinking it's time to put my new camera to use."

After lunch I used a Sharpie and fixed an "N" to the EAR Sears on the posters. I watched the tapes I'd recorded, wincing at the sound of my voice. I thought about Julie and how she was making the most out of things. And even as I did my best to block it out, I spent a lot of time wondering what Tara would think of what I was doing. I guess I already knew what she thought of the contest, but I couldn't let that stop me now.

It was time to *Sell Myself*, to quote my favorite halfway-read business article. Only I didn't have much to offer. Tara had seen that all too clearly when she went off to college. But maybe, if I became someone else, like Julie had, I could bust out of my moping and find that angle I needed.

That evening, as the stores closed and the mall fell quiet, I positioned the camera on the minifridge and worked on my image. I set the Clean Car hat on my head and pressed record.

"Max Miller here, from Clean Car Wash. And I'm telling you now, buy some sodas, get me out of here, then come see me at Clean Car." I stopped and dropped my head. "Weak."

I needed more urgency. Something that would make people feel like they *had* to come and see me. I tried again, then another time, stumbling, whining, pleading to the camera for help. As the skylight turned from yellow to orange to a dusky purple, I worked on different voices and accents. But the message stayed the same. *Please come buy some drinks.* Only now it was too desperate, plain begging, and it wasn't working. Each take got worse. Another glance at the dorky poster. I threw the hat to the ground. I was destined to fail.

It was late. My cashier was gone. I'd managed twenty-two six-packs for the entire day, easily dead last out of the four contestants. I paced the yard, for exercise or pent-up energy. It was close to ten, and no one was around. I'd noticed three different security guards. They made their rounds every half hour. I walked around the castle, ignoring the puny dent where twenty-two six packs had stood. It was 10:28. No sign of security.

It was tempting to walk, to roam the empty mall. Not that there was much to do; all the stores were closed, chained up, and once the movie theater closed, things really went dead. But I was dying to move my feet, get my legs working again. I shook them out, rolled my neck. I did some stupid dance because I was in an empty mall and no one was watching. I glanced at all the Pepsi cans I still needed to sell. Pepsi. Pepsi. Pepsi. And then it clicked.

I went back for my Clean Car hat and set it on backward. Another dance, this time the running man. Yeah, whatever. I set up the camcorder on the ledge and pressed record.

I popped the top on a Pepsi and guzzled it down, slammed the can to the floor. It echoed like a gunshot. I cracked another one. Some fizz got me in the eye, but I rolled with it.

"This is Mad Max, coming to you live from the bowels of RiverView Mall," I spat out in a dramatic whisper, my eyes darting left to right. "For those of you who don't know, I'm stuck here until I sell all these Pepsi products. That's right, that's right. Trapped. Imprisoned." I leaned in close. "*Detained.*

"Anyway, thanks to my peeps at Radio Shack, I'll be documenting my stay. So stop by and get you some good old-fashioned Pepsi, or Mountain Dew for those who like it wild." I turned up my head and actually howled, then slugged down another gulp until it dribbled down my cheek. "And Diet Pepsi, which you can't really tell is diet, or at least your mom can't. So come by, buy some, and free your main man, Max. Out."

I recorded a few more, tweaking it some and doing different voices for each soda. Maybe I was crazy with boredom, desperation, a maniac in an empty mall, but it made me laugh, and for the first time, I didn't feel like everything was a waste of time. I did one where I lay on the table and recorded myself upside down. My voice echoed off the walls as I plugged the carwash, Radio Shack, Ford, and then kind of went wild talking about nothing until I had to charge the battery.

With the camera on the table, I ran around, rolled, slid across the floor. I did jumping jacks, then managed to do the worm two entire times around the castle before I hurt my hip. It wasn't exactly the urgency I was going for, but something felt different about it. Or maybe it was me. I felt different. I performed my best Michael Jackson dance, worked in my Bart Simpson impersonation. Anything to pass the time. The only time I stopped was when security made a pass through and asked me why I was yelling. I played up the bad boy angle, pretended I was on the run. It was stupid, but what did I have to lose?

12

D ay Two. I woke up to my favorite cashier banging around outside as she set up shop.

"Good morning," I said, still wiping the crust from my eyes.

"Mmm-hmm."

She'd remembered her paperback this time. I smiled, because today, win or lose, I was determined to do better. And things were better. A couple guys from the wash stopped by and bought a few cases, then some of Mom's work people. I surpassed yesterday's total by first break and was feeling kind of good about myself, until I trekked across the mall and found the mass of patriots cheering on their favorite marine.

Sarge was actually doing pull-ups. I grumbled in disbelief at the sound of a bugle blasting from the boom box. He already had a line snaking around the castle.

Poof went my morning inspiration. Sarge had half the second wall knocked out, so everyone could watch him work out. And I hadn't noticed the other day, being that he was all dressed in fatigues, but the dude was massive—even for an old guy. His veiny arms bulged with the work as he exhaled loudly, like he didn't know he had a hundred people watching him.

I walked right up to the open wall, now sectioned off with yellow tape.

"Looks like you're doing okay."

He got his chin over the bar, which, where'd he score a pull-up bar, anyway? He dropped down, smacked his hands together. A roll of the neck and he was back at it again. "Yeah, I should be out of here by Thursday, according to my sources. What about you?"

It was annoying, trying to talk with someone doing pull-ups, even if he was doing them effortlessly. Still, I wasn't about to give him the satisfaction. I played it close. "Hmm, well, to be honest, I'm not so sure I'll be here by this evening, the way things are going. Thought I'd drop in to say goodbye."

He laughed. "Right."

The sound of the cash register dinging, the murmur of his crowd, the bugle music, it was working on my nerves. I had to get out of there. "You seen Julie?"

Sarge didn't miss a pullup. "Nah, too busy selling soda."

This dude, I swear. I looked off, about to head back, but I couldn't resist a parting shot. "Well, you might want to check her out. She's not doing so bad. Signing autographs and stuff."

Sarge dropped from the bar again and grimaced. I thought I had him stumped, until someone asked for a picture. Zap, the tiny seed of worry in his eyes was gone. His back stiffened, and he gave a salute and said it would be his honor.

I sighed, failing to hide my eyeroll.

And this time he caught me. "You got a problem?"

I laughed. "Nope."

The man who'd wanted the picture glared at me. "Rolling your eyes at a hero. You some sort of commy?"

"What?"

Bodies turned, walling me in. Harsh stares, pointing, some whispering and head shaking. Time to make a retreat. I threw a wave to Sarge, who crossed his arms and grinned. A quick step back as I side-stepped a group of old dudes who looked like they were on their way to a Civil War reenactment. "Okay, well, see you around."

"Thursday," he said with a sly smile. "Could be Wednesday night."

"Right, okay. We'll see."

To my left I found an opening. I managed to squeeze through the mob and bounced right until I was free from the pageantry surrounding Sarge. I sprinted back to the quiet safety of my castle.

Most of the day I spent fiddling with the camcorder. I did more impressions, worked on my pitch. Things were still slow, but customers were trickling in. I recorded everything, interviewing shoppers, and found that people brightened when the lens was on them. I did more skits, a few promos for Radio Shack, quoting hot bargains and deals from the morning paper. I also paid more attention to security. The routes, the times they came and went. It gave me something to do.

It paid off. By lunch I had my own line going. Nothing like Sarge or Julie, but a group of kids clamored around, like something important was happening. I asked dumb questions in more horrendous accents. I quizzed them about their favorite stores at the mall, favorite movies or TV shows and so on. Maybe I was caught up in the moment, but it felt like I finally had a bit of a buzz going on.

Even Cashier Lady seemed impressed, or irritated, it was hard to say. I made sure she never cracked open Grisham's latest.

At breaktime, I popped the tape and took off for Radio Shack, where I asked for the manager. I was sent to a middle-aged bald guy with bulky glasses, a wrinkled, short-sleeved shirt, and a plaid tie—pretty much *exactly* what you'd expect. "Hey, I'm Max over there in Castle One."

He never looked up from the keyboard he'd disassembled on the counter. "How are you?"

"Good. Look, so um, one of the corporate guys, uh, Willie?" I tried and failed to remember his exact name. "No, Williford? Anyway, he gave me a camcorder, told me to take some videos." Shoot, what was his name. "I think it was Wilbert, Mil...uh..."

He dropped the keyboard, scattering bits and pieces of it onto the floor. "Wilford Milders?" he said, snapping to life. His eyes bulged from behind his tinted glasses. "You *spoke* to Mr. Milders?"

"Yeah, and uh..." I looked around. Was he going to pick that stuff up?

"*Wilford?* Wilford Milders was here at the mall. At *this* mall?" His voice squeaked.

I raised my brow and threw my hand up. "Yep, that's it. Yes, he was."

The manager hurried around the counter, crunching on keyboard bits as he fixed his shirt and wiped the strands of hair on his head. He looked over the tape. "That's an 8X-ERL. We don't even carry that yet. He gave you that?"

"Yeah, well, as a loaner." I tried not to laugh. I'd thought this was a longshot, but the guy was basically panting. Clearly, this was going to work to my advantage. So I went big.

"Yeah, he said you guys would play the tape at the store. Like, put it on a loop and stuff. I gave you some shoutouts and mentioned today's sales." Then, remembering all the goofball stuff I'd done. "Oh, and some silly promos and interviews." I shrugged, then added, "It's what Wilford wanted. He specifically asked for it."

The guy nodded. "Yes, of course. Of course," he said, now

fully engaged in our conversation. "Yes, so you're one of the castle contestants? The King of the Mall thing?"

"That's right. Max Miller, Castle One." I raised an eyebrow. "I'm surprised he never mentioned it."

"No, right. I'm sure corporate sent out a memo. Yes, absolutely."

He was still bobbing his head as I gave him the tape, which he handled as though it were an archeological find. With my work done, I sauntered out of the store, pretending my knees weren't wobbly and my heart wasn't racing at how I'd managed to pull this off. Safely out of the store and around the corner, I bolted for the food court.

At Sal's, I scarfed down two slices and a lemonade, thinking how my luck was about to change. On the way back, I passed a block of pay phones but resisted the urge to call Tara and tell her all about Radio Shack, how things were going. Talk like we used to do.

I got back to Castle One with time to spare.

Cashier Lady noticed. "You're getting better," she said with a smirk.

"Yes, I am." And it was true. I was going to turn this thing around. I chased out thoughts of Tara, of going home, even of Sarge doing so well on his end of the mall. Nothing I could do but my own thing. Which, come to think of it, where was everyone?

My line had dried up. I looked left, right, as people strolled past my castle like it wasn't even there. I sighed. Cashier Lady opened her book when something occurred to me: she was there for me, not the other way around.

I popped my head out of my castle. "Can you not do that here? Please?"

She glanced back, then made a production of searching for a

customer to ring up. I sighed and surveyed my surroundings. There had to be customers somewhere.

Cashier Lady grinned. "So, where's your fine looking friend?"

"Gross."

Cashier Lady cackled as I retreated back to my castle. I fell into my cot, the sun streaming through the skylight. I'd done everything I could think of this morning, and it wasn't enough. It was quiet outside my castle, no shuffling feet, no clicks and dings of the cash register. Nothing but the gurgling fountain somewhere in the mall where not a single person was in line.

King of the Mall. What a joke. I might as well leave, only I had nowhere to go. This was my home until Sarge, Julie, or freaking Percy sold out of soda. So here I was, in my own personal jail.

Wait. Jail. Bad Boy. Extreme. I thought back to how I'd played that manager at Radio Shack, his excitement when I handed him the tape. Time to build on that. No time to waste. I sat up, popped another 8X-whatever tape in the video recorder. I cracked open a Pepsi and got back to work.

It was Mad Max time.

13

Day Three and Sarge was down another wall. By Wednesday afternoon he was left with only the front and back to go, along with the turrets, continuing his pace to be done on Thursday. Julie was a distant second, also exposed, as bystanders watched them like hamsters in cages all day. You could go watch Sarge do pull-ups, then head over and catch Julie laze around in a bikini top. Because apparently that was her thing, showing flesh and pretending to be a ditz.

And then there was Percy.

He talked to anyone within earshot. And now that someone had brought him a rocking chair, he'd stumbled upon his own schtick—that of elderly grandpa. Other than that, he was sort of a mystery, but the sympathy thing was working well for him. He had a wall down and sat solidly in third place.

After another day of lackluster sales on my end, I'd started to accept my fate. In a day or two, this would be all over, and I'd be left crashing with Jason. I shifted my focus to thinking how I could save up some money and figure it out. Because this whole Mad Max thing was nothing but a bigtime bust. It was just as well. I should've known it wouldn't work.

And if I was going to lose, what *was* there to lose? That night, I snuck out of my castle.

It wasn't difficult. Midnight meant I had twenty-eight minutes until checks. I also knew Gary, the whistler, walked at roughly the same pace as a salted slug. If nothing else, my boredom had given me ample time to take in my surroundings. At the stroke of twelve, I set off like a ninja, scampering past the fountains, ducking my way through the little kid playground. A quick check left to right. My heart raced, the adrenaline flowed, and it felt good to do something—anything—other than sulk on my cot.

I skittered my way down the main pass, the most exposed part of the mall, dashing into the open and expecting someone to call out after me. I was almost high with the thrill of it all as I dove to a stop and surveyed my surroundings. When nothing happened, I hung a left for Julie's castle. What was left of it anyway.

The low, faraway sound of a radio, otherwise it was clear. I crouched and darted to the back, leaving me open to the Hecht's.

"Psst."

Julie sprang from her cot with a scream. Her hand flew to her chest. I dove to the ground, counted to five, then peeked up and looked around. "Hey, it's me!"

"Oh my gosh," she exclaimed, eyes wide, her voice lower now. "You scared the crap out of me."

"Julie, you all right?"

I dove back to the ground. A jingle of keys. A familiar wheezing as Gary hustled over. I laid still, my stomach to the floor, taking cover behind the back wall. I whispered at Julie. "Don't tell him I'm here."

"Yeah, you think?" she hissed back at me.

Gary's sliding shuffle came to a stop.

Julie instantly switched to ditz mode. "Oh, aha, a bad dream. Sorry."

Gary ducked into the castle roughly four feet from where I hid. "Are you, uh, are you sure?" His voice went soft, and I covered my mouth.

Julie kept up the breathy Madonna routine. "Yes, I'm sorry. I was, well, you know." ·

"All alone, huh. I hear you. This place can get kind of lonely."

I squeezed my eyes shut. Things were getting uncomfortable. Julie tried to tame the old hound. "Yeah, but I'm okay. Really, but thanks for checking on me." She tacked on a little giggle at the end.

Gary's feet shuffled. "Okay, well if you need me. Call the desk, 8859."

"'Kay, thanks, Gare."

Once he was gone, I raised my head. Julie turned to me, and I couldn't hide my smirk.

"What?" She took a quick peek to make sure Gary was gone, then she flung her head back around to me. "And what are you doing here?"

"*Gare?*" I said, eyebrows raised.

Julie shot me a *don't mess with me* glare.

I shrugged. "I don't know. I was wandering. Just bored." I came around the wall.

Julie smiled. "You're so going to get kicked out of the contest."

"Probably," I said, thinking how the oversized t-shirt and shorts she wore now was more than she'd had on during the day. I looked around. Her castle was so weird without walls. "Not sure it matters. You and Sarge, even Percy, are way ahead of me. I'm losing my ass."

She cocked her head to the side. "Aww, poor baby. Did you come here to pout?"

I laughed. "No, not to pout," I said, but couldn't think of anything else.

Julie took a seat on her cot, both of us keeping an eye out for security, knowing old Gary was lurking in the shadows.

"I'm going kind of stir crazy I guess."

Julie smiled. "Yeah. I miss Haley." She saw my confusion and let out a small laugh. "My daughter."

"Oh... You have a kid?"

She nodded, smiling at the thought. "Yeah." She picked up a small picture frame of a little girl and offered it to me. "She's three. You look surprised."

I *was* surprised. Julie seemed too young and carefree to have a kid. But as I took in the picture there was no denying that the little girl, with the strawberry blonde hair and striking green eyes, was a mini version of the person in front of me. I handed it back. "Is that why you're doing this contest?"

Julie bit her lip, nodded. "Yes. This could change our lives. We could start over."

I wondered if mini-truck guy had something to do with the life-changing. The way she'd been crying the other day. But I didn't want to come out and ask.

Julie nudged me. "I mean, I guess that's why we're all here though, right?"

"Yeah, well, I'm only here for the free soda, it seems."

She set the frame down. "Ha. Well, you should change that. I mean, instead of roaming around all night. Aren't you worried about Gary?"

"You mean *Gare*?" I checked my watch. I still had ten minutes. "Nah, he's too worried about you."

She smirked. "Whatever. You'd better get back."

"Want to go exploring with me?"

Julie cocked her head with a squint, as though she'd solved a mystery. "Ah, okay. Now I get it. You want to get me bumped? Is that what you're doing, knocking off the competition?"

"No." I laughed. "Well, maybe. So, you in?"

She glanced at the picture, then her eyes met mine. "Maybe tomorrow."

"Okay," I said, starting off. I looked back. "See you then."

She moved the hair from her face. "You're crazy."

I hopped over the half-wall and posed. "Call me *Mad Max*."

"Dork."

Getting back to my castle was cake. I spotted Gary a few hundred feet away, sitting on a bench with his chin on his chest. I could practically hear him snoring over the fountains. I laughed. The guy had to be the worst security guard in the history of malls. I breezed past him and decided to go check on Sarge's place. Just to do it.

Even laid out on his cot, sound asleep for all to see, I approached Sergeant Cardwell with caution. Peeking out from behind what was left of the side of his castle, I couldn't help a quiet chuckle, as all those pushups must have wiped him out. A quick fantasy came to mind of lugging my six-packs to his castle and rebuilding his walls while he slept. I could see it now, Sarge waking up, wondering what happened, griping to Marissa about a conspiracy.

No way I'd ever go through with it, though. One, I wasn't going to cheat, and besides, Sarge struck me as the kind of guy who slept with a pistol under his pillow. I bid him a silent goodnight and got moving.

I got back to my castle but was too worked up to sleep. It was dark and quiet, a perfect time for the memories of Tara to haunt me for the next six hours.

On our first real date, I picked Tara up in my mom's Honda, as I was too embarrassed about the Rabbit. It wasn't much of an improvement, but anything was better than asking my date to help pop the clutch. We had dinner at a local restaurant, where Tara filled me in on Tina's latest drama with the guy she was seeing.

I nodded through it all, gazing into Tara's sparkling blue eyes, wondering how I'd ever gotten so lucky. Looking back, maybe it would have been better for me had she cut me off right there. Thanks, but no thanks and all.

At least then the memories wouldn't sneak up on me, knock me over and gut punch me at random moments. Although then we never would have cuddled close under a cold, starry sky, her cheek on my chest as I kissed the crown of her head and breathed in her herbal shampoo. I thought about all those times she told me how great I was, as though she were the lucky one, how she always said she loved the way I listened to her, right before she'd crane her neck and kiss me so perfectly.

I sat up, wiped my face, and shook it off. I couldn't do this to myself. Not now or ever. I found my Clean Car hat, slipped it on backward, and hit record. I cleared my throat and kept my voice low and foreboding. The little light shone blue on my face.

"Mad Max, coming to you from the depths of Castle *Numero Uno*. While the mall is quiet and resting, I'm plotting." I rubbed my hands together like a movie villain. "That's right, I may be trapped in my castle, but I have plans, big, big plans. But first, to make this work, I need your help. I'm urging you, my great legion of fans, to come out and support me. I'm running out of time, and what I want to know, *need* to know, is, where *are* you guys? Come buy some sodas. Stop by Radio Shack and check me out."

I took a dramatic slug of Pepsi then looked around wildly. "Come get a piece of my castle."

14

I awoke Thursday morning to a bustling commotion outside my castle. The sky was bright, and the bleeps and dings of commerce combined with the squeaks of shoes and kids laughing had me up in an instant.

Peeking out, I found a line wrapped around the castle. Some kids saw me and pointed, they started cheering, so I ducked back in, wiped my face, and jerked on my Clean Car hat to cover my bed-head. Was this for real? Was my plan working?

Cashier Lady seemed to think so, as she struggled to keep track. She managed a harsh glance my way, as though she'd been expecting to coast these next few days. "Nice of you to join us."

I shot her a beaming smile and went to work. "Well, all right," I called out, in my best Mad Max persona. "You guys trying to get rid of me?"

They whooped it up. A huddle of middle school-aged boys cheered before one asked for my autograph. I shot him a look, figuring he was joking, when someone mentioned the ads I'd done at Radio Shack. I did my best to nod and smile, still wondering how in the world I'd pulled that off.

I signed the kid's *King of the Mall* flyer. "What's up, guys?"

They nodded. "Dude, you're on every TV at Radio Shack."

"Wait till you see what's next," I said with a smirk, trying not to freak out. I had to own this. I was Mad Max, my own brand now. I nodded and gave the kid a playful shove. "Buy some drinks and get me out of here, okay?"

They did. And more kids filed in and started clamoring, asking about my big plan, what stunts I was going to pull next. I had no idea, but I acted like it was some big secret. I'd think more about it later. But for now, I worked the crowd.

Things were still going strong around ten when I took off to call my "probation officer." Actually, I needed to call Dre, and maybe Mom. On the way over to the phones, I cruised by old Percy's castle when another pack of kids ran up behind me. "Hey, it's the Radio Shack dude."

I turned around, and they stopped, looking at me like I was some kind of star. "Mad Max, right?"

I laughed, remembering I still had my Clean Car hat on backwards. I set my finger to my lips. "Shh, keep it on the down low."

They're eyes glazed over. "Righteous."

"Now go buy some soda, get me out of here."

"Rad," one of them squealed, popping a bubble before they tore off for Castle One. "Right on, dude!"

I watched them rush off, shaking my head in disbelief. No one had ever listened to me, did what I told them to do. I was a guy with fourteen dollars in my wallet. I owed more than that in late fees to Blockbuster video. Now these kids thought I was someone worth looking up to. It was my first brush with celebrity status, and I wasn't sure how to take it. Things were looking up. At least until I stopped by to check on Percy's castle.

Every geezer in Linwood was lined up to buy some "pop" as they called it. They came by way of walkers, canes, motorized scooters. And there was Percy himself, in his rocker, lovable as ever, smiling and waving to his adoring fans.

I wasted precious minutes stewing in jealousy. The old man had the side wall sold off and was working his way to the back. His cashier guy—someone who actually smiled—even helped haul six-packs to the front. It was an operation.

About to leave, Percy saw me and waved me over. With a twinkle in his eye, he got to his feet and hobbled to me. Funny, I didn't remember him limping around like that. "Ah, Max. How are you?"

I shrugged.

He waved to a few fans.

I looked around. "I'm okay. You seem to be making out."

"Yeah, can't complain. Got some nice people here campaigning for me at the bank." He leaned in. "My wife is sick you know."

I exhaled. Great. The last thing I wanted to do was take pity on this guy. "Sorry to hear it."

"Yeah, she needs surgery. Figure five thousand and whatever I can get for the truck ought to help."

Dammit, old man, stop it. First Julie with her kid, now this guy with his wife. Before I could dwell on it, I was recognized again.

"Hey, it's Mad Max." This time it was some kids gathering around, looking out of place with their backward hats and baggy jeans.

Percy smiled and said he had to get back to his rocking chair. I knew it wasn't helping my image, hanging with the geezer, but I couldn't help it, the guy was likable.

I waved him off. "Well, I hope it all goes well. I gotta get back."

"Oh yes. Good luck to you, sir."

I turned to the middle schoolers. Five, ten, then like fifteen kids asking about my record and probation, reaching for high fives as they followed me back to my castle, where there was an actual crowd. Even my cashier lady was busy, but not too busy to scold me.

"'Bout time you got back. People are asking to see you." She nodded toward the line. "I don't know what you did," she said, pausing to count six-packs, "but it's working."

A kid in line called out. "Yo, Mad Max."

Cashier Lady grimaced, then cocked her head at me. "You couldn't think of a better name? And what's with the hat? You look delinquent."

I raised my hands in the air to a rush of applause. "Oh, remember that camcorder you didn't like? Well, I did some promo stuff for Radio Shack. I guess people—"

She held up her hand and got back to the register. At least she was busy, even if she was still rude. Someone trounced over, slapped my back and asked if they could get a picture. Only then did I notice how many kids were wearing their hats backward. I smiled. Guess it was time to play the role.

I posed for a ton of pictures. Someone even asked Cashier Lady to take a pic, and I smiled ear to ear at her irritation as she actually had to get up, accept the camera, and snap the picture. My crowd grew as people kept coming. Someone would slap an arm around me and then there would be a flash—it happened again and again. It went on like that for a while, with a mob around me, raising six-packs of soda and cheering me on. Cashier Lady kept snapping away as more rushed in, and then she announced she couldn't take pictures *and* ring up customers.

Cases of Mountain Dew vanished. Pictures. Pepsi. Snap. Diet Pepsi. Flash. Smile. Repeat. I did pictures for another hour as the boom continued. I managed to knock out half a wall of cans before lunch, when Julie stopped by with her own gaggle of fans trailing behind her.

My place was rocking. Kids huddled in groups, chanting my name and chugging down Pepsi between rounds of hacky sack. A few of the braver ones skateboarded while others flipped through magazines or did battle on their Game Boys. Julie's eyes lit up as she took it in. "Well, this is quite impressive."

"Yeah?" I said, looking over my legion of maniacs. It did look like something was going on, I just wasn't sure what yet.

"Uh-huh. Nice." Julie nodded.

I felt a tinge of guilt at how she seemed happy for me when I was rooting for everyone to lose. I took off my hat, wiped my forehead and set it back on. "It's crazy."

She smiled. "Well, want to grab some pizza?"

On the way to Sal's, we stopped in at Radio Shack, where I was surprised to find that they had rolled a couple big screen TV's outside to play my video on a loop. It was super weird, and a little embarrassing, having my mug on every screen in the store. Then again, it wasn't really me, it was this Mad Max lunatic, guzzling cans of soda, howling at the moon, his midnight plots echoing throughout the store. *While everyone is sleeping, I'm busy plotting...*

Julie turned to me with a smile. "Or sneaking out."

"Shh."

She smacked my arm and I laughed. Still holding to my arm, she pulled me into the store where I was surrounded by my face. Again, normally I would have been mortified, even as I fed them the tapes, I never thought they'd actually show them to the public, at least not on such a big, loud scale. But whatever, it was working.

The manager guy from yesterday looked up and abruptly abandoned his customers.

"Max!" He came shooting out from behind the counter.

Same tie, same shirt. "We've been playing your tapes on a loop all morning," he said, motioning around the store. "This is great, huh? I've called corporate and they're thrilled. This is..." He took a breath, trying to find words to convey how big this was. I was just glad corporate went with it. By the looks of things, I must have gotten him a nice raise.

Julie cocked her head at me as a group of teenagers stopped when they spotted us. They made a line for the store. "You're that dude, right?"

"And Julie," another one said.

The manager guy nodded. *Yes, he is. He sure is. You guys want to buy a pager?*

I looked at Julie and she winked at me.

"Umm..." I stammered.

She didn't wait for me to answer the kids. She scooted over and presented me like Vanna White showing off a washing machine. "Yeah, it's Mad Max. In the flesh."

I rolled my eyes as she shoved me forward and dove into the bubbly flirty act. I swear, she could turn it on and off in a second, but truth be told, even with the bikini top, I sort of liked the real Julie better.

From there things got loud, between the promos and the Mad Max chants, it was all Julie and I could do but pose for a few pictures and make our escape. Even the manager chased after us so he could snap one of me outside the store. *I'll get this to corporate!*

I turned to Julie. "Can we go eat now?"

She laughed before waving to our fans. "Well, make sure you buy some Pepsi. Byeee."

By the time we got a slice of pizza, fought through the crowd, we had fifteen minutes left to eat and get back. I walked Julie to her castle, now without walls one and two.

Julie raised her drink. "Ah, this is living, isn't it?"

I laughed. "How are you going to go back to normal? I mean," I motioned to her bikini top. I was doing all I could to keep my eyes chin level.

"I'm only trying to win, Max." She lowered her head. "Or should I say, *Mad Max?* You know, like you and your videos."

Fair enough. I had asked for the camera, made the videos—even if I hadn't known why—then given the tapes to the Radio Shack manager. A quick glance at the bikini top, straining to keep things PG. I turned my head away with a cough. "Yeah, good point."

Julie smiled. "What about you? If you win this thing. I mean, obviously a truck is nice. But what would you do with the money?"

"Ha. Well, I need to get my own place. My mom sort of kicked me out. And my girlfriend dumped me." I tried to laugh it off but failed. "I guess you could say I had a rough week leading up to this."

Our steps slowed. "Oh, wow. Yeah, sounds like it," Julie said, her face soft, eyes big like she was soaking up my story.

I was about to say more, but I changed the subject and soon we were at her castle.

Julie seemed to have something on her mind. She blinked it off and turned to me. "Want to hear something funny? I don't even like soda. Never drink the stuff."

"Really? Feel like I've heard that before."

"It's true. The stuff is poison."

"You sound like Tara."

"Is that your girl—well, your ex-girlfriend? The one who…"

"Yeah." I smiled, realizing I'd dampened the mood. "Hey, I should go tell everyone you're a phony. You don't like Pepsi."

She aimed a cute little scowl at me. "Do it and die."

15

I spent the rest of the afternoon working the crowd, doing stunts and impressions and even judging a hot dog eating contest. The more I acted like an idiot, the louder things got, right up until the crowd thinned out and the shops closed up. As the mall cleared, I felt a pang of envy as the employees pulled down the gates, joking and making plans while locking up.

Silence settled in like a thick, ghostly fog. I was left alone with my thoughts in my lonely castle. The only places that stayed open were the movies and Bailey's, a little bar on the south end. With nothing else to do, I did more promos for Radio Shack, then a few for Scottie Snyder, thinking maybe they would play the audio on air. I shouted out Flash 102.9, Ford, Radio Shack, and of course Pepsi, plugging the car wash a few times along the way.

And then it was time to roam.

Last night there'd been another stretch between checks, not the midnight one, but a two-hour gap between one and three am. Maybe it was a one-off, or something had come up, but I was too bored to stay put.

At twelve minutes past one I ducked out of Castle One and

plunged into the eerie quiet of the mall. Once again, I crouched, darting between kiosks until I got to the fountain, although most of my fears were gone now. The way Sarge was selling cans, so what if I got caught? Even with my newfound fame, I wasn't exactly in a position to win. The best I could hope for was second place, so why bother?

Two and a half minutes later, I arrived at Julie's castle, where she'd sold off the entire backside and was working her way around the side. No wonder she was happy for me and my little crowd; she was crushing it.

No time to dwell, I glanced around for Gary, then slid into position behind the cans.

"Psst."

Nothing from inside. I looked in, like a creeper. "Julie," I called out, popping up from where the side wall was half down. She was snoring something crazy. "Julie," I called again, laughing. Then, louder. "Julie!"

"Ahh!" She whipped her covers off and sat up. "Dammit, Max, you did it again! Stalker much?"

"Shh." I glanced around. "Want to go for a walk?"

Her short, reddish hair was tossed to the side, over one eye. She wiped it back and stifled a yawn. After a quick glance around, she narrowed her eyes. "What if we get caught?"

I was prepared for this question. "Oh, come on. Where's your sense of adventure? Besides, Gary would never rat you out."

She looked ready to argue, but she knew I was right. Another glance around and she smiled. "Yeah, okay."

She pulled on a hoodie, and we set off for the movie theater. If the mall was quiet right after closing, at almost two in the morning it was like living on another planet. The theater lobby was wide open, and we were free to roam. Julie took in the movie posters, the bulbs around the frame casting a glow on her face as she turned to me. "Okay, so what's your favorite movie?"

"Hmm." I gave it some thought. "I don't know. Either Friday or Dumb and Dumber, I guess?"

She covered her mouth to keep from laughing. "Wow, that's deep stuff."

I followed her, and we ducked into the Airplane Racer game and sat side by side. "What, are you some kind of movie buff?" I asked.

Julie giggled. "No way. I like scary movies."

Ugh. It reminded me of *Tremors*, which reminded me of my late fees, which reminded me of Tara.

I was sulking about it when Julie knocked me with her shoulder. "You okay over there?"

"Yeah." I nodded, trying to force myself to believe it. Julie smiled and my face warmed up. Even though she was older with a kid and there was no way she could be interested in a guy who'd recently been kicked out of his mommy's house, I couldn't help being drawn to her. How cute she looked in her hoodie, how a perfect curl of strawberry blonde hair fell on her nose. Her eyes found mine, and I couldn't say what I was doing or thinking about doing, but before I could try anything, Gary came jingling into the lobby.

Julie mouthed, "Oh, crap," and we took cover as Gary turned right, thankfully, where the Ski-Ball machines lined the wall. The racing game strobed with police lights. Julie grabbed my hand and gave it a squeeze, as we were trapped on one end of the lobby—only the ticket stand to our right and beyond that, the dark corridor that led to the theaters.

I held my breath as Gary swung back around, the sweep of his steps so close I could hear his fingers tapping on his leg. Gently, I tugged Julie out the other way and we crawled into the photo booth and slid through the curtain. Julie fell onto my lap then quickly slid off, covering her mouth as we sat shoulder to shoulder as old Gary waltzed right up to us.

We stayed close as Gary's whistling came to a sudden halt. Only a thin black curtain separated us from his raspy wheeze, the friction of his polyester pants, his soles sliding along the floor as he ambled by so close that I caught a whiff of beef jerky and Old Spice aftershave. The curtain moved as he brushed up against it, and Julie nearly crushed my arm in her grip.

For two or three pounding heartbeats, all was still. Julie and I sat frozen, staring at the curtain and waiting for it to sling open. But it never did. A few seconds later, Gary turned, his keys jingling, still huffing as he moseyed off and out to the mall.

We exhaled. Julie let go of my hand and slammed herself back with a huff. "Oh my gosh, that was close."

She opened the curtain, sort of crouching as she surveyed the lobby, before she turned back to me. "I swear, I would have killed you."

A crush of guilt hit me hard. She had her little girl and whatever else going on in her life that had left her in tears Sunday night. But as she stared into my eyes, only the dim blue light from the photo booth on our faces, I thought we might be having a moment. Until she slapped my arm and leaped out of the photobooth.

"You almost got me kicked out of here."

I shrugged. "I didn't know he'd be out so late."

She turned and huffed off, but I didn't realize how upset she was until I caught up with her and she blinked a few times, her mouth tight. Her head fell, and she studied the floor, then looked up and faced me full on. "Seriously, is that your plan, to get me busted?"

"No. Honestly." I spoke to her back as she'd already turned away. I tried to lighten the mood. "And besides, I'm sure you could've talked him into something."

She spun around so fast her hair fell in her face. "What's that supposed to mean?"

"Nothing," I said, backtracking. I was still caught up in the thrill of almost getting busted, the way she looked at me. Speaking of Gary, I looked around to be sure he wasn't on the way back. I lowered my voice. "I was kidding. He sort of likes you, in case you haven't noticed."

Julie pulled the strings to her hoodie, then set off. "Well, I need to get back. This was stupid. And..." She shook it off.

"What?"

"Nothing. Just," she took a breath, "I know you think I'm some sleazeball hooker, but I'm not, okay?"

"What? No. I didn't say that."

"You didn't have to." She shook her head. "Whatever. I gotta go."

"Okay. Can I walk you back?"

She sighed. I took it as a yes, and we stepped out, careful and quiet. I wasn't sure what I'd said to upset her so much, but I repeated the conversation in my head.

As we made it back to her castle, she shrugged. "Sorry I lashed out at you. It's, I don't know. I'm stressed. I really wanted to win this thing, but it looks like Sarge has it in the bag."

"Yeah, no. I'm sorry I said that about...Gary."

"Okay." She let out a deep yawn. "Well, thanks for a good time. It was, if nothing else, exciting."

"Yeah. Hey, wish me luck getting back. I'm going to go check out Sarge's place."

"You better be careful." She smiled. "Actually, don't be careful. I hope you get busted."

"I'll be as noisy as possible. And then you can figure out a way to beat Sarge and be King of the Mall."

"Queen."

"Queen. Right."

Julie turned and went straight to her cot without a word. She flopped onto it and that was it. I set out for the next wing. I figured Gary would be a while getting to Sears, so I had time. Then again, he had surprised me once. But I was feeling reckless.

I took cover behind a train at the kids' playground, then, seeing the all-clear, took off into the dark. I was still buzzing with adrenaline—from thinking I had a chance with Julie, for almost getting busted, then the strange fight we'd had on the way back. There was a lot going through my mind when I decided to take that chance and check out Sarge. I breezed past the gated stores and the empty benches, still thinking about Julie. So I wasn't quite prepared for what I saw when I got to Sarge's castle.

Because there was no castle.

16

What remained of Sarge's castle was all the way down to the studs. Only a few turrets were intact. It looked like he'd called in an airstrike and decimated everything but his cot, where he now slept, arms crossed, sans blanket, content to lie out in the open, victorious in his olive-green military issued tank and shorts. Even his deep, rhythmic breaths were disciplined, more like mini drills for his lungs than rest.

My steps slowed as I broke from my crouch. I was too stunned to care. It was all over anyway. Minutes passed. I stared at the sparse remains of his quarters. The extension cords duct-taped to the floor, the chin-up bar he'd set up. Even as I'd known Sarge was going to win, seeing it like this—all the empty space—hit me hard. I might as well start packing. This thing really was over, he'd be done with this by morning.

I shook my head, dropped my shoulders, and turned to leave.

"Max."

I jumped, stumbled, and nearly fell on my face. When I recovered, Sarge was sitting up, his back straight and his eyes clear already, as though he'd been awake for hours. He set his feet on the floor, and I was about to take off running, but he only grinned.

"Not bad, huh?" he said, palms up, looking around.

I sighed in relief, beckoned by his softer tone. For once he wasn't rough and gruff. In fact, he sounded almost normal. And, had he just smiled? I slid back to the ropes.

"Looks like the platoon came to your rescue."

Sarge reached high and stretched, the pride in his eyes shining even in the dark. He took me in with those laser brown eyes. "What are you doing out, anyway?"

"Oh, couldn't sleep."

"Aren't you worried about patrol?"

"*Patrol?* Have you *seen* Gary?"

He nodded. "Yeah, he wished me well."

Maybe I was trying to impress the mighty military man, or maybe it was that I knew it was over, but I ducked under a two by four and kicked at the extension cord taped to the floor. "I've learned their schedules," I stated proudly. Then, looking off. "I mean, it's not exactly recon or anything."

Sarge laughed. Again, not something I would've thought he was capable of until now. But there, in the wee hours of the morning, he didn't seem much like himself. He rubbed his eyes, then hung his head.

I inched closer. "You okay?"

He glanced up, nodded. "Yeah. Well, I guess I can tell you. I've been called up. They gave me twelve hours. I'm set to leave in the morning."

I stumbled back. "What? Like, win this thing and leave, or...?"

His mouth was tight again. "Bosnia."

"Oh." I struggled with a map in my mind, where Bosnia was —somewhere near Russia was as far as my brain took me. "What about..." Here we were talking about halfway around the world, some soda contest sounded dumb. "So," I checked for security and lowered my voice, "so what are you still doing here?"

He smiled, gestured toward the turrets. "Thought maybe I could finish this thing off first. But it looks like I didn't make it."

I cocked my head, still trying to understand. "So why..."

"Why am I still here?" Sarge wiped his massive hands on his legs. When he looked up, I saw nothing but pain and loss in his dull stare. "I've got nowhere else to go."

I wasn't sure what to say.

He saw my confusion and shook his head. "No, I've got a home, but... Well, I've spent twenty years in the military. When I come home, the house is empty and..." He shrugged. "Nowhere to go."

Ten minutes ago, I had no idea I could feel sorry for the guy. But now, seeing him slumped on the cot, the soda cans, the porta-potty and fridge, it felt so...sad.

"You're not married or anything?"

"My wife died ten years ago. Car accident. I was in Libya when it happened."

Damn. "Man, I'm so sorry."

He nodded solemnly. "Night before I found out, we had a strike. Didn't get back until five days later. Haven't wanted to be home since."

"Oh."

"Since then, I kept deploying. And almost hoping..." He threw his arms out.

Chills ran down my arms. I couldn't believe what I was hearing. Then again, it was clear this machine-like man had seen some stuff, had his heart broken, and kept diving back into conflicts to avoid having to stop and think about it for too long.

Sarge must have seen my reaction. He chuckled. "Hey, this gives you a chance, though. Right?"

I was too caught up in what he'd implied. I nodded,

shrugged, stared at the floor. "Yeah, I mean, well, it puts me in third place."

"Ha. Come on, kid. Those Radio Shack promos are helping. Keep doing those and play it up. You've never been afraid to look like an idiot before, don't stop now."

My eyes widened. "Was that a joke? Did you make a joke?"

He nodded. I laughed, but it was short-lived. I hadn't checked for security in a while, but it was kind of hard to think about the contest with Sarge confessing things like this in the dark. But when his eyes swept past me, taking in the perimeter, I knew I was pushing it.

I followed his gaze and surveyed the area. "Well, I guess I have to get back. But if I don't see you..."

"Good luck to you, Max. Remember, stay positive, keep hustling. Keep doing the promos. You can pull this off."

"How many cans do you have left?" I gazed at that last wall.

"Less than a thousand. It's a shame, huh? I had this thing licked."

"You really did. And they won't let you finish off?"

"Orders are orders. I've got to go. And between you and me, I don't care too much about winning a mall contest. I was just keeping busy."

"Well, job done, man—sir. Okay, well, good luck with everything." I wasn't sure what else to say after what he'd told me. "And I hope things get better, for..."

"Thanks, kid. Now take off before you get caught."

I managed one last look at Sergeant Jerome Cardwell. He'd taken this contest by storm and now he couldn't see it through. But something about him, about the way he spoke of orders told me he was ready to move on to the next mission. He didn't like being here, in town, in the mall, anywhere but on assignment.

I set off with a newfound determination. If Sarge believed I could win, then I did too. Carefully, I worked my way back across the mall, hiding, ducking, crouching, and sprinting my way to Castle One. Because up until a few minutes ago, I'd thought it was all over. I'd failed, and there was nothing left to do but move into Jason's house. But now, with the news of Sarge leaving, there was a chance.

That is, if Gary hadn't already found out I was gone.

17

Early Friday morning, the remaining contestants were summoned to the back room for cheap coffee and stale donuts. As we gathered, the mood was somber. Security lined the wall, faces drawn as though they'd lost one of their own, while the rest of us stared at each other until Marissa swept through the door, clutching her notebooks as she thanked us for coming to this emergency meeting.

Percy said he had nowhere to be. Marissa closed her eyes and smiled at his joke before she dove in. She regrettably informed us that Sergeant Jerome Cardwell had been called in on a peacekeeping mission and was withdrawing from the contest.

Julie let out a small gasp. Percy didn't seem fazed either way as he sat in his chair, fiddling with a set of keys as Marissa went on about military duty and how they were going to do all they could to support his efforts—whatever that meant.

I did my best to appear surprised but felt like roadkill after all the running around last night. I'd only made it back to my castle when good old Gary hung a left for the bathroom, giving me the opportunity to hustle in and hop in my cot before he shuffled past without a second glance.

Marissa closed her notes and shifted gears with a smile. "So, that leaves the three of you. And we wish you the best of luck the rest of the way."

As we got to our feet, I went for a refill on my coffee. Julie, still bleary-eyed and yawning, leaned in close. "Wow, what in the world?"

I checked to make sure Marissa wasn't listening. "I saw him last night, right after I left your place."

"Did he say anything. Was he upset?"

I shrugged. Percy moseyed off. "Yeah. I mean, not upset, just..." I thought back to Sarge on his cot, looking off, talking about his wife in the dark. It seemed so private. "I think he was ready to go. You know how he is, all military all the time. And hey, lucky for you. He would've easily been done today."

Behind us, Marissa cleared her throat, her way of telling us it was time to get back.

Julie pulled away and shot me a smile. "So, then there were three."

"Yep."

She smirked. "And I think Percy is up to something."

"Like what? Whittling?"

Julie slapped my arm.

Marissa nodded our way. "Hey, guys, time to go."

I went for a donut. Julie fixed a cup of coffee. She glanced back. Marissa went over something with Gary and security. Julie ducked her head and whispered. "I don't know what he has planned. But we should find out."

"Tonight?"

Julie gave me a quick nod and a smile before she switched back to the ditzy routine. "Well, looks like I've got some sodas to sell."

She flounced off, and I snagged another donut for the road. When I turned to follow, I caught Marissa staring at me. She raised an eyebrow, as though to tell me she knew all she needed to know.

I got on my way.

Scottie Snyder looked like he needed a shave and a nap as he stopped by to pick up my latest promo tapes. Since Radio Shack had been airing them, the radio station and possibly WLET had expressed interest as well.

We joked some about the Mad Max routine, but Scottie looked to be in a hurry. He promised to run the audio every hour on the hour. I asked if it was a violation of the rules, and he shot me a look. "Are you kidding? Mention the station and we'll run ads from anyone who has them. We're not playing favorites."

His face was puffy, with dark cycles under his eyes and a five o'clock shadow at ten in the morning. He was always hustling on the side—nightclubs, dances, weddings—whatever he could find to pick up a few bucks. And as always, he enjoyed the perks of his profession—like, well, drinks on-the-house.

I almost asked about the rigged alternate position but let it pass. He seemed a bit grumpy for questions. He was on his way out when I told him about Sarge dropping out.

"Really." He shot me a smile. "Well, that's good news, huh?" He regarded my castle and grimaced. "You need to get moving on this. That hot chick has sold two walls already."

"Two?"

"Yeah, she's out there in a bikini," he said with a pervy grin. "Got the old folks all worked up about it." I wasn't sure what he meant, but before I could ask, he held the tape up as a goodbye.

"Oh hey, I'll be spinning records at Bailey's tonight. Stop in and I'll give you a shoutout."

I shrugged. "We can't exactly leave."

"Oh, right," he said, only half listening. "Okay, well if you change your mind, come on in." He shook the tape again. "I'll get these on."

Mom arrived around eleven. She was all put together and more chipper than usual—something I attributed to me being out of the house. Her cruise sunburn had tanned, and she'd done something to her hair at the salon. She glanced around and smiled. "I can't believe this. They have you on at the Radio Shack."

"Yeah." I told her about the radio ads, and her eyes brightened.

She smiled the way she did for customers at work, never for me. It was like she was seeing someone else. "Max, I think you might have a future in advertising. You know, you should talk to Mr. Snyder about a sales position and maybe you could take some courses and—"

"Mom," I laughed. "I'm only trying to win a contest."

Her smile fell. "Well, it wouldn't hurt, is all I mean."

So much for that. I sucked in a breath, allowing her to have the last word.

She adjusted her pocketbook straps. "Rob is here, somewhere. I think he popped into Sears. He wants to buy a couple of cases of Mountain Dew. Isn't that sweet?"

"Very sweet. Lots of sugar in those things," I said as a joke. But Mom wasn't listening. "I mean, thanks. That's really cool."

"Well, make sure to thank *him*," she said.

"Hey, look at it as an investment. If you guys buy me out, you won't have to worry about me coming home." I don't know why I couldn't let it go, but that one did it.

Her eyes sharpened, and it was back to normal for us. "He's trying to be nice, Max."

Cashier Lady rang up some kids buying sodas. They held them up to show me. "Yo, Max."

I pumped my fist like a dork. "Right on. Thanks, guys!"

Mom raised her brow. "Right on?"

I shrugged. The kids started with the howling, then came the chants, spreading down the line until I came out and took my ovation. I waved and thanked them for coming out. I wasn't about to howl with Mom in there. Maybe I'd tell my fans she was my lawyer or probation officer or something. Not too far off on that last one, anyway.

If she'd been star-struck earlier, all that shine was gone. She was looking much too Mom-ish with her high-waist jeans and her big purse and her hand on my shoulder. "I always knew you could do something with your life if you tried. Where did you come up with that anyway? Sounds like something your dad would have done."

I snapped back to attention. My mom hardly ever mentioned Dad, who'd remarried a few years back and lived in Ohio.

Rob swooped in before I could respond, saving us from any further awkwardness. He ducked in my castle and set his arm around Mom. "Well, this is it, huh? Your humble abode."

Say what you wanted about the guy, but he could diffuse any situation with his corniness. He took a big breath and looked around. "Nice bachelor pad, chief."

I glanced at Mom, still hung up on her mentioning Dad, while Rob marveled at the can placement, the way they were stacked, going on about the engineering of the castle design or something dorky. When he came upon the gaping hole where I'd actually sold some sodas, he whistled. "Nice going, champ. This is wide enough to drive a car through."

The kids continued with the howling. People outside huddled around. Now that I was moving soda, I'd have to get used to living in a glass bowl. I was all set to kick Mom and Rob out when Rob went for his wallet.

"Tell you what," Rob said, rocking back on his heels. "I'm going to take twenty six-packs off your wall, what do you say?"

"Oh Rob, that's so nice." Mom's eyes grew with surprise. I knew she was doing the numbers on how much that would cost. But it *was* nice. My biggest sale yet. Too big actually.

"Seriously? Thanks, Rob. But there's a ten six-pack limit."

"Oh really? Well okay, I'll take the max, Max."

I winced, as it physically hurt to stand there and laugh at Rob's jokes. Even Mom's face tightened before she forced a lopsided smile. But a sale is a sale, so I helped Rob take some six-packs to the front, and Cashier Lady rang up his total—$24.13, after taxes. Good old Rob loaded up a hand truck and hauled them out to the parking lot. Mom hung back as he left.

"He thinks this is so neat that you're doing this, Max. It's all he talks about."

While Mom thought it was neat, a line was snaking around my castle, fans chanting, howling, all worked up over the Radio Shack ads. I was caught between playing Mad Max and coaxing Mom out as the six-packs came down from all directions. Mom watched it all with a smile, still prattling on about my future, excited that I might actually win the contest and would be out of her hair for good.

I didn't have the heart to tell her about Julie doing so well at her castle. Still, I needed to tamper down her high expectations. "Just so you know, I'm probably not going to win. Julie's way ahead, and Percy too. Maybe."

Mom chided me, told me to stay positive, advice she never heeded herself. Eventually Rob came back, breathing heavy and looking awfully proud. He nodded and smiled at the middle schoolers. He even threw his arms up in victory, revealing two matching pit stains on his short-sleeve plaid button-down. But I had to give the guy some credit. He made Mom happy.

"Thanks again, Rob."

"My pleasure. The guys at the office will love me for it."

Mom adjusted her hair and nodded. "Well, I have appointments. I'll come by tomorrow, okay, sweetie?"

I watched Mom take Rob's elbow as they left. She leaned in and said something into his ear, probably gently scolding him for spending so much money on her loser townie son.

Time to get to work. I went full tilt on the Mad Max, shoving the camcorder in the faces of unsuspecting customers, mall walkers, and security guards alike. I ran down the line, giving high fives, dancing and yelling and howling until I stumbled upon Dre at the back of the line.

He was lugging a huge box that he nearly dropped he was laughing so hard. I waved him over, and he entered my castle, Cashier Lady's eyes clinging to his every move.

Dre set the box on the floor. "Yo, I've seen it on TV but never in person. Where'd you come up with this little act?"

I laughed. "I don't know, bored one night, I guess. So what's in the box?"

"Well, it's working, whatever all"—he waved a hand in my general direction— "this is. Anyway, Frank, the regional manager guy, wants to 'pounce on this publicity,' so he sent a hundred of these down."

He had a box full of brand-new Clean Car trucker hats. He pulled one out and set it on his head. "How do I look?"

"Good to me," Cashier Lady purred from outside. She had a line of kids to ring up and still her head was on a swivel.

Dre shot her a smile. "Thanks, Bonnie."

Bonnie? "Hold up." I stomped out to the entrance. "One, gross. Two, he knows your name? I don't know your name."

She shrugged, all but looking through me.

I threw my hands up. "Can we get some privacy in here?"

Dre waved me back in. "Lunch?"

"Yeah." I shot Cashier Lady—*Bonnie*—one last nasty look. "Let me charge up my camera."

We took a quick detour by Percy's castle. Dre was all jacked up about the news of Sarge leaving, calling it my second chance, spouting all kinds of crazy promotional ideas, until we arrived at Percy's castle. Then he saw for himself how far behind I still was.

Dre only shook his head. "So dude sits on a rocking chair, fiddling with keys, and he's *still* beating you? You gotta do more."

"Like what, give out *hats*?" I said, gesturing to the five or so hats he'd brought along. I took a breath. "Look, sorry, man. I'm stressed. I know, I suck. I did give some promos to Scottie Snyder. Hopefully, that will help. How's Carol, anyway?"

"You don't want to know." He shrugged. "She's huffing and puffing like always. When we get busy, she likes to say 'Well, at least Max is nice and comfortable at the mall.' She's threatening to hire someone."

I stopped in my tracks. "What? She gave me two weeks. And she's still mad? Even with management backing me?" I nodded at the hats.

"It's Carol, man. What can I say?" Dre nudged my shoulder. We were getting noticed now as we walked, kids pointing, some asking to take my picture. I posed for a few photos, and Dre perked up. "This is more like it. See?" he said, handing out a couple hats. He uncapped a Sharpie and gave it to me. To my disbelief, the kids' faces lit up. "It's all about the swag."

I was signing hats when I heard a familiar voice. "Hey, Max."

I glanced up to find Adam, Tara's little brother, with some friends. He wasn't smirking or giggling and seemed almost sheepish as he stepped forward, his hands clutching the knotted sleeves of the sweatshirt tied around his waist. "This is rad, man."

"Yeah," I said, noting his change in tone.

Again, no smirking or snorting. He dropped his gaze to his scuffed Airwalk sneakers.

I snatched a hat from Dre. "Hey, you want a hat?"

His face lit up. "Yeah, dude. Awesome. Thanks, man."

"Yeah, here." I gave his friends hats too. They closed in around Dre and me. Then, because I couldn't resist. "Tell Tara I said hi."

Dre closed his eyes, but Adam only nodded, still smiling at the hat. "I will. I will. Hey, could you, like?" He nodded to the Sharpie in my hand.

"Oh, sure."

I was feeling good about myself as I signed Adam's hat, his friends' hats, until they set them on their heads backward and Adam told everyone how I used to date his sister. It was still like a punch to the gut. *Used to.*

Dre got me turned around, talking about how this was all working out. He was laughing and carrying on about it right until we came up on Julie's spot.

She was on full display in her bikini top, her jean cut-offs leaving little to the imagination as she paraded around what was no longer a castle but a pile of cans.

Dre, being ever-so-helpful, set a hand on my shoulder. "Well, I can see why you're losing to her, at least."

"I don't believe this."

"Hey. Don't hate on the girl because she's got a plan. It's working too."

"I have a plan."

"Oh, yeah. I saw it too. Begging Tara's little brother to help you get back with her. Nice."

Julie waved at us. We waved back as she took a running start and did a cartwheel. The crowd ate it up.

Dre shook his head. "You got work to do, homie."

I reminded him once again of the ads, how they were going to do the work for me.

Dre waved to Julie. "Yeah, that's right. The ads. I guess we'll see."

Whatever Dre thought about my plan, the ads aired later that day. I heard the first one when I got back to my castle.

This is Mad Max coming at you live from Castle Numero Uno at RiverView Mall. I'm asking you, Flash 102 fans, to come out and show out, buy some Pepsi and set me free. Mad Max, out.

All I could do was cringe at my voice. I sounded like a tool. But something happened. That afternoon the line formed and wrapped around my castle, twice. I quickly ran out of hats and had to hustle to entertain them, seeing how everyone could now easily see all the way inside to my cot. If this is what it took, I had to go all in.

"What's up, party peeps? Who wants a Pepsi or six?"

Again, my "fans" were mostly middle school boys, so I did what I had to do. I slapped hands, made fart jokes, and otherwise continued to be as obnoxious as possible. And while Dre was content to laugh at me, the side wall of Castle One was reduced to a waist-high barrier as the boys moved in closer, even if it did feel like we were gathering around a Boy Scout campfire.

"Okay, so I've been here what, five days, right. Let me tell you some of the things that go down here at night."

Bonnie kept giving me the side eye, but she was busy ringing people up, as sales were soaring and kids were proudly wearing Clean Car hats, taking polaroids, and eating up all the nonsense I was spouting. "I was riding my motorcycle through here and—"

A kid, maybe fourteen, looked up. "You rode a motorcycle? Like, in the mall?"

"Yeah, man, do it all the time. You can see the scuff marks. Here and here." I pointed to some tire marks as evidence, marks probably left by the bucket trucks when building the castle.

"Whoa."

They hung on my every word, eyes rapt with hope and anticipation as they begged me to show them, speak for them, until I almost felt like I was something more than a townie who didn't have the motivation to register for a couple of classes at community college. I was something like a leader. To them, at least.

Mad Max didn't play by the rules. He bucked authority. He snuck around, chugged down soda, slung the can, and rode wheelies through the mall. Caught up in the moment, I continued, "Security tried to catch me, but..." I glanced off, where Bonnie shot me another smirk. I shot it back at her. She smiled, as though proud of me for finally putting something together. "Pfft, they can't catch me."

I gazed out to my legion of fans decked in Clean Car gear. I spotted Adam in the mix, and I gave him a nod. He joined in as they started chanting my name.

All I could do was smile. Finally, I was getting some attention.

18

Later that night, I lay in my cot, staring at the skylight. My brain was like Jell-O from playing Mad Max all day, but I was feeling good about how things were turning around, dreaming of a new truck and money, when Julie strolled through the front arch of my castle.

"Get up."

I scrambled to my feet. It was only around ten, so I was looking around for security but at the same time thinking about how my hair must look after wearing the hat all day.

Julie smirked at the stupid poster. "What's this?"

"Oh, nothing."

"*Ear* the Sears?"

I pointed to it. "Can't you see where I fixed it?"

Julie snorted, watching me as I rolled up the poster.

"Yeah, yeah. It's dumb."

Her black hoodie was zipped to her neck. She'd ditched the short cut-offs for black jeans.

I fixed my hair the best I could. "So, what's going on? Why are you dressed like a cat burglar?"

She glanced down at herself, then popped up with a smile. "I was thinking we could all have a little fun." She called over her shoulder. "Right, Perce?"

"What?" I craned my head to see outside. Sure enough, there he was, counting the floor tiles.

Julie smiled at my confusion, as though reading my thoughts and fears of getting busted. "As I told Percy, I don't plan on getting caught, but...in the event we do, it's better that all of us are out. Because what are they going to do then, right?" She crossed her arms and cocked her head, awfully proud of herself. Her dazzling smile reached her eyes, and she must have known neither Percy nor I would stop her. Besides, she had a point.

I put on my shoes and started for the entrance when she called me back. "Here, take some old clothes." She gestured to my dirty clothes on the floor and wrinkled her nose. She motioned to the cot. "You know, put some under the covers. Didn't you ever sneak out before?"

I bundled up the clothes. "Oh, right. Of course." I stuffed a sweatshirt and pair of jeans in a lump, pulled the covers up high, and looked at Julie. "Is that good enough?"

"Sure. Now come on."

Percy was nimbler than I gave him credit for, and a tinge of irritation came over me watching how he hustled to keep up with Julie's swinging strides. I shook my head and mumbled, "Rocking chair, my ass."

Julie glanced over her shoulder. "What's that, Max?"

"Nothing."

A faint thump of music carried to us as we approached the south end, and I remembered Scottie Snyder was DJing tonight. "Wait." My steps slowed as I pieced it together. "We're not going to Bailey's, right?"

Julie turned to me, walking backwards. "We are going to rock some karaoke."

"You've got to be kidding me."

"Nope, not kidding."

She wasn't. Percy and Julie strolled right up to Bailey's, where a bouncer the size of a Volkswagen sat slumped on a stool. I glanced back to the open mall, about to tell Julie to forget it, when she took me by the elbow and whispered in my ear. "Relax, we got this."

I started to protest, but she broke off and sauntered over to the door. Reluctantly, I followed while Percy hung a few steps back.

Julie jump-stopped in front of the bouncer and greeted him with a smile. "Hi."

I noticed the zipper had found its way down some on her sweatshirt. The bouncer gave her a full once over. His mustache curled as he grinned. "Hello, princess."

Julie laughed as though he'd made some fantastic joke. "We are here to own karaoke night."

The bouncer's grin fell flat. He looked to me, then to Percy. "I don't think so."

She cocked her head. "And why is that?"

To my disbelief, the guy waved right past me to Percy. "The guy's like a hundred. I can't be responsible for him giving out in our bar."

The way Julie's leg bent at the knee, the tilt of her head as her lips puckered into a perfect pout, made me think she'd done this kind of thing before. She knocked her head back. "That, is my grandfather, and you should hear him sing."

The bouncer sighed. Inside the bar, someone was murdering Montel Jordan's *This Is How We Do It*. Julie nodded a bit to the beat while Bouncer Dude mulled it over. Then his eyes snapped open. "Wait. Are you three, the uh? Yeah. Ya'll are the mall contestants, right? That King of the Mall thing."

"Queen," Julie said with a smile. She did another little curtsy bow. "Queen of the Mall. And yes. It is us. We are they."

Mercifully, the song ended to some scattered applause. I glanced back, hoping Gary had decided to stay clear of all the noise, when the bouncer, now sitting a little straighter, a bit more interested, gestured to the entrance.

"Okay, well, in that case, have a good time."

Julie squealed.

We started inside when the bouncer pulled me to the side. "Stick with Sprite, kid."

"Yeah. Sure. Well, probably Pepsi, if you know what I mean," I said with a laugh. The bouncer stared me down until I looked away.

He turned to Percy. "You too, old man."

Percy smacked his lips. "Okie dokie, karaoke."

With that, we entered the dark into a crush of smoke and bodies. Julie weaved and bounced, bobbing her way to the bar while Percy and I fought through the bodies.

Julie slipped into a spot between stools, where she set her elbows on the bar and read from a drink menu. I tried to play it cool, although the only bar I'd been to was a dive near downtown where they didn't card and served flat, lukewarm pitchers of Natty Lite for three bucks. While I might not have been accustomed to the bar scene, Julie had the bartender's attention in seconds. It was clear she knew what she was doing.

Percy and I eventually managed to push our way to her. "Okay," Julie said, flipping through a notebook on the bar, the pages in plastic sleeves. "What should we sing?"

"Nope." I shook my head. "I'm not singing."

She continued scanning songs. "Perce, what do you think? Disco era? Modern? Help me out here."

Three frozen drinks arrived on the bar. Julie popped up from the song menu and beamed. "Ah, Virgin Daiquiris."

I nodded at the drinks, realizing I had no money. "Very responsible."

"I'd say." She pinched the straw to her drink with a slight hitch to her smile. "I don't drink. I know all too well the stupid superpowers of a drunk."

I was about to ask why we'd chosen to sneak off to a bar in the first place when the bartender, who looked around Julie's age, announced our drinks were on the house. Julie winked at me, then asked Percy to make a toast. Percy hoisted the ridiculous pink glass and nodded to the bartender. "To the confusion of our enemies."

Julie's smile broadened. "Yes, I love it. Good one, Perce!" She held her drink up and looked at me. "To your confusion, Max."

"Wait, what? How am I—" Before I could protest, Julie reached out and tipped my glass up. We all took a drink.

"Tasty," she said, slapping the notebook shut. She snatched a pencil, filled out a scrap of paper, and waved it at Percy and me. "Okay, gentlemen, we have a song."

There was no stopping her as she took her drink and spun off in the direction of Scottie Snyder.

Scottie was busy chatting up a couple ladies when he saw us approaching. "Hey, guys, you made it. Enjoying the field trip?"

Julie handed him our song. "Something like that."

Scottie looked at the selection and frowned. "Ah, well. You're a little late on that one."

"What do you mean?" Julie asked with a pout. The light flashed over her face, and I found it hard to look away—the way her freckles bunched together when she wrinkled her nose.

Scottie nodded to the stage. "Well, that's Griz's song. You can still do it," he grinned, "if you dare."

I nodded to Scottie. "Griz? Do what song?" I turned back to Julie. "What did you pick?"

Julie shook her head. "It's a surprise. Well, it was."

The lights dimmed to a spotlight as a middle-aged man with a half-tucked button-down shirt stumbled onto the stage. He was flushed, obviously drunk. The crown of his bald head shined like a bowling ball while the hair on the sides was swept up like a fin. He looked like he'd dressed for work in the office only to fight through a hurricane.

Scottie whispered to us as the man adjusted the microphone. "That's Griz. Guy thinks he's a rock star. It was hilarious the first time. Now it's just annoying."

"Oh?" Julie sipped her drink, holding the straw with her thumb and forefinger, her gaze trained on Griz, who had his head bowed and his hands on his hips as the room fell silent.

"Prepare to be wowed," Scottie said, covering his mike. He rolled his eyes and pressed play on the CD player.

"At first I was afraid, I was petrified..."

I staggered back a step, spilling some daiquiri as a high-pitched shriek erupted from the short, plump, intoxicated banker. So many thoughts, but first...

"You wanted us to do *this song?*"

"Shh." Julie smacked my arm, her eyes wide. She let out a hoot, then started dancing. And it wasn't only her, the crowd ate it up. I wasn't sure what I was seeing as suddenly, the beat kicked in and Griz threw his head back and threw his hips into it.

The guy was a complete diva. Julie grabbed my forearm and leaned in close enough that I could smell the strawberry sweetness of her breath. "I'm going to change the song. No way we're following this."

I couldn't help laughing as she hustled off. I caught Scottie Snyder watching me with a raised brow. I quickly diverted my eyes, sipped my drink, and set my attention back to the stage.

Onstage, Griz shuffled and bopped and did his thing. Percy took it all in stride with a lopsided smile. Griz spun, dipped, and all but threw his back out as he became a disco legend. By the time it was over, he was back in his starting position, head bowed and hands at his hips as he awaited the applause. But the crowd seemed to be over it.

"All right, give it up for Griz," Scottie deadpanned. "The guy never fails to impress, does he?"

Griz was drenched and heaving as he swung off stage, where he'd left it all out there. A few people patted him on the back in passing as he marched straight to the bar and started flipping through the notebook.

Scottie waved me in. "The guy's wife left him last year. Since then he comes in and does like five songs a night," Scottie said, rolling his eyes. "Takes it wayyy too seriously."

Before I could respond, Julie was back. One look at the smile on her face and I knew we were in trouble. She handed Scottie a new card. "We're switching it up."

Scottie looked down at what she'd handed him and nearly spit his beer out. I glared at Julie, but it's hard to look imposing while holding a Virgin Daiquiri. "What did you choose?"

Julie smiled at me. "Relax. Just follow my lead, okay, boys?"

Percy, having drained his daiquiri, was looking a little loopy. I wondered if he'd gotten the real deal by mistake. No time to dwell on it though, because Scottie Snyder was calling us up.

"Okay, we've got a real treat up next. You may recognize these three from our very own King of the Mall contest. Give it up for Julie, Percy, and Mad Max."

The crowd came alive as we stepped up on stage, which was basically an eight by ten platform about six inches off the ground. I shot a glance to Julie, who took the microphone and addressed the drunks in the crowd. "As you know, there can only be one winner in the King of the Mall contest. So that means..."

The loose strumming of a guitar took the room, and I turned to her. Before I could say no, or stop her, or light myself on fire, Beck's *Loser* scrambled to life in the small bar. And without even a glimpse at the scrolling lyrics on the screen, Julie sang every word.

She killed it from the opening. I stood laughing until the chorus approached and she shimmied over to Percy and nudged him along. She pointed to the screen and showed him the words, which he read like a bedtime story as the song bumped along and left him behind.

"Oh, let's see here. 'I'm a loser baby, so why don't you kill me.'"

Julie and I fell into each other laughing. She hung on my shoulder, hardly able to keep any sort of composure before she gestured to the mike and mouthed "Your turn."

I shook my head. She shook hers. I stepped forward and attempted to get things back on track. "*Soy...un perdedor...*"

It went like that the rest of the way. Julie would speed rap to catch us up, then Percy would wander through a line, and I'd get the mike and try to keep a straight face as Julie performed the running man.

The crowd loved it. They moved in, hands in the air, singing along and cheering us on. At one point, I managed to catch sight of Griz, slumped at the bar, sipping on a tumbler. He shook his head and muttered in disgust at our lack of professionalism. Then Julie and I faced off and we broke into an old school kick step.

The song faded, and I was drenched in sweat. My face hurt from laughing. Percy was still alive, and Julie had shed her hoodie and stood glistening in a tank top.

The crowd roared in delight as we stumbled off stage,

smacking hands and dizzy from dancing. Julie clasped her hands and looked from Percy to me. "Okay, what next?"

"Next? Um, I hate to be a stick in the mud, but we should probably get back."

Julie shot me a devilish smile. "Actually, we've got all night."

19

Before I could ask Julie what she meant, we were mobbed, as bodies knocked against us in the dark, drunks hugging our necks and cheering us on. In all the commotion, I lost track of Percy, then Julie, as we were swept up in the tide. It was hard to tell what was up or down. I made my way forward, calling for Julie and Percy, when someone grabbed my hand. Julie, with Percy in tow, led the way as we snaked through the rush and started for the door.

Leaving the bar, I nodded to the bouncer, who looked away from the four college-aged guys he was carding. "Have a nice night."

Julie waved and kept walking. The air was cool on my face after the crowded, smokey bar, and it took a second to adjust to the screaming silence of the mall after the blaring music. It had to be after midnight by then, as I left Percy behind and hustled to catch up to Julie, who was still humming and swaying as she walked away.

A quick glance back to make sure the old man was still following, then I called ahead to Julie. "Hey, can you wait up?"

She turned, her feet scraping to a stop. I waited on Percy, still checking around to make sure we were in the clear.

"Want to tell me what's going on?" I said to Julie. "You've been so worried about getting busted, and now?"

Percy whistled "Loser."

Julie's cheeks were flushed and she looked like she was about to bust.

I was coming undone. I threw my arms out. "What?"

She rolled her eyes playfully. "Okay, so, Gary will be out of commission tonight."

"What?" I asked as Percy shuffled past us like a robot set to SLOW. He was meandering more left to right than straight ahead. I turned back to Julie. "What do you mean, *out of commission?*"

She giggled. "Well, he had a dentist appointment and he was on the gas." She cupped a hand to her nose. "Like, laughing gas? His wife dropped him off for work."

"Gas?" So many questions. For starters, how did she know that? But first, "Why is he working?"

She shrugged. "It's a security guard gig, not like he has sick days. I'm sure he clocked in and hit the sack. He'll be out all night."

"And Gary just came out and told you all this?"

At that, Julie cocked her head with a defiant smirk. "Yes. Yes, he did."

"Oh, okay." I took a breath, feeling the stress leave as I exhaled. I checked on Percy. "Okay, so what now?"

Julie followed my gaze to Percy, then bit her lip. "I don't know, but the night is young. Let's have some fun. Come on."

I glanced over my shoulder to Bailey's where Griz was back at it. *When a Man Loves a Woman* from the sound of things. Julie and I looked at each other and busted out laughing. Then we hurried to steer Percy clear of the jewelry store.

Hecht's department store stood at the south end of the mall, where the bay doors were pulled down, but the lights were on. The mannequins lining the walkways were dressed to impress and looking to mingle. Julie led us to the left, then pointed to a side door. Percy, without saying a word, walked up and wiggled the handle, finding it locked, of course. He grinned.

Julie smiled at me, wiggling her eyebrows as Percy went to work. Not for the first time, I wanted to know more about her, starting with her boyfriend and what happened the other day. But she was so alive and happy, buzzing with too much energy to stand still.

Two minutes later and the door swung open. Percy bowed, a proud smile on his face as he held the door for us. Julie nodded her thanks. I asked if he'd ever thought about cracking bank safes or if he'd pulled any heists. He pleaded the fifth.

A faint murmur of elevator music wafted overhead. I eyed the dark semi-globes holding the security cameras and waited for the alarm bells. I thought about Gary and the gas. I hoped Julie was right about Gary. Meanwhile, she strolled up to a rack, snatched a scarf, and threw it over her shoulder. "Look at all these old people clothes." She laughed and started flipping through the hangers of flowery blouses. "Sorry, Perce. No offense."

Percy, all twinkles and smiles, shook his head. "None taken."

I rolled my eyes. It seemed everyone was enamored with Julie. Again, I thought about how Sarge was gone, and I should be more focused on winning the contest. I had a real chance now, a chance I might blow doing karaoke and whatever we were doing now.

"Hmm, what else?" Julie said as she glanced over to the men's suit department. Her eyes lit up. "Okay, Max, ready for your fashion show?"

I backed off. "What? No."

"Yes, why not? Got some big plans tonight?"

Before I could answer she took my hand and led me to a rack of suits. She rifled through the sports coats before snatching one off the rack and pressing it to my chest, just under my chin. "No." She went back to work, this time she set a charcoal one up to me and smiled. "There. This one."

I laughed. "Julie, really." I looked around. "What if we get caught?"

"I'm not saying you should steal the suit. Just try it on. This was your idea, wasn't it?" She found a shirt and a vest and thrust it into my hands. "Go."

"Well...no. This was not my idea," I said, holding up the clothes. "What about Marissa?"

She set her hands on her hips. "Come on, Max. Do you honestly think she would cancel this thing? No. Way. Things are just getting interesting."

Clutching the clothes, I started for the dressing rooms. "This is nuts," I muttered to myself, shutting the door. Outside, Julie chatted up Percy.

I changed quickly, surprised at how the shirt, vest, and jacket fit perfectly. I buttoned up and finger combed my hair before I stepped out of the room, completely unprepared for what I found, which was Percy in a baggy hoodie, stocking cap, and sunglasses.

"Look, it's Gangster Percy." Julie laughed, but when she turned to face me, her eyes widened. "Oh, wow. Nice, Max." She nodded. "Very nice."

My cheeks warmed. I glanced down at myself. Button-down shirt, tie, suit. I fiddled with the jacket buttons. "I feel like a tool."

Julie shook her head as she approached. She bit her lip and looked me up and down. "No, you look fabulous."

Percy, however, had a golf club over his shoulder. I couldn't help laughing. "Seriously. What did you do to Percy?"

"We hit the sports and leisure department."

"Okay, so I can change back now." I turned for the dressing room when Julie grabbed my arm. I spun around quickly, and we drew close. A gust of her breath hit my chin. Her face flushed before she backed off with a smile.

"Nope. No changing," she said, tapping her chin with her finger. "Hmm, now it's my turn."

Julie dashed off for a dress, leaving me alone with Percy, who was still in his stocking cap and sunglasses. He regarded me with a smile. "You clean up well, young man."

"Umm, thanks."

Worried as I was about getting busted, I got caught up in the thrill of roaming around a closed department store in the middle of the night, decked out in half a suit, chasing Julie around. It was all so weird—the day, night, the week for that matter—but a good kind of weird.

Percy lost the sunglasses in our rush, then shed the stocking cap and the hoodie. At some point, I turned around and realized he was nowhere to be found. I had to double back where I found him sitting on a bench, trying to tug on a pair of loafers. I sat down beside him when Julie appeared out of the shadows, shimmering in a full-length, silk dinner gown.

I got to my feet in a rush, until I realized I'd forgotten what I was going to say.

Green, low cut, and clinging to her waist, the dress caught the lighting as well as my breath. She twirled around, pulled her hair up on her head, then craned her neck, glancing down to her feet. "Well, I suppose this will have to do."

"Marvelous," Percy supplied.

Julie thanked him graciously. She pursed her lips and looked at me. "Well?"

I nodded. "Yeah."

She rolled her eyes, then slid across the polished floor like she was floating, humming along with the elevator music. It was quite a transformation, from the girl in the zip-up hoodie who'd gotten on stage and sung the wheels off of "Loser," to now, this beautiful aberration before me.

Percy got the loafers on his feet, and we followed Julie to the escalator, which was turned off, so we climbed it like stairs up to the Home and Kitchen section. Even in the dress, Julie was like a kid at an amusement park, marveling over blenders, microwaves, taking calls on cordless phones. Everything she touched became magic as she presented the most mundane items with flourish. When she caught me staring as we arrived at the linens, she shot me a sly smile, then took off running and leaped onto one of the beds on display.

She patted the spot beside her, and I followed, leaving some space between us. Percy settled in on the other side, and maybe it should've been weird, the three of us laying on a bed in some dark, closed department store in the middle of the night, but then Percy leaned over to the bedside table and clicked a button and a mini star projector whirred to life. Suddenly, we were laying beneath a starry sky.

Julie gazed up at the manufactured constellations with a childlike wonder on her face, still heaving and smiling. Again, none of it seemed real, how I'd gone from begging Jason for a favor after getting kicked out of Mom's place, to laying here, in a suit, with a gorgeous woman in a dinner dress. Oh, and there was Percy.

With a grunt, he announced that he needed a nap. He rose, then fell onto the extra fluffy pillows arranged on the queen-sized bed beside us. He was snoring within seconds.

Julie reached over and took my hand. She let out a gusty

breath. Her eyes shone in the starlight. She wasn't crying, but she was close to it.

"So, how are you doing? I mean, with the other day and all?" I asked.

Her smile fell and her hand left mine. She flipped over on her side to face me full on. I did my best not to glance down even as she was basically spilling out of the dress.

"I'm okay. I mean, I knew I was doing this for my little girl, not Bryan. So, if he wants to call me a slut or whatever," she shrugged, "so be it, you know?"

Bryan. Mini-Truck Guy. I looked off, then back to Julie. "Can I ask you something?" Her eyes narrowed, and I should've stopped right there. And maybe it was the dark, the stars above our heads, the dress, but I continued. "Why are you with someone who'd make you feel like that?"

I was asking some really bad questions. But I didn't understand it. Julie was so lit up, so fun and amazing. It killed me to think she was with someone who didn't appreciate her.

She glanced over my shoulder, then into my eyes. Five or ten seconds, like she was thinking about what to say. Then she flopped onto her back. "It's not so easy, Max."

I wanted to ask her more about it. About her daughter. Where she lived or what she wanted to do. But before I could figure out how to approach it, she rolled the other way, out of bed, and started off in the dark.

"Julie, wait." I took off after her, which wasn't far. I found her in the dark, clutching herself at the stomach. "Look, I'm sorry, I didn't mean to—"

She flung herself around. "You think it's what I wanted? That it was my plan to live in a trailer park and date a jerk? Because it wasn't what I wanted. Not at all."

"Julie, no, I didn't mean it like that. I'm sorry."

She started sobbing. I reached for her, but she shook her

head and tore away from me. "I wanted to do all sorts of things—travel, go to school, see people and things, and figure it all out. Teach. I've always wanted to be a kindergarten teacher. It's my dream. But I never got that chance. And it's okay, totally okay. My whole life is my girl."

The traveling thing made me think of Tara. How Julie had those same dreams but didn't see any way to achieve them. Sure, she had a kid, but that didn't mean she couldn't do things. "Julie, you can still do...whatever. Look at you. You're going to win this contest."

Soon as I said it, she turned to me, her lips parted. Then she looked away. "It's not so easy. Even if this worked out...I don't know what I'm going to do, either way."

I set my arm around her, and she fell into me, wiping her face. "I just miss her so much. It's funny, it's only been a few days and it feels like months."

"It kind of does, huh?"

"Yeah," she sniffled.

"I think it's the lack of sunlight messing with us. But you're doing better than me. My mom kicked me out. How loser-ish is that?"

She giggled, still wiping her eyes. "You're not a loser, Max. Not even close. Trust me on this one. I know a loser when I meet one."

"Well, I..."

When she looked up, we stared at each other. I fell into her eyes, green and captivating even in the dark. I held my breath. I wanted to console her, help her figure this out. But more than anything, I wanted to kiss her. And it was then that it hit me. For the first time, I realized I could live without Tara. I could care about someone else.

Julie blinked and I laughed. "I think you'd make the best kindergarten teacher."

Her smile drew me in, closer. I shuffled forward, and her smile fell, and her eyes widened, and I probably would have gone for it when something crashed behind us.

We jerked apart and found Percy up and shuffling around. "Say, you folks want to take in a movie?"

Julie pulled away, still looking at me, her smile in full bloom again. "Ooh, hear that? Percy wants to take in a movie."

"Aren't we sort of pushing things a bit?"

Julie slapped my arm. "Oh, stop being a lump." She turned to Percy and offered her arm. "Lead the way, sir."

He hooked his elbow with her arm, and they started off. I looked around, wondering how this night was going to end.

20

W e changed back to our old clothes and left Hecht's for the most part the way we found it. Percy shut and locked the side door, and we waved goodbye to the mannequins as we started off for the movie theater.

Personally, I'd had enough fun for the night. Gary or no Gary, it felt risky to stay out. I was caught up in the almost kiss, and I was still thinking about what Julie had said about her daughter and all those things she'd said she couldn't do. And yet I followed along, looking out for guards until we reached the cinema, where Sandra Bullock's giant face watched me from a movie poster.

Julie was back to bouncing and giggling as I checked for guards for maybe the thousandth time while we slunk through the entrance.

"Wow. So we're really doing this, huh?" I said, rocking back on my heels.

Percy eyeballed the candy behind the glass counter. Julie furrowed her brow in confusion, as though I were the one making no sense instead of being the lone voice of reason. "Yes, we are. Live a little, Max."

"Live a little," I repeated. Like this was the master plan, watching a movie at—I checked my watch—1:13. Julie and Percy breezed past the ticket booth, and I thought about ditching. This wasn't going to end well. Instead, I chased after them. "And how, umm, are we supposed to...oh, right."

Percy dug in his pocket and came out with some kind of tool. He went to work on the door, and I turned to Julie for help, as I'd given up talking to him directly. "What's he doing?"

Julie watched with glee. "Well, Percy here worked at a movie theater for what, three years? Is that right?"

"Yes, dear. That's right. I worked the Grand Theater over on Fifth Street back in forty-eight. I think it's been gutted and turned into condominiums."

Julie kept an unfaltering smile trained on me. "Sooo, there. A locksmith *and* a projectionist."

I rolled my eyes. "Projectionist?"

She clasped her hands together and jumped. "Yay. Now, what should we watch?"

Percy wasn't done reminiscing. "Oh, yes. For years we did films down there. Then I volunteered at the Holden Cinema over off of...uhh, oh my mind fails me."

"Holden Road," I supplied, trying to move things along. My impatience was showing because this was ridiculous.

The old man's bushy eyebrows wiggled. "Yes, that's the one."

Julie shot me a stern "be nice" glare, and I sent it right back to her. She'd gone back to humming "Loser" when Percy said, "There we go," and the door swung open. We found ourselves looking up a flight of stairs. Julie squealed.

Percy rolled a hand toward the stairs. "Welcome to RiverView Cinema."

I took another glance at the entrance. "This is undeniably stupid."

"*You're* stupid," she said, cocking her head.

Upstairs it was all canisters and fans and vents and discarded drinks on the floor. Percy looked around as he got himself situated. "Ahh, standard changeover configuration, this should be a breeze."

My jaw clenched. I kept an eye on the door, waiting for *someone*—if not the police—to storm the stairs with guns drawn. Seemed we were taking things a bit far, relying on one guard's dental visit to run rampant all over the mall. Percy didn't seem to care one way or another.

Julie and I continued to wage our silent argument until I broke away from her and found a seat near Percy. If I was going down, I was at least going to get the scoop on this guy and what motivated him—besides his wife's illness, of course.

"So, uhh, Percy. Looks like you've got quite a few fans."

His tongue peeked out from his mouth, his gaze fixed on the reels. "Yeah, it's quite a turnout. Gladys would be happy with it."

"I'll bet," I said. I felt the heat of Julie's glowering but plowed ahead. "But *you* seem to be healthy, at least tonight."

Julie sighed dramatically.

Percy looked up from the reels. "I'm feeling okay, I suppose."

I picked at a cardboard cover. "Yeah? That's good. You're really working that rocking chair thing too. And the cane, what's up with that?"

To my surprise, Percy grinned. "Well, it seems we all have our little roles to play in this thing, no? You with the Peppy Max thing. Julie with the...cartwheels."

"Mad Max," Julie supplied. "He's Max, the Pepsi Slugger."

Percy snapped his fingers. "Ahh, that's it."

Julie winked at me before she turned and studied the posters on the wall. Percy wiped his hands on his pants and faced me full on for the first time that night. "Well, I figured I'm an old man, so I'd play an old man." He looked down. "It's all I have left."

So there. He'd admitted it. But I wasn't feeling any better about myself. I got up and paced. "I guess you're right. And we all would have lost big if Sarge hadn't gotten called up."

"That's the truth," Percy said, getting back to whatever he was doing. "Ahh, here it is."

It took some tinkering. Percy suggested we leave him to it. Julie, with a straight face, suggested we go find seats. When we got down the steps, Julie turned to me, one eyebrow cocked. "Went a little hard on the old guy, wouldn't you say?"

"Hey, all is fair in a mall castle competition, no? And you heard him, he admitted it."

"Admitted what? That he's trying to win a contest? Wow, Max. What a revelation." She rolled her eyes, and I thought she was angry, ready to tell me to get lost or even slap my face, but instead she took my arm. "Well, come on. I'm scared of the dark."

We pushed through the doors into a void of darkness without aisle lights or curtain lights. Nothing but an all-encompassing blackness that felt like a weight on my skin. Eventually, my eyes adjusted, but not much.

Banging noises came from overhead. Julie jumped, then laughed, excitement rolling off her as Percy worked in the projection room. A flicker came from the booth as the screen came to life. In a flash of light, I made out Julie's profile before she turned to me and smiled. Our arms still locked, she led me down the aisle to what she called the best seat in the house, about halfway up, slightly to the left of center.

We fell into our seats as the opening credits rolled to life. Julie kept turning from the projector to the screen as though it were some magic trick, before she arched her back, something crinkling as she reached into her pocket.

I laughed, and she leaned her head closer. "What? You can't watch a movie without snacks. I have Skittles. Want some?"

"Well, yeah." I nodded and she poured a few into my hand. The movie was funny, probably, with Michael Keaton cloning himself to get more done, but I was too distracted between keeping an eye out for security, checking the window back there for Percy, and sitting next to Julie, who grabbed my arm when she laughed.

Again, I thought about her life outside of the mall. I tried to picture her doing mom things, like making breakfast and getting her daughter ready for school. And then Mini-Truck Guy—Bryan—how he made her feel. It was too much.

Trying to get my mind off Julie and her issues took my thoughts back to where they always eventually ended up: Tara.

What was she doing right now? Was she asleep, studying, partying? Thinking about me? Probably not that last one, not after how things had ended.

A shuddering flash of embarrassment passed through me. I used to imagine our future together. Sometimes, when I was washing cars, or driving, or sitting up in bed at night, I'd fantasize about how Tara and I would somehow stay together until she finished college. I'd figure out whatever it was I was going to do, and we'd find a place together. We'd have friends over, get a dog, a cat, or both. Who knew what else might happen?

Wow, and to think the whole time she was plotting her escape. All those times she'd told me how much she cared about me but stopped short of the L word. Not me, I was a gushing goofball, happy to tell her just how much I loved her. When I had, she only closed her eyes with that sweet, soft smile I could never resist. In hindsight, it was all laid out for me. I guess I just never wanted to see it for what it was.

Julie giggled at something in the movie. I'd been so preoccupied with everything I hadn't followed anything on the screen. I swallowed my shame and heartbreak and forced myself to live in the moment, and when Julie bumped my elbow and offered me Skittles, I was doing okay with that–right up until the door flung open.

"Hey. Who's in here?"

We jerked around to find a flashlight. Julie yanked my arm and we fell to the floor.

"Hello?"

Poor Gary sounded a bit loopy and warbled, but it was clear he meant business. He'd definitely been asleep, but I guess he felt like doing his job tonight. That or a midnight matinee wasn't so inconspicuous.

"Who's here? That you, Max?" he called out again.

I jumped at the sound of my name.

"Stay still!" Julie whispered, still unable to contain her giggles as we crouched, peeking over the seats. Gary clung to the door like he was too afraid to go any farther. Meanwhile, the movie blared through the speakers. No wonder he'd come looking for us. We'd woken him up.

In the commotion, Julie dropped the Skittles, and they clattered across the floor. I started to pick them up when she slapped me and nodded to her left, where we shimmied across the sticky floor toward the other aisle as a beam of light splayed over our heads. On screen, three Michael Keatons argued about something as Gary finally made his move down the aisle.

Julie and I crab walked up the aisle on the other side as Gary hobbled down to the front row. Julie shoved me in the back, and I flung the door open. We sprinted out of the theater, our feet slapping the bricks of the mall floor until Julie stopped on a dime and spun around.

I bumped into her, and she took my arms, our bodies still stuck against each other as Julie looked up at me, her fruity Skittles' breath in my face. I tried not to notice how her boobs were pressing against me as she craned her neck to see over my shoulder. "What about Percy?"

I half-turned around. "What? We can't go back."

We clung to each other, still in front of the theater, unsure if we should bolt or rescue the old man. Julie bit her lip. "What if he gets busted?"

A bang of the theater doors. There went that. We tore apart and raced out of the lobby for the mall.

Around the corner, Julie hesitated for a split second before she hung a left, for her castle. I bolted for Sears, sprinting as fast as I could while still trying not to let my feet slap the tile. Every sound was amplified in the stillness of the empty mall. I was just hoping Percy had found a place to hide. Something told me he had a few tricks up his sleeve.

I ducked into my castle and threw the clothes off the cot, still keeping watch for Gary, although there was no way he could've covered so much ground that fast. I smiled, the sugar and adrenaline coursing through my body. I wasn't sure if he'd seen us or what might happen next, but one look at the camcorder and I knew I had to send a message to the public. I found my hat and went to work.

"This is Mad Max, and this might be my last video…"

21

In a blink it was morning. I woke up disoriented, confused because I thought I was still dreaming about a crowd chanting my name before I realized it was real. I got to my feet and snatched up my hat. Another glance outside to the swarm of kids. There were kids with parents. Kids without parents. Kids with skateboards and kids with *Ear the Sears* posters. And they were all cheering for Mad Max.

Soon as I stepped out of my castle, the place erupted. Even during summer, Saturday brought a different kind of vibe with it, and I was mobbed as my fans clamored for an autograph. I signed away with a smile, because it wasn't something I would ever get used to. Me, Max Miller, sorry waxer of cars—and these kids wanted *my* autograph.

I ducked back in for the camcorder. Time to go to work.

They went nuts all over again as I leaped out, one hand on the camera, the other like a maestro raising the tempo. I cleared my throat, winked at Bonnie, then summoned the masses.

"How are you feeling out there?" I panned the crowd with the camera. I was getting better at working the focus, zoom, and other features. I turned the camera around and spoke into the lens. "This is Mad Max, coming to you from RiverView Mall, where the fans await." I spun the camera back around and addressed the crowd again. "Let me ask you something? Do you like Pepsi?"

They went crazy. "Yes!"

I cupped a hand to my ear like a cornball. "I can't hear you!"

More cheering.

"Do you like Mountain Dew?"

"Yes!"

"What about Diet Pepsi?"

Clapping. Hooting. Cheering. I swung the camera from one end to the other, and all the way back around to my own face. "Now, let's ask them about Coke-a-Cola."

"Do you like Coke?"

"Boooo!"

As long as I had the camera and the hat on, they'd do whatever I asked. But it worked both ways, because something happened to me too. With the camera and the commercials, it was like I was no longer myself, but someone or some*thing* that belonged to them. Spoke for them. Lived through them. Or maybe the other way around.

Bonnie informed me that *Flash* 102.9 had been running my promo three times an hour. I couldn't help cheesing. It was really starting to work out. I had rabid sixth graders lining up and buying drinks, all jacked up on caffeine and sugar. Another glance at my favorite cashier. I smiled thinking about all those jabs she'd taken at me. For the paperback books and nail files. It was payback time.

"And here she is," I announced, sounding more like a circus ring master than some kid living in the mall. "The one and only Bonnie!"

Her eyes widened as she looked up in horror. I popped up from the camera and gave her my best grin as I nodded to my fans. Bonnie turned to them with a tight smile, set her hand up in a mechanical wave as she muttered to me, "I'm going to kill you."

"Once again, give it up for Bonnie!" I announced, and they roared with delight. Bonnie took her seat, flushed but almost smiling. "Bonnie, I see you forgot your book. And how are those fingers feeling? Because they're about to get a workout. We're going to sell mad Pepsis, right?"

"Bonnie. Bonnie. Bonnie."

It was almost scary how many of them had shown up. They stood before me, a small army trailing out toward Sears, lining the kiosks and climbing the ledges. And the crowd was growing, following the chants, gaining momentum as shoppers had to stop just to see what the fuss was all about. Me, I was the fuss. People were all about Max Miller, their faces red and flushed with madness.

I took a breath and let it sink in. That I'd stumbled on something that worked was new to me, and the fact that maybe I hadn't stumbled on it at all but actually put it all together was almost too much to consider.

It was hard not to get swept up in the buzz. So I didn't. I kept right on recording everything, high fiving kids as Bonnie did her best to keep up. And it was then, in the midst of my finest moment, that I finally let myself believe I could actually win this contest.

Then I saw Marissa, marching toward my castle with her security guards in tow.

I lowered the camcorder. The crowd was still worked to a frenzy, a massive body of fist pumping and screaming, oblivious to the terror rushing through my limbs and down my spine. I thought back to Gary chasing us around the movie theater.

This was it. She was coming for me. And while Marissa's

face was completely blank—no smile, no flare as she stared me down—I knew it was over.

Marissa stopped to survey the scene before she marched up to me and nodded. "Good morning, Max."

I glanced over at the daytime security guards. Two beefy, no-nonsense guys looking like they had a score to settle. Part of me thought this was good, it would only bolster my bad-boy image. But as Marissa motioned to the entrance of my castle, I turned the camera off and followed her inside.

After a quick look around, Marissa announced, "I'm calling an emergency meeting. I've informed the other contestants." Her eyebrows went up as she regarded my adoring fans. They seemed to sense something was going on. Security turned to face them, chests out and arms crossed. Marissa walked over to the shorter of the two.

"Tell Bonnie to take five," she instructed, then turned back to me. "We'll have to delay your morning a bit until we can settle this matter."

"What *matter?*"

She cocked her head as though to say, *Don't even try it,* before she caught herself. "If you would accompany us, we can discuss it in the auxiliary room."

I set the camera on my cot and followed her out. This was it. We'd gone too far and now it was over.

The crowd grew suspicious as we filed out. Someone threw a wad of paper, and I feared things were going to get messy. I made sure to smile, let them know it was under control, and they applauded. Security edged forward as they cut a path through the bodies, looking back at me as though they'd love nothing more than to cuff and mace me.

In truth, my mouth had gone bone-dry, and my back was covered in a sheen of cold sweat. But I tried to keep myself together as I was led away. If I managed not to get the boot, this would do wonders for my image. I even played it up as kids were asking where they were taking me. Security held up their hands and told them to keep back.

With nothing left to lose, I went for it. I placed my hands behind my back like I was cuffed. Marissa rolled her eyes. But it was too late, a "Free Max!" chant sprang to life, and a few kids even marched behind us.

Security did their best to keep things orderly, even when a few of the faithful followed us all the way to the auxiliary doors, where a guard was stationed as I was taken to the back.

Once we were shut away from it all, Marissa broke with an irritable shake of the head. "Seems your publicity stunts are working. Is this what you had in mind when you asked for the camera?"

"No, but..." I shrugged. "Hey, I'll take it."

My bravado faded without the crowd. Now, in the quiet hallway, with the mop buckets and a few boxes of cleaning supplies, the lights buzzed, and it was starting to feel more and more like an interrogation. With these new security guards around, looking to pepper spray anything that moved, it was hard to keep the Mad Max persona going. My frustration turned to Julie. This was all her fault.

But then again, they had no proof, at least I hoped they didn't. For now, I'd play innocent. "What's this all about?"

Marissa whipped her head to me and crossed her arms. "Oh, please."

"What?"

"Come on," she gestured to the door with a nod, "right this way."

Through one door and out to another. We walked into the breakroom, where we all first met. Percy fiddled with his keys. Julie sat at the table with her head propped up on her arm. She glanced up with a weary smile, and just that quickly, I didn't blame her. She hadn't forced me to come out last night. Well, maybe a little, but still.

Marissa slapped her notebook on the desk. "Okay," she began, all the life drained from her voice. She glared at Julie, then me, and even a little at Percy. "Let's talk about wandering."

"Wandering?" Julie repeated, her brow crinkled. She looked around the room.

Marissa closed her eyes. She rubbed her temples and exhaled loudly. "Can we..." She glanced at the guards then back to us. "Can we all just cut the crap? Please?"

Julie shot me a sidelong glance. Percy seemed unaffected by Marissa's frustration as she ran a hand through her hair and fought to keep her composure.

She clasped her hands on the top of her notebook and nodded to an empty chair. "Max, have a seat."

I plopped down beside Percy.

Marissa took the time to gather her thoughts. Maybe it was the harsh lighting, but she had some new lines around her eyes. Her mouth was tight, and she looked like she hadn't slept in days. When she spoke, her voice was low and restrained. "Look, when I took on this promotion, it was supposed to be a few days, okay? And things were great when Sergeant Cardwell was about to wrap things up nice and neat. Mr. Patriotic, a soldier, everyone was happy about it. But now, since he took off, the station is getting calls. People are filing complaints. Lots of complaints."

Julie removed her head from her hand. "Complaints?"

Marissa cast a level stare on Julie. "Okay, Miss Julie. Let's be blunt. As a woman, I respect your right to...hmm. How should I say this? Do whatcha' gotta do, girl. With the queen stuff and all. But we're being flooded with calls from the churches, religious types, and you're parading around half-dressed and, well, it's making the prudes uncomfortable."

Julie's cheeks reddened. Her gaze fell to the table before she looked up and opened her mouth like she was about to protest, but Marissa simply held up a hand and moved on. "Percy, I don't know what to make of it. I find it hard to believe you could be so easily influenced by the likes of these two."

Percy stopped fiddling with the keys. "Oh, well, I…"

Marissa turned from Percy to me. "Max. Oh, Mad Max. Finally found our shtick, did we?"

I kept my mouth shut. Marissa wasn't looking for answers. Or responses. She'd brought us in here to lay us out, and she was doing just fine.

"Here it is, okay? There will be no leaving the castles, got it? No Karaoke. No dress up, and absolutely no freaking *movies*, which, we're lucky the cinema is being so cool about, all right? We've convinced the mall to put an extra security guard on night duty. Which means extra man hours, which means the station will be billed for those hours. All because you three wanted to take a field trip in the middle of the night."

I raised my hand, about to plead innocence, when she narrowed her eyes on me. "No? Wasn't you? Got Mr. Locksmith right there, and you're going to tell me it just so happened to be someone else? That security footage from Hecht's was just some lookalikes? Were some other people in the mall last night, picking locks and catching a flick? Just stop. If you want to quit, then quit. But if you are in this contest, you have to follow the contest rules. Is that much clear? Does everyone understand?"

I looked down, silently pleading the fifth.

Marissa sniffed, a show of victory before she moved on. "Okay, that's what I thought. So…as of now, Julie you have a nice lead. Percy, you are in second, but now Mad Max is surging, recording his own commercials—which seems dicey, but I found nothing in the rulebook against it, so you might have some competition. After some deliberation, I've decided we'll let this thing play out." She threw her hands up. "I honestly don't care one way or another who wins, but let's make a push and get it done in the next few days."

She set her hands on the table, looking us over like a teacher having finished scolding her class. "Are we clear?"

Julie gave her the bitchiest smile. "Oh, quite."

22

I was happy old Gary didn't get fired after our sneaking around. But Bucky, his new muscle, was big and burly and liked to stare me down as he made his rounds.

Whatever my troubles with security, sales were booming. With the walls coming down, it was like living in a fishbowl, people peering in whenever I tried to catch my breath or grab a quick nap. They'd yell my name, chanting or sometimes just gawking, waiting for me to entertain them. So, I did.

Radio Shack supplied more blank tapes. I got to work with my camera, roaming my boundaries, playing up all the trouble I was in.

"Security is after me. I'm on probation. They're trying to kick me out of the contest. So, I need your help, and fast. Come down and buy some sodas right now. What are you waiting for? Get me out of here."

I was filming one of those type of promos when Dre showed up with two young ladies on his arms. They might not have been twins but definitely sisters, wearing black midriffs with identical hair and makeup. I nearly dropped my camcorder. They could've been models for all I could tell, and for a crowd of mostly middle school boys, it might have been the only time they were quiet all day.

Strolling in, Dre smiled from one to the other, then nodded to me. "Here he is, in the flesh. Ladies, I'd like you to meet Max Miller."

I lifted my hat and fixed my hair.

Dre smiled. "They wanted to meet you. So, Max, this is Dina and Devin. Dina, Devin, this is my man, Mad Max."

"Hi," Dina said as she came forward and offered a manicured hand.

I was flushed, without a word to say. Dre watched as I tried to play it cool. "Nice to meet you."

Dina looked over my castle, which now smelled of hair product and makeup. "Do you really live here? I thought Andre was making a joke."

"Yeah," I said, smoothing down my hair. I shot Dre a look. *Andre?* I'd get back to that later. "Well, for now at least." I caught a couple kids standing at the ropes, ogling the girls. Others were standing on the bench, playing hacky sack. It was nuts.

Dina smiled, and I was overcome with the urgent desire to start tidying up all the trash, clothes, three or four Dorito bags laying around the castle—which again, was no longer a castle but a shelving structure running low on Pepsi.

Dre had been trying to organize a bikini car wash for the past few months, and Carol had promised him it wasn't going to happen. Now I saw the gears turning, Dre knew this would be great for publicity.

It worked too. But as the crowd took notice of two beautiful girls in my castle, for some reason, I thought about Julie, down at her castle strutting around in a bikini. I remembered how Marissa was getting complaints about it. Then, before I could stop myself, I was thinking about how Julie's nose scrunched up when she laughed at a joke. How her shortish red hair curled at the ears. How she was covered in freckles, but it worked for her. Wait, what was I *doing?*

Julie was my competition. A mom. She had a boyfriend, and she was what, twenty-three, twenty-four? And after last night, who knew? Maybe she was using me to win the competition.

I needed to take advantage of what was happening in Castle *Numero Uno.* I fixed my hat and clapped my hands. "Hey, would you ladies like to be in a commercial?"

Devin and Dina were up for it, and with no time to waste, I handed the camcorder to Dre and showed him what buttons to press. We moved out to the front of my castle, Bonnie rolling her eyes as she saw what we were doing. Dre gave me the thumbs up, and I counted down—three, two, one—and rolled with it.

"All right, I'm here with the coolest dude I know, Dre Barns. Dre, say hi."

Dre flipped the camcorder around. "What's up, what's up?"

He turned the lens back on us. I set my arms around both girls. "And I also have with me, the ever so lovely, Devin and Dina. Welcome to *mi casa.*" I had to fight not to cringe at my own words.

As though they'd rehearsed, both girls flung their hair back and beamed. Two identical white smiles.

"Dina here says nothing beats a Diet Pepsi on a hot day, isn't that right?"

"Mmm-hmm."

"And Devin always goes to Radio Shack for her needs—cell phones, computers, cameras, TVs. Am I right?"

"Absolutely," she said, so sultry I thought I was watching a soap opera.

"Okay, well, just remember, stop by Castle *Numero Uno* and grab a six-pack, or three. Or more! Mad Max, out. Say bye, ladies."

"Byeeeee."

Dre set the camcorder down, and the girls smiled.

Devin—she had a rounder face than Dina—looked to me. "Was that okay?"

"Yeah. That was great. Perfect."

I still had my arms around the girls when I saw Julie near the sunglass hut, with Percy of all people. She looked over at us and I waved, but she turned and started back. Percy waved then followed Julie off. I was about to rush over and say hi when Dre chuckled.

"How's that going?"

"What?"

"Psh." He laughed, shot me a look. "*What?* Yeah, okay." Dre shook his head. "Okay, man, we're going to bounce." He grabbed a six-pack of Mountain Dew and held it up. "Here, let me help you out."

"I appreciate it."

Bonnie glared at Dina and Devin as she rang him up. Then he was gone, laughing it up as he strolled off with the girls.

***

Soon as I got my next break, I hurried over to Julie's castle. I was surprised to find only a few people hanging around. No one was buying any sodas, and she didn't seem at all interested. She was fully clothed, back in her zipped-up hoodie, flipping through a Cosmo magazine—Karen Mulder on the cover. No radio and no cartwheels. Nothing like her bikini top days.

I slunk around back, stopping at the frame of her castle where I set my elbows down and held my chin in my hands. "Hey, Julie."

"Hi," she answered without looking up.

My smile fell seeing that her bags were stuffed, zipped, and looked ready to go. My heart skipped. Was she leaving? Quitting? Did she know something I didn't?

I tried to play it casual as I straightened, stuffing my hands in my pockets. "Want to go sneaking around later?"

A gust of perfume from the magazine as she flipped another page. "I don't think that's a good idea."

Her eyes were red and puffy. My smile faded, as it was clear she'd been crying again. I dropped the act. "Are you okay?"

She shrugged, sniffled, then wiped her cheek and went back to the Cosmo. "Yeah, peachy."

"You sure?"

She looked up and cocked her head, glaring at me with glassy eyes. "Yes, Max, I'm sure."

"Okay, umm, sorry," I said, eying the clock. Four minutes and not a second to spare. Marissa was probably looking for reasons to get rid of us by now, so I turned to leave but stopped. I thought back to how Julie had looked at me at lunch today with Dina and Devin. "Hey, earlier, over at my castle. That was all Dre. He thought it would—"

She lowered the magazine. "What?" Her eyes narrowed to a squint, as though she was trying to understand something. Then she laughed. "Max, I don't care what you do to sell sodas." Then, to be clear, she added. "Or otherwise."

"Oh, I just meant..."

Her sigh came out like a hiss as she glanced off, past my shoulder. She fought back the tears, blinking as her eyes moistened all over again. "These people, they were harassing me again. Gary and Bucky had to run them off."

I looked over my shoulder. "What people?"

She shook her head. "The holier-than-thou ones. The people Marissa was talking about."

"Okay, but," I gestured to her clothes, "you're not...I mean, you aren't thinking about..."

She waved it off. "Doesn't matter. Then Bryan stopped in to see me. It's been a day, all right?"

"I'm sorry," I said, because I couldn't think of anything better to say.

Julie set her hair back then let it drop. "He didn't even bring Haley. He called me a whore. Said I should be ashamed of myself. He couldn't believe I would embarrass him like that."

"Oh, that's..."

"Embarrass him, can you believe it? He got arrested for being drunk in public at the bowling alley a few months ago. He's been doing real fine embarrassing himself for the past five years."

"That's, wow." I felt like a jerk. Here I was thinking she was, what? Jealous? When this was something totally different, so much deeper. A quick glance at the clock. Two minutes.

"Julie, I'm so sorry. What can I do?"

"Nothing, Max. It's fine." She buried her nose in the magazine. "You should get back."

"Okay, well. I'll stop by later. But, hey..."

She looked up again. "Yeah?"

"Don't let them decide for you, okay?" I backed off a few steps. "All right. Bye."

I turned and sprinted back to my end of the mall. All I could think about was Julie's bags, all packed and ready. Yeah, I wanted to win the contest, but not like this.

"Mad Max. Mad Max..."

My little army erupted as I dashed past Bonnie and through the little entrance of what was left of my castle. I was moving so fast I nearly ran right into my mom.

Great.

23

Things between Mom and me had been rocky since my freshman year in high school. She'd been pushing me all summer to join the ROTC, and so I did, reluctantly, only to quit within the first week. She pouted for a month, scolding me about how I'd never make anything of myself if I didn't see things through. I didn't have the heart to tell her I'd never wanted to join the ROTC in the first place.

When I stumbled upon honor roll later that year, she told everyone she knew. My report card landed on the fridge and stayed there. It served as a reminder when the next one came in with straight Cs. She would point to the fridge when she went on one of her rants about goals and responsibilities. I swear, that one report card, along with ROTC, became the focal point of every argument since. To this day, whenever she wanted to remind me of how I wasn't living up to my potential, she brought up freshman year in high school. When I was fourteen.

When I turned sixteen, I got a job at Pizza Hut. Mom urged me to save for college. I maintained a low two-point something GPA, just enough for Mom to keep the dream alive but not enough to continue with the scholarship nonsense.

From there we reached an understanding. Or maybe we didn't, but Mom worked a lot, and I was content to drift through school without thinking too much. Mom spent the remainder of my high school years counting down the days until I could leave. But I didn't leave. And things got ugly.

Mom quit speaking to me. She did the bus fare/classified thing. She ate dinner in her room. It was almost impossible to believe a whole year had passed since graduation. All said, I guess I was lucky Rob came into the picture. Mom had become almost unbearable at that point.

Now, back in my castle, Mom was all smiles and compliments. "I really can't believe all this."

This, meant a lot of things. Could be my fans or the latest promo. Radio Shack looped the Dani and Devin video the next day. The mall went wild. The crowd around my castle was like a rock concert atmosphere. Between the videos and the radio promo, it attracted news teams from as far away as Richmond.

I didn't know where Mom and I stood now. It felt like I was caught somewhere between her pride and her ultimatum. It wasn't easy though, standing with my mom in what was left of a castle made of soda cans. I threw my hands up and smiled. "Yeah, it's hard to believe."

"I saw your latest commercial. Umm, who were those young ladies?"

Young ladies. My mom was forty-three and playing the role. I went with it. "Oh, they were friends of Dre." I waved to some kids looking in the castle. They giggled and got back in line. "Rock on, dude."

I fixed my hat, really not wanting to discuss this with her now, not really wanting her around at all as it was killing the mood. Especially when she picked up a pair of my dirty socks and frowned. I jerked the socks out of her hand. "Mom."

She pulled a tissue out of her purse and cleaned her

hands. "Well, they sure like that video at Radio Shack. It's drawing a crowd." She craned her head to look around the castle. "Here too. This is all so hard to believe. Max, you could win!"

The way she said it, the way she smiled at me, it was like my report card was back up on the fridge.

I wiped the back of my neck. "Yeah. I'm trying." I popped open a Mountain Dew. I had to get her out of there. Might as well get the show on the road. "Well, I gotta get to work," I said, motioning outside where my fans were awaiting Mad Max. Not this guy getting a pep talk from his mother.

"Right," Mom said, fiddling with a button on her blouse. "Work. So, I was thinking..."

And here I thought she'd come to say hello. "Yeah?"

"Rob and I have decided to... Well, Rob's going to move in."

I choked on the Mountain Dew, coughing and spraying it all over the place. "What? When did you decide this?"

She found a napkin on the floor and used her toe to slide it over the spray. She clutched her pocketbook and looked over her shoulder. "On the cruise. He's not moving in today or anything, but we thought you should know." When I didn't say anything else, she shook her head and kept explaining. "It doesn't make much sense, us having separate places. This is best, for everyone."

Sure, I'd recently turned nineteen, old enough to fend for myself, but still. I fell back into the cot; the weight of what this meant sat heavy on my shoulders. There was really nowhere else to go from here.

Mom quit toe wiping the mess.

I did my best to keep it together. "Okay," I said. "Well, I'll get the rest of my things out after this finishes up."

Another pack of kids at the window. "Yo, Max."

I leaped up, glad to have a diversion from my pending

homelessness. "What's up, fellas? Going to buy some drinks or what?"

Mom shook her head, muttered a quiet goodbye, then made her escape. What else was there to say anyway?

From there, I threw myself into being Mad Max. It was easier, screaming and dancing and acting like an idiot. It was like a stress reliever and took my mind off what would happen out in the real world after the contest. There was a new sense of urgency now, and so I took it up a notch. I screamed until my voice went hoarse. I climbed up on tables, fell, and nearly broke my ankle. I rapped every Beastie Boys song I could remember, starting with "Paul Revere" until I came up short on "Sabotage."

Meanwhile, my third wall was on the way down, only the entrance left standing. Bonnie worked feverishly to keep up.

It wasn't even lunch, and I was tearing into the turrets—my castle crumbling before my eyes as sodas were snatched up from the walls. With three sides fully down, only the wooden frame was left. It was like living in a hamster cage and I had no choice but to perform. So I kept at it. I went all out for the passersby, like a maniac, so wrapped up in the Mad Max-ness that I didn't see Tara until she was standing right in front of me.

Tara. Here. Smiling at me.

I stopped. Gawked. My thoughts whooshing out of my head. I dropped the camcorder to my side and rubbed my eyes. Was I dreaming?

"Well, look at you," she said, her lips curling into a smile. She was as gorgeous as ever, the sunlight streaming through, finding every strand of her silky hair. The middle schoolers giggled and hooted and kept right on with all the mayhem as I stood motionless, staring into Tara's hazel eyes that shined the way they had on the night we met.

"Tara." My voice came out high, loud. I snapped out of it, looking around. "Wait right here, okay?"

"Okay." She giggled, the sound of her laughter soaking into my skin and stirring my blood with tingly magic.

I asked my fan club to give me a second. Once they backed off, I ripped the stupid hat off my head and brushed my hair in place. "Hey. What are you doing here?"

She shrugged, her eyes darting around the castle. "This is wild. I heard you on a commercial. Then Adam called and said you were getting mobbed by fans. It's all so..." Tara took a breath, as though she couldn't find the words to describe what she was feeling.

I knew exactly what *I* was feeling. Adam, oh sweet Adam. My boy had come through for me. But wait, she'd heard me? "You heard the commercials on 102.9, in town?"

"No, at school." She bit down on her smile, something that always drove me crazy.

"Really?" I laughed, out of excitement, out of shock, out of everything because Tara was actually standing before me. Plus, whoa. Was I on more stations, like, regionally or something?

Tara nodded, narrowing her eyes, nudging me with her shoulder. "You're kind of famous."

"Yeah?"

Kids shuffled past us, occasionally reaching for a high five. I slapped hands and Tara gushed. "So this thing is crazy. They're talking about it at school, everywhere, really. Do you have some time for lunch? I'd love to hear all about it."

Bonnie hawked us closely. I started away from the castle, shooting my nosy cashier a nasty look before I smiled at Tara. "Yeah, we can get a slice if you want? I can't really leave the mall. I haven't been outside in days. Seems like years."

The way Tara was looking at me, her star-struck eyes crinkling at the edges, I couldn't help babbling. It couldn't be real, Tara, gushing about the commercial—on TV! It only added to the craziness I was feeling, even as a tiny little tingling part of me wanted to stay the course and skip break to finish this thing altogether. I was on a roll.

Wait, what was I thinking? Tara had driven all the way here to see me! And it *was* lunch, so we started off for Sal's. It was all I could do not to take her hand like old times, but kids kept approaching, rushing up to slap my hand or ask when I was getting out. I nudged Tara and we hung a left, a slight detour to see Percy's castle where he was working on his third wall and making ground.

Again, a squeaky little voice in the back of my head whispered how I should be staying the course, working the crowd. A wriggling down my neck, the pressing urge to get back at it... For the first time in my life, I was inspired.

Percy smiled and tossed his hand up to us. I waved back and tried to forget the contest for a few minutes and enjoy what was happening. I smiled at Tara. "So, how's school going?"

She shrugged, then launched into a story about all the parties she'd been to and how much fun she was having. I took it in stride, mostly, as she gushed about her new friends passing out at random houses, even who they'd hooked up with, her roommate who was seeing a new guy every week.

"I don't know," she said, throwing her hands out. "I guess I needed a break from it all." Again, she bumped my shoulder. "I wanted to see you, how you were doing. Is that weird?"

Nope. Not weird. Not to me, at least, as my chest flushed with warmth at the thought of getting back with her again. And yet, yes, weird. She'd torn me apart, then stomped on the pieces only last week. Then with all that "corporate slave" stuff. I hadn't forgotten that, but I shook it off and smiled, told myself that was all in the past. Even while Percy was back at his spot, selling sodas. Even while we passed Julie's castle, where a few protestors were hoisting signs and yelling about sin and burning in hell.

I stopped walking.

Tara stopped. "What's happening over there?"

All we had to do was go right to the food court. There weren't many protesters, if you could call them that, but they were angry and loud and keeping customers away.

"I wonder where Gary is?" I muttered.

Tara asked again what was going on.

"These people." I nodded toward Julie's castle. "They keep harassing Julie."

It was hard to watch, as Julie was all zipped up in a hoodie and shorts, and still they kept at it, yelling and calling her names. Tara asked who Julie was, but before I could answer a group of kids swarmed.

"Yo, Max. Can I get an autograph?"

Tara beamed as I signed a few autographs. Eventually we got back on our way to Sal's where we ordered pizza. My stomach rolled at the smell. It was hard to imagine I was getting tired of pizza, but the thing with Julie had me all mixed up.

I pushed it out of mind. As Tara sat across from me, smiling and shaking her head in disbelief, I realized she was finally looking at me the way she'd looked at all those world travelers. I'd become one of those people she admired. It was working. My wildest dreams were coming true.

And all I'd done was entered a contest to live at the mall.

Between bites, I asked questions about school. About her classes, what she'd learned. She already had summer plans. I resisted asking if those plans involved me. In fact, I did a lot of resisting. I didn't ask what changed her mind about the contest or taking a break. I resisted the panic of losing the contest, of rushing back to my castle to work the crowd.

With ten minutes left in my lunch break, I suggested we get back. I helped Tara to her feet, an excuse to take her hand, and as we stood face to face, she leaned in and kissed me on the cheek.

"I'm really proud of you, Max."

I laughed, to relieve the pressure—the breath I'd been holding since that disastrous day at her house. Tara's hand grazed mine and sent more shockwaves of hope up my arm. Again, I would have thought I was dreaming had some middle school twerps not pushed past and snickered about how Mad Max was going to get some.

On the way back, we passed the tuxedo rental place, and Tara started talking about the lame Fall Formal coming up at school. I glanced back to the tuxedoes, the silk dresses. I pictured her on my arm, her hair pinned up as she smiled at me.

I waited for her to ask if I wanted to go. She didn't. So, as slick as I could manage, I said, "Ha, well, if you need a date?"

She turned to me, her eyes wide with surprise. But it was short-lived. "Max, dances are so old fashioned and only perpetuate gender stereotypes. Even if I did go, I would never go with an actual date."

"Oh."

"But," she added, keeping me on the hook, "I'm sure my friends would love to meet *the* Mad Max. In person."

I couldn't keep myself from smiling like crazy. "Ha, well, I'd love to come and see you. And your friends." I pulled her to me, caught up in the dizziness of emotions. My mind spun in all directions. She'd driven to town, come to the mall, touched and kissed me. I gazed into her eyes, and she giggled, then gently pushed me away.

"Max, I, umm, I don't want to give you the wrong idea here."

"Huh?" I let go of her hand. Someone slapped my back in passing, and I flinched. "Oh, I thought..."

Tara fixed her hair, blushing some as she glanced left then

right. It wasn't until she looked at me again that I realized I'd fallen into another Tara trap. "You know what I've learned this year in college?"

Great, now I was getting a lecture.

She took my hand, but this time there was no magic. Nothing. I took a deep breath as she went on. "Our society puts too many labels on things. On relationships and goals and jobs and..." She looked off. "We should live free. Especially now, in the nineties, while we're young."

I could hardly pay attention. I was too amazed at how she'd managed to do it all over again. Here she'd come back to lull me in, only to shove me down the hill again. I felt like a yo-yo, up and down, helpless to her whims as I nodded through the rest of whatever she was talking about—the World Wide Web, the euro, Tibet, Boris Yeltsin, Sandra Day O'Connor, Hillary Clinton, women's rights.

By the time we arrived back at my castle, it felt as though I stepped off an emotional roller coaster. But the scene was like a festival. Beach balls took flight, a silly-string battle was waging, and a few skaters did kick flips off the ledge, skateboard wheels slapping on the tiles. And once again, it was exactly what I needed. Something about the way those little middle school hooligans erupted into cheers and came racing for me as I approached put me back together again. It was where I needed to be, here, at the mall, where I was destined to be king.

"Yo, Max."

Tara grinned. Another shoulder bump and she set me free. A tiny part of me still wanted to run after her, ask when I'd see her again. But the urge wasn't as strong anymore. It wouldn't do any good. If I understood anything now, it was that I would *never* understand Tara and her ways. Her mind was a puzzle I would never solve. And strangely enough, as I was surrounded by middle school maniacs, urging and pleading for me to lead them on, I was okay with that. Again, I knew exactly what these crazy kids wanted, and I was more than happy to oblige.

With one last gaze over her shoulder, Tara set off, having conquered me all over again. I stood with my little army, watching her stroll away, before Bonnie mentioned that I should probably get back to work. And so I did. I snapped out of my brooding and became Mad Max, the sort of guy who would never get hung up on an ex-girlfriend.

I'd ducked into what was left of my castle, changing out a tape in the camcorder, when Marissa walked in unannounced. She consulted her notes and almost smiled. "Looks like you're on your way out."

I shut the tape in and smiled, before I remembered how upset Julie was yesterday. How she was getting badgered by those idiots at lunch. I set the camcorder down. "How's Julie? You guys keeping those hillbillies at bay?"

As usual, Marissa was all business. She clutched a clipboard in one hand and a pen in the other. I set my hat on my head and followed her around as she stepped out and walked the perimeter of my castle, studying things from all angles. She made a quick note before she glanced back at me. She clicked her pen a few times. "You know I warned her about that, didn't I? I believe I made it abundantly clear about how she should carry herself."

"And she took your advice. But they're still..." Bonnie turned to get a better view of us. The whole crowd was watching our little showdown. I gripped my camcorder, about to storm off, when Marissa relented.

"Max. Finish this thing and be done with it. That's my advice to you. Don't worry about your girlfriend. Just win."

"She's not my girlfriend. She's a contestant being harassed. Seems like that would be of concern to you."

Marissa's eyes flew open. She swallowed, looked to the clipboard, but ultimately didn't take the bait. She glanced at what was left of my final wall, maybe a few hundred six packs. What had started as thousands, an inconceivable number, was now whittled away to a single wall. I was actually going to win the contest. It wasn't a joke anymore. And Marissa must have known that's what I was thinking.

"Get this done, Max. Then we can all go home."

"Okay, but you should be taking this more seriously, protecting Julie. What happens if one of them attacks her?"

"Oh, now you're the expert on all things serious, is that right?" She gestured to my fans, one of whom held a whoopie cushion over his head with both hands and squeezed. Marissa turned back to me with raised eyebrows.

Point taken. I slunk back into my castle, slid the old tape into the case, my newest promo for Radio Shack.

Marissa followed me in. She took a breath. "Look, I'll note your concerns and talk to Gary. How about that?"

"That would be great. And hey, can you drop this off at Radio Shack on your way out? Or is that against the rules?"

Marissa smiled at the tape. "Sure, I can do that for you. Anything to speed things along. Is there anything else I can get you, Mr. Miller?"

"Nope, that will do it," I said, sitting back, propping my feet up. "Thanks, Marissa."

A busy day got busier. Dre arrived with more hats. Mom dropped by again on the way to the movies with Rob. "The one with Patrick Swayze in a dress. What a hoot," she said with a giggle.

I plugged away, determined to work the crowd and keep the momentum going. And everything was going great right up until my good friend Chip Banner showed up with his camera crew.

Oh how the tables had turned. I set my hands on my hips, smiling broadly as the crew got the tripod set up. This time, Chip came bounding for me like I was the prize of the day.

"Well, hello again," he said, offering up that orange hand of his. "I was hoping you had some time for a quick interview?"

He was practically begging. Funny how last time he was here, Sarge was taking the mall by storm and Chip wanted nothing to do with me. But now I was the leader, and my fans were cheering and snickering loudly, jacked up from all the Mountain Dews they'd chugged (we'd had a contest to see who could chug down a can the fastest, the cleaning staff was not amused). Everything had changed. I turned to my small army lining the walls, sprawled out on the benches near the fountains, and I smiled.

"Yeah," I said, nodding my head. "Sure. We can do an interview, Chipper."

Without hesitation, I picked up my camcorder and zeroed in on Chip, who stopped cold, his hand out, somewhere between a smile and a snarl on his face. His camera guy was filming me, and I was filming Chip.

Ever the professional, he powered through it all. "Umm, right. Yes, so we've been following your videos. They're very raw and real."

Raw and real. Wow. I popped up from the camera. And yeah, I probably should've taken the high road, but I wasn't in the mood. Instead, I improvised. "Chip Banner with WLET.

Here to interview me." I turned the handheld to the crowd, and they went crazy. Chip's eyes darted to his cameraman before he blinked and nodded stiffly, gripping the mike like it was a baton.

"So, Max. Can we do this or no?"

"Did you interview Julie?"

"Julie Cannon? The other contestant? Well, we couldn't get the interview, but we did get some footage. Quite the scene down there."

I looked up from the camera. "What do you mean?"

Chip frowned, a gesture I was sure he'd practiced in the mirror. "Things were a bit intense." He said with his usual flourish. Then he took the reins. "But we thought we'd come here, to Castle One, where it looks like you might wrap this thing up today." He gestured to the remaining sodas, the trail of receipts, empty cans, candy wrappers, and a few random socks.

Bonnie was snooping nearby, smirking at old Chip as he dove right in with his list of questions. I didn't hear a word of it, too busy thinking about Julie and those protestors trying to chase her off.

"Is that true, Max?"

"Huh? Is what true?"

Before he could tell me, I was walking away from his camera. Julie needed help. An idea hit. I checked the clock.

Perfect.

"Hey, Chipper. I have a few minutes for my break. Care to do some investigative journalism?"

His forehead creased, giving away his age. "I'm sorry? I don't follow."

I turned to Bonnie. "Hey, it's break time, right?"

She nodded. "Sure is, boss."

I smiled. At last, she had my back. With little time to spare, I worked my mind tricks on Chip Banner. "You have to be tired of these puff pieces. Pets, the circus, this mall contest. How about we do some real stuff?"

Chip's mike dangled precariously in his hand as he glanced off. "Real stuff?"

"I'd like to take a trip to Castle Three, interview some of these hillbillies."

He covered the mike. "You can't say hillbillies on the air."

"Why?"

"Well, I don't know. It doesn't seem friendly."

"Come on." I started off, leaving Chip to watch in confusion as I marched away, my crowd cheering as they filed in behind me.

Left without much choice, Chip Banner and his crew followed along as I walked backward, cupping my hands to my mouth. "You guys want to help me out?"

An eruption of cheers. Enough to rouse Bucky, the new guard, who had been nodding off near the vending machines. He sprang to attention, saw the commotion, and came jingling over to us. "What's going on?"

I shrugged. "I'm taking my break. Chip Banner is coming with me."

He glanced at Chip, then back to me, unsure whether to trust me or not. "Where are you going?"

"For a walk."

The matter settled, Chip Banner, his cameraman, a moonlighting prison guard named Bucky, and about fifty rowdy middle schoolers descended upon Julie's castle, where the scene was worse than I'd imagined.

Around thirty protestors, armed with homemade signs that looked like they were made by first graders, stood around shouting at Julie. To her credit, she had shed the hoodie and was back in the bikini top, doing somersaults.

I wanted to cheer her on for not giving in, but things were

getting heated. Gary stood stoically between Julie and the angry mob, but he was vastly outnumbered. While Julie was ignoring the unruly locals, when she saw us, she froze, her hands above her head, one foot in front of the other.

The protestors took notice and turned, still shouting and still thrusting signs in the air as I stepped into the fray. I did my best to smile, to appear unaffected, even as every muscle in my legs went stiff and rigid.

I had a bad feeling about this, as things had gotten downright nasty since lunch. I turned to the flushed faces with bulging veins and gritted teeth. My confidence waned. Still, for Julie's sake, I powered through. I had my camera and Chip had his.

I swallowed down the little voice in my head telling me to run. We were young, loud, and had the numbers. Besides, these kids were looking for me to lead, and whether I'd signed up for this or not, here we were. At least we had the town's favorite local celebrity standing by. Chip Banner spoke low and solemnly into the mike, as though he were on the frontlines of a wartime crisis.

With a deep breath, I checked the battery on my camera. If there was ever a time to be Mad Max, it was now.

"Don't you people have anything better to do?"

I gripped the camcorder as I yelled over the protestors, Bucky, the busy hum of the mall, and my own fears. All of it.

A guy with a bushy ZZ Top beard stepped forward like he wanted to take a swing at me. "We don't need this hussy out here hardly dressed, prancing around and corrupting our youth." He motioned to the middle schoolers. "Matter a fact, we don't need a punk like you around these kids, either. Ain't that right Chip?"

Somewhere behind me, Chip cleared his throat, clearly torn between his viewers and a story. As always, he did his best to stay neutral. "Well, this is a very conservative town, after all..."

I shook my head at him. It sure didn't take much for old Chip to crumble. Before he could continue, I cut him off, getting back to the man with the beard. "So you come out to the mall, *for the children,* to harass people and call them names?" I made a show of reading a few of the signs. "*No Whores,*" I gestured to another sign, "*Shame on the Slut.* You think that's what the kids should learn?"

"Son, this is wrong. What she's doing," Beard Man pointed to Julie. "It's a sin."

Bucky shouldered his way through the crowd to better assist Gary. I was hoping Chip Banner was getting this, but he was all but frozen. I handed the camcorder to one of the middle schoolers and told him to keep rolling. Then I snatched Chip Banner's mike and motioned to his camera guy. "Hi, this is Mad Max, here at RiverView Mall, where a group of 'concerned citizens' have gathered to badger a contestant in the *King of the Mall* contest." I made a beeline for the bearded guy. "Sir, what is your name?"

His eyes doubled in size. "I don't, uhh..." He shook his head. "No comment."

I laughed. "So you can call other people names but can't give your own. Wow, what a hero, huh, folks?"

The middle schoolers let out an "Ooooh!" like I'd just won a *Your Momma* contest. A buzz spread as the kids found their voices and piped up, shouting down the protestors. Not to be outdone, the protestors shouted back. Seemed all I'd done was make things louder. But the thing about middle school boys is that it's hard to compete in the noise department, and soon we began to crowd them out. I pressed on, continuing to place the mike under chins until finally the protestors began a steady retreat.

Beard Guy said he'd be back as Gary made sure they found the door. I waved to Julie, who tilted her head with a smile.

Even after I'd stolen his mike, Chip was content to stay out of the way as Gary and Bucky worked to get the stragglers out of the mall. I made a show of wiping my hands, then got back to the camera. "Well, it looks like the Blue Bird special is starting over at Golden Corral."

My job done, I tossed the mike back to Chip, who fumbled it and had to go chasing it under the stampede. A quick check of the time. I was supposed to be back at my castle, but that would have to wait.

As the crowd exited, I collected my camcorder, and with the tape rolling, I started for Julie. Seeing her through the little pop-out screen, something in my chest clutched. She looked ready-made for TV, with a smile that dazzled and those freckles that showed up nicely. I used a rolled-up flyer for a mike. "Hi, Julie. How are you feeling?"

Gary and Bucky had a handle on things. My middle schoolers clung to the wall, smiling and buzzing from all the excitement. Still breathing hard from the gymnastics, Julie watched her detractors make their exit. "Better now, thanks to you, Mad Max."

I glanced up from the camera. Julie smiled, but it quickly vanished. I turned to find Chip. He wedged the microphone between us. "Well, now. That was something. A heated moment here at RiverView Mall. Julie, would you like to issue a statement to the public regarding this matter?"

Julie scrunched up her nose with a giggle. "What does that even mean?"

Chip stammered, then switched gears. "Well, uhh, as sworn enemies, what do you think about Mad Max taking on your protestors?"

I turned, ready to get rid of Chip Banner once and for all, when Julie set her arm around my shoulders and shot me a smile that lit up the mall. She tossed back her hair with a dramatic wave of her hand. "Max here is no enemy." She gave me a squeeze. "He's more like a brother."

Chip's obnoxious smile doubled. I did my best to keep my own face intact. Julie gave my shoulder another squeeze, and we were wrapping things up when some commotion erupted at the door.

"Julie!"

Her arm slid off my shoulder. No one had to tell me that the guy coming for us was Bryan. His hair bounced with his strides, and while he was yelling at Julie, his bloodshot eyes were trained on me.

Julie gasped. Chip took a step back, his eyes darting to his cameraman as he let out a salacious, "Oh."

"What in the hell you doing, Jules?"

"Bryan, what are you doing here? Go home." A slight quiver slid into Julie's voice. Between the protestors and now Bryan, Julie looked like she might start hyperventilating, but she did her best to face the crazy man who'd entered the mall.

Bryan puffed his chest out. "I can't believe you, out here parading around like a slut."

My jaw clenched. It was bad enough she had to take it from the beard brigade. Now this buzzkill was making things worse. Julie's eyes brimmed.

Bryan glanced from her to Chip Banner, then finally to me. "And you. The hell you think you're doing, messing with my old lady?"

"*What?*"

He gave me a shove. "You heard me."

I staggered back. Chip nodded for the camera guy to keep rolling. Bryan rolled his neck, his chest heaving. He was a few inches shorter than me but wider, with a nose that suggested he'd been in his share of fights. He came in hard with another shove. I tried to sidestep him, but he adjusted and caught my shoulder.

I dropped the camera as I knocked into Julie's castle, causing a six-pack to tumble off the wall. A couple cans busted open.

Julie shrieked. "Bryan, what are you doing?"

"What's your problem, man?" My voice sort of squeaked.

He was in my face before I could finish, reeking of cigarettes and beer. "*You* are my problem. What, you trying to push up on my girl?"

Julie ran up behind him. "Bryan, you're being stupid. Really, really stupid. Where's Haley?"

He slung an arm back in her direction, still glaring at me. "That it, huh? You're trying to get with my girl?"

He poked me in the chest. I held my hands up, confused, still flustered from the protestors, now this guy busting in here and shoving me.

"Bryan, stop." Julie reached for him again, but he turned and pushed her, and she slipped on the spilled soda and fell to the ground.

I pounced. "Hey!" I planted both my hands on his chest, but it was like pushing a wall.

His eyes flashed, then he charged into me. We crashed to the floor, and I rolled over as he grabbed my hair and swung at me with his free hand. Drunk as he was, I saw it coming and managed to dodge his death blow.

A piercing scream. Julie leaped on his back. He staggered a step then shed Julie and came chuffing at me, plowing ahead, his face maroon with anger. I managed to catch a glimpse of Chip, who couldn't contain his glee at happening upon such an event, but there wasn't much time to dwell on it as a drunken maniac tackled me again.

Gary rushed in, yelling for us to cut it out. I'd just gotten to my feet when Bryan deflected Julie and lunged for me yet again. We hit the floor, rolling over extension cords and knocking over the table that held the cash register. I rolled free as the register hit the floor with a clang, but Bryan was on top of me as we banged into what was left of Castle Three.

Soda cans rained down, some on my back as others went rolling all over the place, spraying like geysers. The crowd closed in as the middle schoolers cheered me on. But Bryan kept coming through the fizz and bodies, and at some point managed to get the upper hand by sitting on top of me.

"You son of a—"

He reared back to pummel me when a geyser of Mountain Dew caught him in the eyes. "Arghh!"

His hands flew to his face. I snatched a soda from the pile, gave it a shake, then popped the top and blasted him all over again.

He fell back, gurgling, wiping his eyes. The middle schoolers "ooohed" again as I wiggled my way out of the mess and went for another can of soda when a huge hand grabbed my shoulder from behind.

"Max." A jingle of keys. Gary grumbled, yanking me away from the wreckage. Bucky wasn't so fortunate with Bryan as they scrambled around the empty cans, slipping as they tried to get their footing, shoes squeaking for traction until some bystanders finally rushed in to help.

Bucky's fist found Bryan's ribs a few times, and that was that. Bryan cried out and Bucky swung him over and cuffed him. Gary turned me around, a mix of concern and anger in his eyes. "What was all that?"

I wiped my face. My clothes were soaked, and my hands and arms were sticky. My fans bounced around, chanting "Mad Max!" until Gary shut them down with a glare. I waited for him to turn his ire on me—after the other night, and now this.

I motioned to Bryan, being dragged by Bucky to a bench near the fountain. "That guy came in and attacked us." I explained the best I could how he came storming in, shoving off Julie and starting a fight with me. Gary nodded, told me not to move, and stalked over to Bryan on the bench.

He jabbed a meaty finger at the handcuffed man. "You some sort of tough guy, beating up on girls like that?"

Now restrained, Bryan hung his head and kicked his boots. "Jules, baby. How could you do this to me? Jules, please!"

Julie stood in front of the remains of her castle, her arms limp at her sides, a blank expression on her face. Cans were scattered everywhere. The floor was soaked. The cash register was spilled over on its side, and past that, by her cot, lay the cracked glass of the frame holding her daughter's picture. We'd demolished the place.

I closed my eyes. The fight had washed out of me as I took in all the damage. How it was my fault. If I hadn't come down here and made things worse for Julie, this never would've happened.

Meanwhile, Bryan continued his pleading and moaning. Bucky looked like he wanted to go another round but waited on Gary for direction. Then there was Chip Banner, arms flailing as he described the events to the camera.

It couldn't end like this. But it had. Julie knew it, and it seemed Gary did too as he wiped his brow and sifted through what was left of Julie's castle, wet and destroyed. How else could it end?

I wouldn't have to wait long to find out. The doors swung open and what looked like Linwood's entire police force stormed RiverView mall.

And all I could think about was what Marissa was going to say when she found out what had happened.

As soon as the cops arrived, things started buzzing all over again. Six, no, seven uniforms clearing things out and ready to bust some chops. As they converged on what was left of Julie's castle, Gary snapped to attention. They asked him questions, and he did some pointing. A tearful Bryan was led to a cruiser parked outside.

My arms went slack as I waited for Gary to point my way. This was it, all Gary had to do was say the word. I dropped my head and waited for the cops to take me next. But they never came.

Gary did some grandstanding—the mall being his home turf and all—motioning for people to move along. Chip Banner stood his ground and made sure anyone nearby understood he had every right to be there.

The cops pushed Chip back ten or twenty yards, where he fixed his hair, and the lights came on as he went live to report on the melee at RiverView Mall. A couple officers gave me a nod and a "Nice job" in passing.

Wow. I had to give it to Gary. Even after we'd snuck around and made him look bad, he'd made me out to be more of a hero than a punk. Not like he was ready to hug or anything, but if he had my back, then I had no problem doing what he asked, which was staying put, answering questions, and being cooperative. I had a feeling I'd need him as an ally when it came to the police, and more importantly, Marissa.

Slowly, it dawned on me that there might be a chance. Maybe the contest was still on. If Gary was on our side, then maybe Marissa would take it easy. I breathed a sigh of relief, until I took another look at the wreckage of cans that had been Julie's castle.

Julie roamed about and picked through the mess. Everything was destroyed, and I couldn't imagine what she was feeling after the protestors and her daughter's father outside with the police. With Gary tied up answering questions and working crowd control, I made my way over to her. She didn't even face me as I approached.

"Julie, I'm so sorry."

She surprised me with a laugh. A mirthless, bitter chuckle as she fiddled with the hoodie she'd put on. "I should've known he'd do something like this."

She blinked to catch the tears, and I knew I'd do anything to make her feel better.

I tried again. "I'll tell Marissa it was my fault, okay?"

I picked up a can, still full and intact.

Julie bit her lip and finally turned to me. "I was only trying to do something for us. I wanted to give Haley a better opportunity, you know? With a stupid radio contest." She threw her hands out. "I can't even do that right."

I tossed the can to the side and took a breath. My arms were sticky where the soda had dried. "She'll be really proud of you, Julie. You've done so much."

When Julie finally met my gaze, her eyes were heavier than I'd seen them before, her voice flat. "Yeah, Max. I'm sure she'll be proud. We just played out the Jerry Springer show on the local news. What a wonderful mom I've been lately, really."

"Don't do this, Julie. Don't quit. It's not over."

"What? Not over?" She gestured to the scene, the police, Gary, the onlookers. "It sure looks like it's over to me, Max."

Gary motioned for me to move aside as he marched over to us. He told me to get back to my bench, then asked Julie if she needed anything. I heard something about the cops needing a statement from her, when she was ready. Bryan was still making a fuss outside, he said. More officers were on the way.

I had started back for the bench when Marissa walked through the doors. She took charge with her usual huff. Great, I thought, seeing her wrinkled t-shirt and jeans as she offered a quick nod to the police and spoke to an officer, her razor-sharp gaze surveying the carnage. A few blinks, and she summoned Gary.

He straightened, mumbled "Oh, boy," then gathered Bucky and they hurried over to her.

Even in her funk, Julie's eyes widened as we watched Marissa lay out security. A few pointed stares and nods before she broke free and strode for the castle.

She ignored us completely as she whipped out a pad from her huge tote bag. She wielded a pen from the bun in her hair and began scribbling notes before she spun on her heels and marched through the double doors.

Gary wiped his forehead as he hobbled over to us. "Wow, for such a little lady, she sure is scary."

"What did she say?" I asked.

Gary shook his head. "She's calling the corporate folks now."

Julie blew a strand of bangs from her face and threw her hands up in defeat. "Well, that's that."

Maybe Julie was ready to give up and leave, go get her

daughter and live the life she was predestined to live, but not me. We weren't through with this yet. I was ready to plead our cases.

Roughly five minutes later, we got that chance. Marissa, still with her tote bag slung over her left shoulder, appeared with her notepad and pen at the ready. The look on her face warned us against speaking. She made a V with two fingers and aimed it at us. "Both of you, to the back with me. Now."

This was it. I glanced at Julie, who took a breath, closed her eyes, and slid to her feet. Gary and Bucky hung back with the police and preserved the crime scene as Julie and I were led through the doors and into our favorite little meeting room.

"Well," Marissa began, hefting her tote onto the table with a bang. A baby bottle rolled out and bounced along the floor. "Here we are again."

Julie and I sat shoulder to shoulder, waiting for Marissa to announce how Percy had been declared the winner and we were to gather our things and leave the mall and never, ever come back. Oddly, Percy wasn't around this time, and Marissa seemed content to glare at us under the harsh florescent lights like she wanted nothing more than to leap over the table and murder us.

Instead, she took a deep breath. "You just couldn't get through this last stretch. Have a normal contest. No, we needed more drama."

I leaned forward, about to remind her how it wasn't us who brought the news team to the mall, when it occurred to me that I had video evidence of what happened. It wasn't like Julie had invited her drunken boyfriend to come in and attack me. But before I could say a word, Marissa held up a single finger and stopped me cold.

"Oh no, Max. You're not going to explain your way out of this one. We have police, news, witnesses, and everything else out there, all watching this cluster f—" She stopped short, closed her eyes tight, then took the deepest of breaths.

She paced a few steps, then spun on her heel. She bent down and picked up the bottle, stuffed it in her tote, then set both her palms on the table and glanced down at the pad. "Julie. At last count, you stood at six hundred twelve six-packs. Max, you were at three hundred four."

Marissa let that sit there, as the coffeepot groaned and a faucet dripped somewhere within the bowels of the mall. The muffled sounds of conversations leaked in through the cracked door. Julie stiffened, and I tried to play it casual. I couldn't tell if Marissa was simply giving us the numbers or trying to stir something up between us. Either way, I hadn't known I was winning, officially speaking, how close I was to holding five grand and a truck.

Beside me, Julie scooted back, breaking me from my daydream. "What about Percy?"

Marissa pushed off the table and almost smiled. "Well, funny you asked," she said, placing a hand to her forehead. "Let me say, it's been quite the eventful day. While you two were having your own little WrestleMania out there, Percy quietly bowed out of the contest."

Julie and I nearly sprang from our seats. "What?" we blurted out in unison.

Marissa took a step and turned. "It's true. His nephew drove down from Salem, where Percy lives with him. It seems the old man was on one of his daily walks when he simply wandered off, caught a bus, and didn't return home." She picked up her book and flipped through some notes. "You know, I'd be fine with this contest folding now, this minute, as it's been nothing but an abject disaster. But corporate seems to think differently."

I fiddled with my camcorder, thinking about my talks with Percy. "What about his wife? He mentioned she was sick."

"Yeah, well, she *was* sick. She died in 1986. Percy has been living with his nephew for the past two years. The nephew was not pleased, by the way, especially seeing the police presence here when you all were..." She waved a hand and rolled her eyes. "Anyway, we're not at fault. He was of legal age, entered the contest, and provided ID. Had we not taken him, we would have been sued for ageism, or who knows what else." She took another breath. "I'm so done with this."

Julie's eyes went soft.

Marissa, however, was ready to move on. "So, back to the contest. Will it go on? Yes. Corporate, far removed as they are, is actually quite pleased with all the free publicity. They want to see how this plays out. Go figure."

Julie and I exchanged looks. Marissa caught us. She set her palms on the table and loomed over us. "That's right, it looks like you've been given yet another chance. So, next issue. How many of Julie's damaged cans will count against her?"

We were trying to figure that out when there was a knock at the door. Gary poked his face through. "Excuse me."

Marissa whipped her head to the door.

Gary ducked and lowered his voice. "The police need to speak to Julie."

"One second."

Gary lingered, unsure whether to wait or shut the door. Marissa stared him down until he backed away, leaving it cracked like he'd found it.

Marissa turned to Julie and cocked her head with a malicious grin. "*The police need to speak to you.* Isn't that cute?" Getting back to her notes, she continued. "Anyway, corporate asked if we can fix the castle. I'm going to say yes. But here's the deal. I want this contest finished in under twenty-four hours. Am I clear?"

Julie and I nodded. Marissa set her hands on her lower back

and stretched. "Okay, Julie, you can go talk to the *authorities*. Max, get back to your castle and stay at your castle."

We rose from our seats, a bit weary but determined to go on. I started to say something to Julie, but she turned for the door and shuffled out to Gary, who regarded her the way a father would his favorite child on their worst day.

I watched the door after they were gone, until I caught Marissa staring at me. "What?"

She turned her attention to the table, stuffed her notebook into her tote. She hoisted the bag, knocked her hair out of her face, and sighed. "You're going to do something stupid, aren't you?"

I looked away to the cinderblocks. The faucet dripped.

She sighed. "Yes, you are." And then she marched out the door.

27

By the time I exited the auxiliary hallway, a crew of four workers had gathered to discuss how to rebuild Julie's castle. Marissa set out to supervise, having ditched the tote bag for her notepad and calculator, meticulously tracking how many six-packs they would use. Apparently, there were back-up sodas at the ready, as a pallet of them arrived on a forklift.

I was offered a hero's welcome upon my return to the mall, as sales were halted until Julie's cans were replaced. Unfazed, my middle school fans were electric by then. They chanted from behind the yellow tape stretched across Julie's yard so the construction could start. I tipped my hat to them, but I wasn't in the mood, not as Julie stood off to the side, nodding and talking with police. I wondered if she'd have to press charges and what that meant for Haley.

Bucky basically perp-walked me back to the castle, where a parade was in session.

Upon arrival, Bonnie set her book down and shot me a look. "Are you *trying* to lose this contest?"

I threw up my hands. "Did you miss me?"

She pursed her lips.

I ducked under the frame, no longer a castle but a boundary. Here it was, the last lap of the race. Back when I was selected as an alternate, I never would've believed it would come down to this: me and one other contestant. That I'd have a chance to make this happen. Now, everyone was watching, waiting to see what stunt Mad Max would pull next. But I couldn't stop thinking about Julie.

Even with no place to go after this, no chance with Tara, it didn't seem so earth shattering any more. If nothing else, the past few days had taught me I could make things happen for myself. The promos, the fans—even the sneaking around with Julie and Percy. In less than a week I'd gone from loser townie to Mad Max. If I could do all of that, I could get over Tara. I could find a place of my own. But the whole thing with Julie had me twisted.

"Everything okay at the other end?" Bonnie's question shook me from my thoughts. She'd closed the book and turned around in her chair.

I placed my head in my hands. I'd almost forgotten she was still there. It felt much later than six. I shook my head. "Nope. Oh, and Percy is out."

"So I heard. Also heard you got into a fight."

Lifting my head, I nodded. I rubbed my jaw and opened my mouth, feeling the soreness where Bryan had clocked me. "Yeah, things got a little out of hand."

The kids sat on the ledge like they were waiting for something big to happen. I was done with big. I looked over to them with a smile, remembering the good old days of middle school as I watched them laughing and lip smacking, gobbling candy. Trading baseball cards or comic books. After a while, we got word that the contest was back in session. Bonnie waited at the register, still eager for details.

"So, Julie's boyfriend showed up."

Bonnie nodded. "Ahh, I thought something might happen with that."

"Oh you did, huh?"

"What did you expect, running down there, sticking your nose in things? Why did you do that, anyway? That mob, as you call it, was assuring your victory. Could it have been because..." She raised an eyebrow.

"No. Not that. But they were bullying her. Hey, it's the nineties. Women's rights and all, right?"

She only stared at me. "Look, kid. I'm fifty-three years old. I've made my share of mistakes. I've been in love before. It didn't end well. And while this has been fun and all, we've only got these last few cans to go." She checked her watch. "And it's not quite seven. The mall is staying open late for the two of you. Think you can knock this out tonight?"

"I'll see what I can do."

A few shoppers dropped by the castle. They picked up a six-pack and waved. I thanked them. Once they were gone, I dropped my head. "I don't know. I'm not feeling it right now."

Bonnie grimaced. "Well, you better start feeling it."

I got to my feet and looked over the small pile of soda, all that remained. I thought about Julie and how she was doing. That is, if she hadn't dropped out. My stomach growled, and I realized I hadn't eaten since lunch. I gazed out to the kids lining the walls, feet dangling as they waited me out. I was completely exposed when all I wanted was a few minutes alone.

I was still lost in my thoughts when Marissa dropped in thirty minutes later, her trusty notes in hand. Her face was a mix of irritable determination and fake cheeriness. Although the cheeriness could've been real. No one wanted this contest over more than she did.

A quick hello to Bonnie before she stopped short of coming inside. "Julie's castle is back in place. She's down there making the best of it, selling six packs that just hit the shelves. The mall will remain open until ten tonight. Make the most of it."

"That's great."

She stared at me for a second, then her arms fell to her sides. "How did I know this was going to happen?"

I fixed my hat over my sticky bangs. "What would happen?"

"This thing with the boyfriend. What a mess." She'd calmed down since earlier when I thought smoke might plume from her ears.

I shrugged.

She looked away, to the tiny wall of cans—all that stood in the way of me being King of the Mall. "I'll say this, Max. You have a certain quality I admire."

"Oh yeah? What's that?"

She gave me a once over. I couldn't imagine what she saw. I was sticky and filthy. Marissa smiled. "She's too old for you. Just so you know."

"Mmm-hmm," from Bonnie.

I threw my hands out. "What? I wasn't... It's not like that."

Marissa closed her eyes and smiled. In a flash she was all business again. "Okay, so everything is rebuilt, cleaned, and reset. It's like it never happened. I'm asking you to get this thing done, okay? For the sake of everyone. And full disclosure, I told Julie the same thing."

"Okay, I'll get it done. Maybe even tonight," I added with a laugh, despite everything.

Marissa gave me her own tight-lipped smirk. "Yeah, well. You still have a couple of hours. But I'm done for the day. I'm going home. I trust you will behave?"

I nodded, caught between laughing and screaming. I wanted to stay, and I wanted to quit. I wanted to win, but I couldn't rinse the thought of Julie and her daughter getting a second chance.

Reading my thoughts, Marissa tilted her head. "It was noble of you, to stand up for her like that. I have several eyewitnesses that said you came to her defense. And from what I hear, it's all on video. So, nice work."

Outside, I was surprised to find I had a line of customers. Bonnie went to work as Marissa turned and started to leave. "Don't blow it, Max. And as soon as you win, take a shower, okay?"

I sniffed at my armpits. Marissa rolled her eyes, and the middle schoolers gave one last surge, leaping off the ledge and crowding around the frame of my castle.

Marissa shot me another small smile. Then, with a shrug, she got on her way. "Get to work, lover boy."

Another customer. Bonnie's fingers danced across the cash register. The drawer opened with the familiar jingle. This was it, the sound of winning. The sound of cash. The crowd gathered, sensing something big was happening. And the incident at Julie's castle had everyone wound up. My pile of sodas dwindled. Only a few hundred cans of Pepsi products. I tried to psyche myself up for the moment. From second alternate to sitting on the brink of victory.

Mad Max! Mad Max!

The kids wanted a show. Others had seen the news. With nothing left to do, I pulled on my hat, grabbed my camera, and set off to finish what I'd started. I glanced over my shoulder to the Sears.

A spark of inspiration hit. An idea flickered into being. A bold, adventurous, and completely stupid idea.

So I had to see it through.

28

Bonnie glanced up from the register as I started for the crowd, hoisting the camcorder over my head to pan the scene. "You guys ready for a show?"

A round of cheers as Bonnie's face wrinkled in suspicion. Shoppers exited the stores, clutching bags as they stopped to watch the commotion at Castle One. "I said, *are you guys ready for a show?*"

They jumped in place. Forty, fifty boys, a few girls, all looking for something to do.

Bonnie, perhaps hearing it in my voice or seeing it in my eyes, stopped on the register and turned to get my attention. "What are you doing, Max?"

It was too late to go back. I had a plan, and the plan would only work if done Mad Max style. I shot Bonnie a twisted grin. "I'll be right back."

"No, Max. You can't leave your castle," she pleaded. "And you don't need that stupid camera anymore. We're almost done."

"One sec, okay?"

Before she could argue, I started for Sears, the crowd

cheering and the slap of sneakers behind me as the middle schoolers gave chase. Inside, I headed for the lawn and garden section, not sure what I was doing but following the idea that was forming as I moved.

Some people in the store turned and recognized me and my entourage. A man about Rob's age asked if I needed some help. I told him I was good and kept going.

At Lawn and Garden, I checked out the push mowers, the trimmers, the riding mowers. I set a hand to my chin. Hmm, close but not quite.

Then I saw exactly what I needed.

I found an employee about my age. "Hey, I need a favor."

His eyes lit up. "Max, what's up? Remember me?"

I nodded, trying to place him. His bulky blue Sears shirt was crammed into his jeans, and his nametag read *Eric*.

"Hey, what's up, Eric? Look, I need this." I gestured to the vintage minibike on display. Shiny red, with its fat little tires and long handlebars. It was almost cartoonish, like something a clown would ride in the circus. In other words, perfect.

Eric laughed. "You looking to buy a bike, Max?"

"This bike. I need to borrow it. I can give you guys a shout out." A quick look around. "Does it have gas in it?"

His smile widened with his laugh. "Gas? Oh, wow. Umm, I don't think so. It's a display. We can't run it in the store."

"Can't?" I wiggled my eyebrows. "Or won't?" I held the camera up to my fans. It was scary how good I'd gotten at this Mad Max thing. I was almost starting to annoy *myself*. Back to Eric. "Well, can you score some gas?"

Eric looked left then right as he thought it over. His eyes darted to the camcorder, the fans, the Clean Car hat before he smiled. "Wait right here."

This was it. I'd go out with a bang. I tried not to think too much about what I was throwing away as Eric raced off—either to call security or grab some gas. The mall almost didn't seem real anymore. This Mad Max thing, the cheering, it was all part of some weird world I'd entered only a few days ago. But I'd seen what was real only a few short hours ago, and I knew Julie needed to win this contest more than I did. I'd figure something out. I always did.

I was almost surprised when Eric returned with a metal gas can. He looked around as he handed it over. "Here, got this from the garage. Put the oil in too. Hey, and you didn't get this from me." He motioned to the camera. "Could you not, like, show me on tape?"

"Oh, right. Sorry." I clicked a button and turned to hand the camcorder off to one of the kids, igniting a small argument on who would get to hold it. I pointed to a kid wearing a Smashing Pumpkins t-shirt. "You."

The kid took the camera, and the matter was settled. It was still hard to believe anyone listened to me.

Eric stood on his tiptoes as he looked around. "You really are crazy, dude."

"I think you might be right about that," I said, finishing up the oil and uncapping the gas can.

I tightened my grip on the handle as my hands trembled some. People were starting to notice. *It won't be long now*, I thought, as I filled the tank with minimum spillage.

Eric instructed me on how to prime the engine. Then, with a tug, the little lawn mower motor sputtered to life.

"Hey, you!"

"Dude, it's my manager," Eric muttered, as an older man with a blue shirt and nametag made his way through the bystanders. I kicked the gas can off to the side.

"Look, tell him I stole the gas and forced you to do it," I said with a smile, throttling the engine. It roared like an explosion in the store. Before anything could stop me, I gave Eric a fake shove, and he sold it like a champ, staggering back with flailing arms. No turning back now.

The kids parted to give me some room as the bike roared into action and I got turned around.

"You. What do you think you're doing?" The manager guy called out as he neared. Before he could close in, my loyal army of middle schoolers formed a wall and blocked him off. I found the kid with the camera and stared into the lens with my best Mad Max grin. "Kids, don't try this at home. Mad Max, out."

I pulled back on the throttle. There was plenty of noise but not much kick, or horsepower. I kind of had to shove off with my feet to get going, but then I got the hang of things.

I beeped the horn and shoppers took cover, leaping out of the way and gawking as I waved to them in passing. I had to swerve not to hit a couple of older folks walking in, their mouths flying open as they scooted out of the way.

"Sorry," I called out as I exited Sears and drove out to the mall, revving the engine as the kids trailed behind me. They were still chanting and carrying on as I zipped around my castle, nearly wiping out a few times when I cut the turn too sharp. I hit the little horn and the crowd came to life, pointing and smiling as I beep-beeped until I caught a scouring glare from Bonnie.

"Mad Max, baby!" I screamed for the camera, gaining speed as I did a figure eight then another circle around what was left of my castle. In all my grandstanding, I was astonished to see I was down to a small cluster of six-packs, maybe fifty or less. And people were in line to buy me out. I had to hurry.

Another *beep-beep* of the horn, and I tore deeper into the mall, past the kiosk and Spencer's Gifts as I raced for the food court. I circled the fountains, drawing attention as shoppers lined the stores to gawk as I tried and failed to do a wheelie. I did manage a couple of less than spectacular burn outs before I spotted the person I'd been hoping to find.

Gary shuffled out of the auxiliary hallway like he was looking for a fire. His hair was out of place and a pang of guilt hit my chest as he seemed to be favoring his left knee. I hated to make him do this, all over again, but the plan was in action and there was no turning back.

"Whoo, whoo," I called out as Gary worked to clear shoppers out of harm's way. Bucky ran up behind him, his face flushed as he clutched his belt with one hand to keep his pants up.

When Gary saw me, he stopped in his tracks. I let off the gas. We were about twenty yards apart. He threw his hands out as though to say, *What gives?* But when we locked eyes, it felt like we had an understanding. At least I hoped we did.

I let out a yell and took off, circling Gary and Bucky a few times, giving the middle schoolers a chance to catch up. I wanted all of this on tape.

"What are you doing, Max?" Gary called out.

"Just test-driving this beast," I said, still doing circles around him, closing in. "Whatcha' going to do about it, huh?"

Bucky had a vein flexing on his forehead and didn't look nearly as forgiving about things. His hand settled on the pepper spray holstered to his belt. I cut between them and tried to catch a wheelie, but it wasn't happening. I gave Bucky a wide berth. "Mad Max rides again!"

For all that had happened that day, the crowd at Julie's castle, the fight, Percy being gone, it was refreshing to let it out, ride a minibike through the mall and be done with it all. I smiled, feeling the wind in my face. I let out another yelp. The kids ate it up.

It was on the fifth or sixth time around them when I must've cut it too close. Bucky lunged, and before I could react, he grabbed the handlebar. The bike jerked and turned sharply, and I went with it, wiping out hard, sliding across the mall floor. I'd have a nice strawberry down my leg, but at least nothing was broken.

The middle schoolers closed in, an overcaffeinated gang of rabid kids on a sugar rush. Bucky got to his feet and unholstered the pepper spray. Shoppers gasped as he wielded the can at them.

"Back up, now. All of you just back up."

I was still sprawled out on the floor with the minibike when I caught Gary's eye again. I gave him a quick nod. His mouth parted, as this time he caught on. A slight sigh then a wink before he jumped into action.

"All right, clear out. Hear me? Get back," Gary barked to the kids.

Bucky wielded the pepper spray left to right like he was really itching to use it. The kids took a few steps back. I got to my feet and spotted the camcorder in the mix. I hoped they were getting this, as Gary came in and grabbed me by the wrist. He slung me over with some extra force and slammed me to the floor on my stomach. "As for you, you're done, hear me? Done."

"What?" I managed. The body slam had knocked the breath out of me. At least he was selling it, I thought, as he was sweating and breathing heavy. I hoped he was okay. A jingle as he took his cuffs out. "Are those real?" I asked, being a real smartass. "Or did you get them at the gag store? They don't give you real handcuffs, do they?"

Bucky told me to "can it" as Gary clicked the cuffs on one wrist, tightly, before he jerked me up to my feet.

"This way, punk."

I jerked my head like I was fighting to get free. "But I'm King of the Mall. I'm king!"

"Not today, you're not."

He marched me to the nearest door where I squinted at the evening sun. Bucky worked crowd control on the middle schoolers behind us, my little cameraman filming all the way.

"You can't do this," I yelled over my shoulder. "You're a rent-a-cop. You can't kick me out. I'm Mad Max!" I jerked my elbow as though trying to break free, but Gary shoved me back toward the door.

"You, Mr. Miller, are officially banned from the premises." He uncuffed me, then turned to the kid with my camera and jerked it out of his hands. He shook it at the kids. "And as for you little hoodlums. I will take you all in and call your parents. Now go."

The kids booed but mostly dispersed. Gary fumbled with the camcorder until the door opened and ejected the tape. He took the tape out and slid it in his pocket, then he thrust the camera in my hands. "Take this too. Go be King of the Curb."

With those parting words, he shoved me out the door. A breath of real live fresh air hit me as the door shut and sealed my fate.

I stood outside in the warmth of the August evening. Gary stared me down from the other side, basking in the glory of his finest moment. I gave him the slightest of nods. He did the same.

And that was it. I was officially out of the King of the Mall contest.

29

For a few seconds, the heat outside was a soothing warm balm to my skin after a week of the mall air conditioning. But as I ripped the hat off my head and huffed out toward the parking lot, rubbing my wrist and chuckling over how Gary went a little wild on the tough-guy cop routine, what I'd done started to sink in.

I kept picturing those few cans I had to go. What might have been. I found my car where I'd left it; the keys under the floormat. I set them in the ignition and didn't even bother giving it a try. I moved the gearshift into neutral, and with one hand on the wheel and the other on the door, I placed my shoulder under the frame and gave it a shove. The car slowly pitched forward. With my legs churning, I worked the momentum, picking up speed until I hopped in, shifted into first, and came off the clutch. Boom.

Just like old times.

The sun dipped toward the mountains. There was no plan now. Losing the contest had been my endgame, and as I revved the engine to keep the car idling, I thought about where I could go. After a week in the mall, I needed some open space, someplace to lie beneath the stars, away from stores and people and everything else. I had half a tank of fuel. In the distance, the mountains sat against the smoldering horizon. I set off in that direction.

On the road, I glanced at the rearview mirror, wondering why things always ended like this for me, why I could never see anything through. Then again, I'd surprised myself this week with the Mad Max thing. How I'd performed and the way those kids looked at me. And I'd stood up to Julie's boyfriend. I guess in a way, I had seen some things through.

I'd done the right thing. Julie would win the contest, and I'd figure something out. For now, it was nice to drive. The engine was running a bit hot, and I couldn't remember the last time I'd checked the radiator or the oil or anything at all. I'd been so set on getting the truck and the money and winning Tara back, I hadn't thought about anything else.

A tractor trailer chugged past. I could always ask Carol for more shifts. Maybe I'd register with one of the three or four temp agencies around town. Get some entry level work, then get an apartment. And yeah, I could go to Linwood Community too. I'd do it for myself this time, not to impress a girl who changed her mind every week.

I flipped my headlights on, enjoying the wind whooshing through my hair as I took on the open road. Heading for the parkway, it all seemed possible. I could travel, camp, go to college, or change jobs. I didn't have to crash on Jason's couch. I gripped the wheel. There were opportunities. This mall thing had proven that.

The Rabbit struggled with the climb and winding curves of the Parkway. The radio lost signal. I pulled into one of my favorite turnoffs, with the waterfall, where Tara and I used to come and sit under the moon, seeking the calming rush of the small stream meeting the creek in the background. I guess I should've been down, having thrown the contest and basically becoming homeless. After the way Tara had chewed me up and spit me out all over again. I was just as bad off now as I had been before the contest.

But I wasn't. Somehow, the Tara thing no longer seemed like life or death. I'd always have those memories, but it was clear we were no longer compatible. It was strange and exciting that I could like other girls—ones a little older than me with freckles and reddish hair, girls with a laugh that danced into my ears and made me think I was someone worth impressing.

It was going on ten by the time I got settled. By now the mall was closed. Julie had won. I smiled to myself, happy for her. I looked to the sky where only the brightest stars were visible. All my worries and doubts were cushioned by the constant fall of the water as it felt like I was the only person on the earth. Under the night sky, it was nice being away from things. Away from work, the mall, Mom, Tara—all of it.

And then the mosquitoes came.

They feasted on my legs, my arms, my face as I was completely exposed, on a picnic table using my balled up Clean Car hoodie that reeked of Armor All as a pillow. My thoughts raced. Scratching and cursing, I regretted everything. Then I rolled over and laughed about the showdown with Gary. A minibike through the mall. What was I thinking?

The next morning, I awoke to the waterfall instead of the mall fountain. I was covered in welts and rashes. My back was stiff, and my head felt like it had been through the spin cycle. And thus began Day One of being homeless.

Part of me clung to some early morning hope that maybe this wasn't over, that Gary would let me back in and let me finish the contest.

No. There was no going back. There was only breakfast. Wallet check. I still had fourteen dollars. I needed to eat.

Back in the car, the sky was almost silver, with bright, hopeful flares of orange as the sun began its morning shift. I coasted down the mountain and got a biscuit. I put five bucks in the tank and caught a whiff of myself. What I needed most was a shower.

Since I couldn't go to Mom's house—I wasn't ready for that Q & A—I ended up at Jason's apartment, banging on the door until he opened.

"Yo, Max. What the hell?"

His dreads hung over his face, and his customary stoner smile was missing. Dirty as I was, the powerful stench of trash, weed, stale beer, and general funk knocked me back. Too late now. "Sorry, man. I uh, I need to use your shower."

The door swung open wider. Jason was already stalking back to his room. He threw an arm in the direction of the couch. "Go ahead, man. I'll talk to you during normal business hours."

"Thanks, man."

Jason stopped at the doorway, scratching his belly, his hand sinking into the waistline of his pajama pants. "What happened with the contest, dude? Did you really ride a motorcycle through the mall?"

I laughed. "Well, a minibike. How'd you hear that?"

"Sauce said it was on the news."

Gary had come through for me. My last stunt had made the news. I tossed my head back laughing, apparently too loud as someone banged on the wall from the other bedroom. Jason's hand lingered at his waistband.

I shook my head. "Yeah. I did do that."

"So that's it?"

"I guess so. Julie won the contest."

He smiled. "Figures, yo, with the, you know..." He cupped his chest. "Right? But you were doing okay, those commercials were killing us. Mad Max, that was dope."

"Thanks." I nodded.

He laughed again. "Okay, man. I'm going back to bed. I think there's some pizza in the fridge."

He pulled his bedroom door shut, leaving me where I'd known I would end up all along. I sat perched on the edge of the couch beneath the hippie tapestries, a Peter Tosh poster, and all the Wu Tang paraphernalia and hung my head. I rubbed my eyes. This was it.

The coffee table was covered with magazines, a scatter of ashes from the burned down incense. There was a crushed Natural Light beer can in the cushions. A pile of AOL free trial CDs beside the ashtray packed with cigarette butts, roaches, seeds and stems, and bottle caps. Even that didn't stop me. After sleeping with the mosquitoes on the picnic table, my exhaustion won out and I set myself back, trying not to let my face touch the pillows.

My morning hopefulness leaked away in the dark, dank confines of Jason's apartment. I told myself it could be worse. At least I had somewhere to go. But at some point, as a fitful sleep came and went, I stretched out my hand only to find a wadded-up pair of boxer shorts under the pillow beneath my head.

It was clear I was going to have to figure something else out. And I had to do it in a hurry.

30

It was Dre's plan, and it wasn't his greatest. But after the shower at Jason's place somehow left me dirtier—from the green film around the tub to the slimy black mold on the shower curtain, a collection of beer bottles where shampoo and conditioner should have been, and the spongy pizza crust stopping up the drain—I was ready to take my chances.

Dre thought it was foolproof, covering the basics as we cleaned the pit the next morning. "So we close at six, right? Carol is out of here by six-thirty, seven at the latest because she has to go pick up her mutant babies."

"Her *what?*"

"You haven't seen her kids?" Dre dumped the sludge in the bucket. In a cruel act of vengeance, Carol had saved pit duty over the weekend so I could do it on a Monday morning. Dre, being the friend he was, clocked in early to help.

He balled up his face at the bucket. "Anyway, so all you have to do is hide out in the bathroom for an hour, maybe kick your legs up on the stall, although she never goes in there, then you get the place to yourself. Plus," he added, going all sales tactics on me. "You'll be on time for once the next day."

"So you think I should *live*," I paused, lowering my voice, "in the...lobby?"

"No. I mean not, permanently, but..." He stopped shoveling up the gunk to give me a once over. "No offense, but you're not exactly making great decisions lately. Tell me again what happened? You rode a minibike through the mall and got roughed up by security? Did I get that right?"

"Something like that. It's hard to explain."

On the radio, Flash 102.9 returned from commercial break. *We have some big news coming in this morning. Stay tuned for a major announcement from Scottie Snyder over at RiverView Mall. We'll have all the details coming up. But right now, here's* Hootie and the Blowfish.

"Hold My Hand" strummed to life, and Dre's eyes narrowed. He gripped the shovel and his jaw clenched as he nodded to the radio. "Change it."

Dre was usually an easy-going dude, but nothing set him off more than Hootie. It was hard to explain, but he hated Hootie and the Blowfish with what could only be described as a violent passion. Whenever one of their songs came on, he lost his mind, and not in a good way. But this morning I needed a good laugh, and so I stood up and started singing along with the song.

"Stop it. Please," he said from his place in the pit. "I'm about to knock you in the head with this shovel."

I kept dancing. "Hold...my...hand..."

He scraped the shovel on the ground, shaking his head.

I kept right on dancing, singing louder now. "Come on, Dre. I want to love you...the best that, the best that I caaaaaan."

A scoop of pit mud hit me in the neck. *Thwap.*

"Yo!" I turned away, held up my hands in surrender as the cold, gritty gunk—like wet concrete—slid down my back. When I looked again, I found Dre with another shovelful ready to go.

"Off. Turn it off," he said.

I flipped the switch on the radio, still wiping the cool, gritty mud from my neck. "Wow, dude. You really don't like that song."

Dre exhaled. He let the gunk fall to the bucket, then looked down at his own hands, as though he was ashamed of his outburst. "I really, really don't. If I was a terrorist and the government needed answers, they could play that, and I'd give them whatever they wanted."

I wiped my neck off with a towel, still cracking up over my friend's irrational hatred of a pop band, when Dre stopped shoveling and got a strange look on his face. "Hey, you remember Kendra?"

Without looking up, I nodded. "Yeah, I liked her."

"Yeah," he said. "Me too. I ran into her the other day."

This time I did look up. "And?"

He shrugged. "We're going to hang out tomorrow night. Catch up. Why are you looking at me like that?"

As long as I'd known Dre, this was a first. My smile widened. "Well, look at you."

"Man, we're just going to grab something to eat," he said with a goofy smile. "But okay, yeah, she looked good. What can I say? You inspired me."

I wasn't sure what to make of that when Carol showed up. She set a hand on her hip, her eyes narrowed to slits. "What the hell are ya'll doing? It's time to open."

We still had all the grates off the pit and cars were already lining up outside. Carol didn't give me time to come up with an excuse. "Good to have you back, Max. You miss a week of work and now we're late. Hurry. Finish up." She glared at Dre. "And I'm not paying you to help him. Get on the register."

Things were as slammed as I'd ever seen them. A line of cars from the start, and it never let up. The sun was bright, and the sky promised a clear, hot day. I sent car after car through the wash, and soon I was lost in the midst of it all.

Keeping busy helped get my mind off the contest, even as Julie stayed in my thoughts. I was vacuuming out a car when the news came on, Scottie Snyder teasing out a big announcement about the King of the Mall contest. A winner had been declared, and Linwood should come on out and join him at RiverView Mall tonight, in the parking lot, where there would be live music, prizes, food trucks, and other goodies.

It sounded like a good time, but I wasn't in the mood to show my face up there. Besides, I had to hide out in the car wash bathroom, as I was going to be sleeping in the lobby.

It was around four when the news trucks started up the entrance to the mall, and not long after that the music drifted down from the hill. As the party got underway, I dumped trash and worked on getting things cleaned up and put away. Leaving the car wash, Dre patted me on the back and told me the plan was all set. Meanwhile, he'd go up to the mall and let me know how things turned out.

After closing, I said a quick goodbye to Carol and snuck off to the men's room to wait her out. An hour later she still hadn't left to pick up her mutant babies as Dre had promised. In fact, things were getting weird. I heard what sounded like love ballads leaking from the office. I shifted quietly on top of the stall as my foot was falling asleep from being perched on the toilet in case she came in to check up on our cleaning.

Through the walls, there was some soft humming and Fleetwood Mac on the radio. I set my head on my lap and tried to catch a nap, when there was a knock at the lobby door.

My head popped up. At first, I assumed it was a straggler—we always had people dropping in well after the bay doors were pulled shut and the sign was flipped—but the knocking was followed by the sound of keys jingling as Carol came swooshing down the hall with a squeal.

I straightened my back, craning my head as outside the lock clicked and the lobby door opened.

"Hi, stranger," Carol said, all breathy and seductive.

My mouth hung open.

"Hey, you." A man's voice, followed by the swift rustling of bodies.

My mouth formed an oval as I nearly fell on my face. I'd never heard Carol's voice so sultry—without hostility, annoyance, irritation, or flat out yelling. This was a bit of a growl, a purr, even. I stared at the floor to fully concentrate on what I was hearing, because it sounded like...

I sat up straight, a jolt of terror flooding my head and washing down my spine. OH NO. OH NO. NO. NO. NO. NO. THIS CAN'T BE HAPPENING!

Carol was getting it on. And I had no choice but to listen to it happen.

31

From inside the rust splotched confines of my stall came the heart-squeezing click of the lobby door. We were sealed in. The three of us. I looked around wildly for an escape hatch. A secret portal. In the lobby some sort of wrestling match ensued, followed by laughing, then squealing. I flinched as they banged into the wall with a groan.

In my time sweeping the lobby, I knew all too well the sound a cheap wooden couch made when it went skidding across the floor. Gross. There went my place to sleep.

"I've missed you, baby."

"Yeah, well, let me make it up to you."

I winced at the sucking sounds, moaning, the rustling of clothes being shed as the soap opera kissing continued. At one point I thought about lifting the toilet lid so I could puke. But I held tight, dry heaving in silence, puffing my cheeks out as I focused on the discolored bathroom tiles. Nauseous as I was, one thought was clear: I was going to straight up murder Dre.

The distinct jingle of a belt buckle coming undone. Carol's keys smacked the floor. I covered my ears and rocked in place, helpless as my boss got her groove on in the lobby. I whispered a prayer, trying and failing to rid myself of the images my brain created.

Sure, okay. Carol was human with human needs. A divorced single mom, she was usually rushed and frazzled and in over her head trying to keep us in check. I guess I'd always figured she was too busy to date. She wasn't exactly unattractive, I guess, she was just...Carol. Now, hearing her make-out session, it was clear there was another side to my disgruntled little boss. A primal, hungry, wild side, judging by the growling and grunting going on.

Fifteen excruciating minutes later, the lobby fell silent. I sat perched on the toilet, without moving, *unable* to move, shell-shocked and scarred forever as Carol and her lover got clothed and zipped. After some murmuring came the shuffling of footsteps headed my way.

I went rigid as the door swung open. Footsteps followed. I poised myself to barricade the stall door with my shoulder. It wasn't locked, and I couldn't lock it now without making noise. The steps slid to a stop. A sniff, grunt, some whistling, then a few dribbles at the stall next door. I allowed myself to breathe—until the guy started talking to himself. Or, more specifically, to a part of himself.

"Come on, little buddy. We had some fun, didn't we?"

I squeezed my eyes closed until I saw sparks. I tried my best to get through it. Not to laugh or cry or bust out of the stall and take off running. By the time the toilet flushed and the door shut, I'd had all I could take. I leaned forward until my head hit the stall door.

In the lobby, keys clattered and the lock flipped. Another click and everything fell silent. I waited another ten minutes before I came out of the stall. Five more until I slowly crept out of the bathroom. The lights were off, the room washed amber with the evening sun. The red glow of the Coke machine. Carol's car was gone. I looked at the couch.

Yuck.

It was almost seven. Up on the hill, the party was still going on, and I had roughly twelve hours until we opened. I sat on the floor, snatched up the newspaper, and tried not to think about what the hell I'd just heard.

Twelve hours is a long, long time to be alone on a tile floor. Even after the castle at the mall—*especially* after the castle at the mall—and an uncomfortable power nap on Jason's couch. The minute hand seemed glued to the clock. Every sound, every wash of headlights over the wall and I leaped up, checking to see if someone was trying to steal gas or break in. But I was exhausted. After trying to guess how many Hot Tamales were left in the candy dispenser, I finally crashed in the chair.

I blinked awake. My neck was stiff from being wrenched around. It felt like I'd been wrestling Shawn Michaels. The sky was a dull gray as I got to my feet, stretched, and brewed some coffee. Traffic was scarce out on Mason Avenue, cars out of place as the horizon awoke to a smudgy yellow in the distance.

The clock showed 5:30. The plan was to hide in the bathroom again, as Dre had promised to arrive early to beat Carol to the wash to open. I cleaned up and paced, shook some life into my legs. After three cups of crappy coffee, dumping sugar to blanket the bitter taste, I washed up in the sink and then took my place on the stall around 7:15. About twenty minutes later the front door opened.

"Hey, yo!"

I busted out of the door at the sound of Dre's voice. I stalked over to him. "I'm going to kill you. Like, right now."

Dre threw his hands up, backtracking. I must have looked like a crazy person, with my hair all over the place and my wrinkled shirt. He shook his head but failed to remove that smirk from his face. "What's up with you?"

"What's up with me?" I nodded, buzzing from the caffeine. "What's up with *me*? Oh, I'll tell you what's up."

I didn't hold back. I unloaded every gross detail about grumpy Carol and her romp in the lobby. Dre's eyes doubled in size. He covered his mouth, shaking his head and saying, "No way," when I got to the part about "Come on, little buddy." By then he was folded over, laughing so hard he couldn't breathe.

"Yeah, laugh," I said, although by then I was cracking up too. "Laugh all you want, but I'm done staying here. I'll tell you that. I'll sleep in my car before I go through that again. Or I'll camp. Anything. Anything in the world but stay here again."

Dre held up a hand, almost hyperventilating. "I can't... I can't..."

When he recovered, we stood in the lobby, staring at the couch. For the millionth time, I tried not to think about what I'd given up, how far I'd fallen since having the contest won. Five grand wasn't something I could brush off, flip over like the couch cushion. I really was without a home, living in a car wash lobby. And now I'd officially reached my breaking point.

A few minutes later, Carol pulled into the lot. Dre wiped the laughter off his face as he turned to the window. "Uh oh."

"What?"

"She's going to wonder what you're doing here."

I shrugged. "I came in early. So what?"

Dre raised his brow. "You haven't been on time once since you started working here. Now you're coming in early?"

Carol got out of her car and did a double take at the Rabbit. I was never, ever going to be able to look at her the same. I turned to Dre. "You really think she'd guess I slept here?"

He looked me over. "Yes, because you look like you slept here."

I sipped coffee and tried to finger-comb my hair as Carol stomped across the lot.

Dre laughed. "She ain't acting like a lady who got some, that's for sure."

I nearly spit out my coffee. "I already regret telling you."

"I can't unthink it now." He glanced up. "Here we go. Looks like we've got customers already."

Carol barged in as three more cars hit the lot, some high school kids hanging out the window. Carol stubbed out her cigarette in the ash tray. "Looks like it's going to be—"

She looked me up and down. "What the hell happened to you?"

"I came in early." I gestured to the lot, to divert attention. "Good thing too, right?"

Carol glared at Dre, who only laughed, nodding to the window. "Yo, they're chanting for Max."

Carol checked the window, then leveled a glare on me.

I looked away and held up my cup. "Made coffee."

32

If yesterday was busy, today was straight mayhem. The rush started before eight and never let up. Whatever Carol's suspicions, she was too preoccupied with customers to get after me. Daryl showed up around nine and nearly quit on the spot, as cars came bumper to bumper out of the tunnel and crammed the lot. Meanwhile, the line at the entrance was backing up traffic and making a mess out of the intersection.

It was the mall all over again. Everyone was asking about Mad Max. It seemed I still had fans, older ones who drove, as well as my middle school faithful. Kids spilled out of vans driven by soccer moms. Apparently, the commercials were still airing, and everyone was curious about what exactly happened. Against company policy, I whipped my hat around backward—eliciting several warnings from Carol—and joined the party.

I posed for pictures with people inside cars, on top of cars, one in the middle of the road with a bunch of bikers, and then a few at the car dealership across the street. I signed napkins, King of the Mall flyers, a few hats, and even Clean Car menus. We did nearly a hundred cars by lunch—easily on pace to smash the Clean Car record of one hundred and seventy-five cars held by the store in Northern Virginia.

It seemed every car in Linwood stopped by—vanloads of kids, police cruisers, company cars, a couple school buses, and even an ice cream truck. It was insane from the start. All I'd eaten were two bags of Doritos from the vending machine for lunch, so I was starving when some kids offered to go grab Dre and me a burger.

Carol was nearly foaming at the mouth, rabid and frazzled, yet elated at the record-smashing business. We were overwhelmed by all the cars, and my boss spent every free second screaming at me about policy and bylaws. She chewed me out for leaving the lot, berating me for taking photos with kids, and at one point she nearly beat me with a vacuum hose after I sent a police car through the tunnel with the red and blue lights on.

I was only having fun with it, but the kids wanted answers.

Yo, Mad Max. What happened with the contest?

We heard you got arrested.

Did you kidnap that old dude?

Julie told us to stop by the wash to see you.

We saw you on the news.

"Keep moving, Max," Carol called me out from her place at the register.

Dre seemed miles away, greeting customers at the entrance, pushing wax jobs and clear coats and making bank on commission. Two kids, maybe thirteen, stood to the side as I vacuumed their mom's minivan.

"Yeah, she was crowned queen but said we should come see you. Said she owed it all to you. Called you Evil Knievel."

I stopped and smiled, the vacuum whooshing in my hand. "She said that?"

The chubbier kid grinned. "Yeah. You two were totally

getting it on, weren't you? That's why you fought her boyfriend, right?"

"What? No. We—"

"Max!" Carol snarled at me from the cashier booth.

I still couldn't look at her head on.

By closing, the place looked like a war zone. Towels strewn everywhere, plastic bags, spray bottles, straws, receipts, a random shoe, even a spare tire. We'd washed over two hundred cars, run out of cherry air freshener, and by five o'clock, Carol, with her shirt stained with sweat and soap, was turning cars away with her usual charm and grace.

First time for everything, I guess. Dre said I was in luck; she was probably too beat for a lobby romp tonight. I nearly puked, then grabbed my cup of water. "I'm not sticking around here to find out."

We worked to get everything back in order. My plan was to go groveling back to Mom until I figured out where I was staying. Daryl and Mike smoked cigarettes on the dry-down side, counting tips and laughing. Dre swept a fast-food bag into the pan. "Tell you what. Why don't you crash at my crib for a few days."

"Is Mel up for that?" I asked, figuring Dre's church-loving grandmother wouldn't want me crashing at her house. And if I did, she'd be sure to sit me down for a Bible lesson. Still, the thought of a warm meal and a clean bed after the night I'd had on the lobby floor was appealing.

Dre said it was fine. "In fact, she was talking about you this morning." He dumped the dustpan in the trash, looked me over. "I think she'd be happy to have a *local celebrity* at the house."

I shot him a sidelong glance. "Whoa, hold up. Are you getting jealous on me, Dre? Worried I might mess up your game?"

He shoved me away with a laugh. "Nah, I am not worried at all about *that*."

We headed inside to punch out, where Carol was up to her chin in paperwork. Being so meticulous about the register, she'd probably be here all night getting it straight.

"What a day, right, Carol?" Dre said, falling into the seat across from her desk in the small office.

"You clock out?" she asked without looking up.

We both rolled our eyes and answered in unison. But I wasn't complaining, I'd almost gotten a week's worth of hours in the past few days.

"Yes, Carol."

Then she did look up. "So, Max."

My gaze hit the floor. I felt her eyes on me. "Yeah?" I forced myself to raise my chin.

Dre snickered.

"I gotta say. Today was incredible." Something akin to a smile formed on her lips. One of her incisors was crooked, but I'd never noticed because it was so rare that she smiled.

Still, all I could think about was last night. *That was incredible, little buddy.*

Dre shook his head at me then pointed to the desk. "Did you fax the numbers to corporate?"

Carol shuffled through some papers. "Getting ready to. They're going to flip the hell out. Way to bring them in, Max. Or should I call you Mad Max now?" She wiggled her eyebrows, and I nearly blew chunks.

"Oh, umm...Max is fine." I cleared my throat.

Dre smirked at me.

Carol shot Dre a look, aimed her pen at me. "What's up with him?"

"Tired, I guess. Right *Mad* Max?"

"Yeah. I'm going to get some water."

"Wait," Carol called out.

I stopped at the door.

"Max. If this keeps up, you might get a promotion. I'm serious too." She did the eyebrow thing again, shook the papers at me. "This was a week's worth of business."

A dry swallow scraped my throat. It was all I could do to get the sounds out of my head. Last night, the moaning. But I needed a raise more than ever, if not a promotion too. I forced myself to look at her. "Really? That's cool."

"*Cool?*" Carol huffed. She slung her pen down. "What, are you too good for us now?" She cocked her head at Dre. "Can you believe this? I give him a week off and he thinks he's a star."

The black pits of her eyes scrutinized me, I was looking for a place to hide when Dre got that charm working. "I don't think it's that. We're all tired, you know?"

A few beats before she smiled, tapped her desk. "You're right. Okay, you boys get out of here. I'll see you bright and early tomorrow."

I hit the door before she could call us back. Dre, not far behind me, laughed the whole way to his car.

I tossed my stuff in the Rabbit. "Well, that was weird."

"You better be careful, Max. You could be next on that couch, little buddy."

"Gross."

"Yeah," he said with a yawn and a stretch. "So, you gonna crash or what?"

"Thanks, but..."

I fell into my car, exhausted. The sun was low, and the heat had relented. I loved the car wash lot when it was closed. Everything was nice and cool in the shadow of the mall up on the hill. The mall...

I took a deep breath. "Think I'm going to go check on Mom, break the news to her."

Dre rolled his eyes. "Well, I'm sure she's *seen* the news, so I think she knows. What really happened, anyway?"

I turned to him. "What?"

"Pshh. *What?*" he mimicked. "Man, you had that contest wrapped up. The commercials. The radio ads. You were killing it. Then you got in that fight, and it was over. Why?"

I looked off again. "I don't know. I mean. Julie's got a kid, and she needs to leave that maniac. You saw the news. Dude is crazy." I shrugged it off. "She needed it more than me."

"Says the guy about to sleep in his car."

I shook my head.

Dre dug in his pocket for his keys. "Do your thing, man. But look, you get tired of sleeping in cars and lobbies, stop by Mel's."

"Thanks, man. For real."

Dre opened his door, and I caught a blast of spearmint air freshener. He always kept his Maxima shining, taking full advantage of the weekly free wash.

"Either way, tell your mom I said hi. And find a shower, my man. You stink."

"Tell Kendra I said hi."

"That's tomorrow night. But I will."

Dre settled in the car, and I tried not to seethe with jealousy as he turned the key and the engine hummed to life. He set the windows down. "Let's do it again tomorrow, right?"

"Bright and early," I said. But my heart wasn't in it. I was still thinking about the mall up on the hill. Something felt...unfinished.

With a laugh, Dre set the car in drive and took off. I glanced back to the Clean Car lobby with a shiver. Nope. Not doing that again.

33

The Rabbit must've been inspired, as it cranked and started up with no problems. I smiled, thankful for the little things, until I pictured myself at Mom's townhouse, answering questions about quitting and seeing things through under the heavy disappointment in her eyes. I wasn't in the mood for that, so I crossed the street and drove up the entrance to the mall.

It seemed right, coming back. I was still dizzy, with too many feelings to sort since I'd left my castle. Up on the hill, crossing the lines of the parking lot, I pulled to the edge where I had a clear view of the evening sun burning over the horizon. I got out and sat on the hood of my car, struck by the sense of peace it gave me after such a crazy day. Below lay the car wash, where I'd spent so many hours of my life. It looked small and insignificant.

Everything was the same yet different. Tara was no longer the center of all my thoughts. Crazy how I hadn't thought about her much since the Parkway. I wasn't sure if that was a good thing or a bad thing.

Behind me, the expanse of concrete and cinderblock that was RiverView Mall loomed. Somewhere inside, Gary was making his rounds, checking locks and doorways. Before I could talk myself out of it, I grabbed my bag and searched for some semi-clean clothes. I hiked across the lot, laughing, because technically I was banned from the premises.

The mall looked strange with the castles gone—only strips of tape and electrical cords as evidence anyone had lived there. I walked around without getting noticed, and hung a left, my feet squeaking on the floor as I strode down the hall. At the door, I found Gary in the security office, the country station on a low hum as he leaned back precariously in his squeaky chair, almost asleep.

"And you call yourself security."

His eyes snapped to attention. He blinked a couple of times as he struggled not to smile. The chair whined as he came forward. "Hey, I thought I banned you from the premises?"

I dropped my gaze. "Yeah, you did. No hard feelings?"

Gary rocked himself to his feet. I gripped the straps of my bag. It felt like years, not days, since I'd left.

Gary wiped his face as he came around the desk, adjusting his utility belt. "Course not. I thought it was a nice performance."

"You went a little crazy with the handcuffs. I didn't see that coming."

He laughed like it was the funniest thing he'd ever heard. "I can't believe it. You missed everything."

I nodded. "Yeah, well, things are wild down at the wash."

"The wash?" His gaze fell to my Clean Car shirt. "Oh, right, I almost forgot you really worked there." He shook his head. "Everyone was talking about you."

"About me?" My thoughts flew to Julie. I didn't even know her number. "What do you mean?"

His radio crackled. Something about an all-clear at 214. He mumbled some gibberish in reply, then holstered his radio. He looked me over with a big goofy grin. "You rode a minibike through the mall, you nut. It was all over the news. Bucky wanted to pepper spray you, truth be told."

"Yeah? How's Marissa? I guess she's happy it's all over, huh?"

"You know, I called her as soon as you left, and something in her voice told me she expected it. And your little fanbase, they were going on like you were some kind of hero. They turned out yesterday, you know. I ran 'em off all over again," Gary said, puffing his chest out some.

I laughed. "Wow, wish I could've seen it. But, well, banned."

"That's right." Gary chuckled. "Well, Julie's acceptance speech was...it was really something. She mentioned you."

"I heard the music, from work," I said, nodding over my shoulder. Unable to hold back, I blurted out, "What did she say?"

Gary smiled. "Good stuff. And hey, I wouldn't be surprised if the station got in touch with you. I think they're after an interview. It was a big crowd. They even did your Mad Max chant," he said, swinging a fist in the air. "Those Pepsi suits ate it up."

I laughed. "Yeah?" I told him about all the cars at the wash today.

Gary nodded. "I don't doubt it. Don't doubt it at all."

All that said, we ran out of steam, and things got awkward as I stood in the office. I looked around, at the monitor, phone, desk fan, a scatter of magazines, calendar on the wall. Work schedule. "So, what's next for you now? Nice to have the mall back?"

"Oh, yes and no. Sears was all upset about the bike, until the Pepsi guys smoothed things over. You really got their attention, by the way. Corporate guys. They kept asking questions, wanted to hear all about it. Even asked for the security footage," he said, then frowned. "Bucky's been out, said he sprained his shoulder. Bonnie was glad to be done with it all." He laughed. "Marissa didn't have much to say, but again, I could tell she was relieved to have a winner. I think we would have gotten in more trouble had things not ended right then."

"Well, I'm glad it worked out for you."

He sniffed, held his chest out with pride. "Hope things work out for you too, Max. What's with the bag?"

I hung my head and sighed. "Kind of need a favor." I swallowed whatever speck of pride I had left. "Would it be okay? Would you mind if I took a quick shower? I'm, uh, locked out of my house, and it's been a few days."

His brow furrowed. He recovered quickly and motioned to the door behind the desk. "Uh, sure. Yeah," he said with a nod. "Right back here."

"Thanks, I worked all day, and..." I shook my head, the shame weighing my words down.

"No, no. It's fine." He waved me off. "Hot water is kind of finicky though."

"No problem. Thanks, Gary."

CAMPING AGAIN. This time in the mall parking lot where I'd found a secluded spot on the backside, with the car parked around the side of a dumpster where I figured no one would show. I set the seat back in the Rabbit.

I couldn't imagine rock bottom getting any rockier than this, sleeping in my car, the radio draining whatever juice was left in the battery. At least I smelled better, and I could wash my work clothes in the towel washer at work tomorrow. Sure, they'd come out smelling a bit waxy, but it was better than how they smelled now, stinking up the back of the car.

Pearl Jam's *Black* drifted through the speakers, Vedder crooning with my thoughts. Julie and me, running through an empty mall, trying on clothes, karaoke. How she said I looked handsome in a suit. I smiled at the dashboard. It would get me through the night.

Shifting left then right, the emergency brake digging into my hip, I was second guessing my decision not to stay at Dre's. In the dusky glow of the evening, it had felt right to go it on my own. But now, in the dark, cramped, and uncomfortable car, going it on my own didn't feel so liberating.

I'd be twenty soon, then twenty-five, and while I'd never given much thought about the future, now, as I was all set to go to work tomorrow and do it all over again, one question kept nagging at me.

What next?

34

Morning came and despite my pushing, popping, turning, and shoving the Rabbit around the parking lot, the engine wouldn't catch. I gave up around seven-thirty. I grabbed my Clean Car hat, tossed my keys to the floorboard, and hiked down the hill.

Again, the lot was already at capacity, spilling cars into the street. My steps dragged to a shuffle. Because, *seriously?*

"You've got to be kidding me," I muttered to myself, about to turn around and say forget it, when I was mobbed in the street. Traffic had completely stopped, and amidst the honking and screaming and cheering, I was signing a Pepsi Frisbee when Carol did her famous two finger whistle, frantically directing me over to the vacuums.

"Max, come on. Go clock in and get over here," she barked over the scream of machinery.

I did as I was told, zigzagging between bumpers. Cars were blocked in, angled like some horrible pileup on the interstate. Kids hung out windows, shouting at me as I hustled over to the office to clock in.

It was already busier than yesterday. And yesterday might have been cool, but Carol was shooting steam out of her ears as she slammed the register drawer in place, lit up a Winston, then exhaled with a string of curse words that were drowned out by my fans.

Mad Max. Mad Max. Mad Max.

"Well, here we go again," I said, trying to mess with her. It was four minutes until eight, no sign of Dre yet.

Carol's cigarette bounced between her lips. "It's too early to deal with this crap."

"Ahh, come on, Carol." I ran over to the cars and smacked some hands. Sure, I wasn't really in the mood either, but if it got a rise out of Carol, I was all about it. What can I say? It was how our relationship worked.

More honking and tailgating. I gazed out and took it in. Anyone looking to get somewhere via Mason Avenue would have to wait. It looked like a rock concert was happening.

"Start vacuuming," Carol chided.

I restrained myself from asking if her friend had come for an afterhours visit last night. So gross, yet it would not go away.

I figured it was best not to push Carol. She nearly had a meltdown as people abandoned their cars. She cleared out a guy playing guitar on the curb, then took the sprayer and drenched a guy breakdancing on the hood of a Camaro.

A kid with *Mad Max* scrawled on his headband slapped my back. "Yo, Max, you actually work here?"

"He doesn't do much working," Carol deadpanned.

Everyone laughed but her.

"Yeah, you know, back to the grind," I said, wondering if this was how it was going to be now, people showing up to watch me vacuum up their loose change and french fries?

The kid followed me to a car, talking over my shoulder as I

vacuumed. "That's messed up how Julie won. You shouldn't have been kicked out for that bike stunt."

I stopped vacuuming. Carol glared at me from the booth, and I realized I kind of missed playing the role, being Mad Max. I laughed, set the vacuum to my palm. *Thunk.* "Na, I'm good. She earned it."

"Where'd you go?" a kid with two plugs in his ears asked. "Heard you led the cops on a chase. My dad said you could sue the mall for how that security guard slammed you down like that."

I laughed. "What? No, I mean—"

"Max! Get to work."

"Yo, she's tripping, huh?"

I laughed. "Yes, she's very much tripping." I set my hat backward. "Now, if you don't mind, Mad Max got bills to pay."

I spent the next hour chatting up fans while cleaning their parents' cars. Dre showed up around 9:15 and Carol didn't say a word about him being late. He took his little salesman clipboard and went to work the line. I may have been the main attraction, but he was still the pretty one.

No time for lunch, as things were still humming along. I was vacuuming out what amounted to a bale of straw from the trunk of a Mazda when Carol tapped me on the shoulder. "Max."

I looked up, the vacuum still whooshing in my hand. To my surprise, Carol didn't seem angry or annoyed or even a little put off. She almost looked shy. "There's some guys here to see you."

"Ha," I said. "Tell 'em to get in line." I stuck the vacuum to my other palm, making a *whoosh, thunk, whooooosh thunk,* sound.

She shook her head, then glanced over her shoulder to the entrance. Her voice was calm and steady. "I'm serious. Suits and shit."

I studied her face. While Carol and I weren't on great terms, usually had it out for each other, something in her eyes told me this was for real. "No, not cops," she said reading my mind. "They're in the lobby. I cleared everyone out."

"You did?"

"Yeah, bunch of these hoodlum kids, probably trying to vandalize the vending machines. Now go. You got ten minutes. Eight now. And clock out first."

That was more like the Carol I knew. Still, my heart hammered in my chest. I was too thrown off by her tone to mess with her. And suits? I hoped they weren't lawyers wanting to talk about suing anyone.

I clocked out and made my way to the lobby where the only sound was the tapping of expensive shoes on the tile floor. I was surprised to find Marissa with two guys I recognized from the start of the contest.

"Mad Max." The shorter one rose from the couch and buttoned his fancy blazer. He said my name like we were old friends.

I sucked in a breath at the sight of the couch cushion, working hard not to think about Carol and her after-hours romp. "Uhh, hey, guys," I managed, still sweating from all the work outside.

The taller stood as well. He came at me like a gale force wind, snatching up my hand. Only then did it dawn on me that these guys were the Pepsi suits. The big wigs. Wow. What were they doing in our shabby lobby? What were they even doing in Linwood?

I shot a quick glance at the Coke machine behind their backs. These guys, beaming at me, wore watches that easily cost more than I made in a year or three. What did they want with Clean Car, looking at me like I was some kind of prize?

Marissa was hardly recognizable, her hair pulled back as she was all put together and organized. She looked like she'd caught up on her sleep. I managed to catch her eyes, and I pleaded for direction, but she only smiled.

"So, have a seat." The shorter suit gestured to the worn couch that sat beneath the window to the tunnel.

The couch. Nope. No way. Not even for them.

"Oh, I'm, uhh," I looked to the chair. "If you don't mind, I'll just..."

"Oh, sure." The shorter suit smiled. "That's fine too. It's your house, I guess."

"Clean Car," the taller one plugged, looking around. "I love it. You have to get me a hat."

Again, I shot Marissa a *What in the world?* look. She stepped forward. "Hi, Max. We missed you the other day."

"Oh, I was...here."

The suits ate it up, guffawing the way only rich dudes who don't have to answer to anyone can. The short guy mentioned he wanted a hat as well before they broke into a conversation about cars and wax jobs like I wasn't in the room. Tall Suit nodded to a rippled Lamborghini poster and said he almost took the plunge a few years back.

I glanced from one to the other, thoroughly confused. Maybe they were in town for yesterday's ceremony and figured they'd stop in to offer me a consolation prize. I could use a few hundred bucks for coming in second place. I could use it lots, actually, put it toward an apartment. Then, with Carol's promotion, or raise—if she wasn't playing me—I could make this happen.

I was trying to do the math on a security deposit and first month's rent when I realized they had turned to me with big, bold smiles. Tall Suit was talking, "...and that brings us to you, Max."

Outside, Carol berated a group of kids for playing hacky sack on the lot.

Tall Suit had the floor now. "This campaign was a far bigger success than we anticipated. In fact, we've been flooded with calls. And the preliminary numbers are staggering." He motioned to the parking lot with obvious delight, as the kid with the headband had gotten a hold of the hose and was spraying his friends. Some water hit the window and the suits jumped, then laughed. "As you can see, it has its own energy, this Mad Max thing."

They smiled at Marissa, and she smiled back. Again, I noticed how much younger she looked outside the mall, or maybe it was simply that she wasn't scolding three contestants in a cinderblock auxiliary room. Still, all this smiling had me completely lost. I rubbed my sweaty palms on my pants. "Well, it was fun."

"Fun." They turned to each other. Tall Suit gestured to me. "You hear this? Fun."

Short Suit sprang into action. "Oh, Max. We think the fun has only begun."

He circled the room, eyed the year-old magazines as Tall Guy took a deep breath and things took a more serious turn. "Max. These commercials. *Your* commercials, have been more successful than many of our recent advertisements. I'm talking multimillion dollar ads. The data is coming in. Early studies show this Mad Max thing is grass roots, it's real. And the kids can feel that. And well, that minibike stunt was gold."

I picked at a loose thread on the chair and allowed myself to smile. "That *was* pretty good."

"Better than good. And not only here, Max. Not just this region, or even the state. We think this could be national. Hell, global."

My throat stuck. I tried to follow what they were saying. "Global, like, commercials?"

Two nods. "Max. Have you thought about hiring an agent? Marissa has some information on that, along with legal forms to look over, but... Max, are you okay?"

I wasn't okay. And this wasn't real. It was an elaborate prank by the station. I could see Scottie Snyder playing a part in this. But what about Marissa sitting there with a smile, her notebook on her lap? She didn't strike me as the prankster type.

I started to get up, but my mind was spinning. I fell back into the worn chair as Short Suit came over to further explain. "Okay, we're throwing too much at you. We'll have time to walk you through that. What you need to know is that we're making you an offer. An offer of a lifetime."

I was trying to absorb what this meant when the door swung open and four sopping wet kids came in. "Yo, Mad Max, we need a picture. Is it cool?"

I turned to the suits for permission, who eagerly gestured for me to go right ahead. The long-haired kid handed a camera to Short Suit, "You mind, dude?"

Short Suit took the camera. "Not at all there, *dude.*"

Four kids crowded around me, damp arms on my shoulders, all posing and beaming. Short Suit held the camera up, then lowered it. He grimaced. "Uhh, could you maybe slide to the left?" He motioned for us to move, so the Coke machine wouldn't be in the background.

The long-haired kid laughed. "Oh, right on."

A few high fives and they were off, back outside, snatching up towels and whipping each other. Carol was going to have a coronary. Tall and Short Suit laughed about being young. I tried to make it make sense. The stale chips in the vending machine. A scatter of crumbs beneath the fake fern in the corner. The ancient

ProWax poster that had been there since this place was built in the eighties. All of it swam past me in the room, circling me. It was all I'd known. Sweep floor, mop floor. Pick up the trash. Close down the shop. Go home. Fight with Mom. Hope to see Tara.

And more recently, sleeping in a mall, then the bathroom, then in my car. I'd known it couldn't last, but none of it was as scary as what was happening now.

These guys and their analytics, studies. Their corporate jargon. "Max, do you understand what we're proposing?" Taller Suit lowered his head to get my attention, as I was still staring at the walls.

"No, not really." I laughed.

They sat and crossed their legs. The mood changed. Outside, Dre strode out to the street, selling washes. Tall Suit clasped his hands, exchanged a glance with Marissa, then got down to business. "Max. We have some products that could use a boost. In the big city markets, but the rural markets as well."

Tall Suit snapped his fingers. He frowned and glanced at Short Suit. "I'll be honest with you. Some of these products aren't doing the numbers we were expecting. At least domestically. Probably why they weren't included in the mall contest."

I did my best to follow, or at least pretend it wasn't weird they'd come to the car wash to discuss failed business ventures.

Like a tag team, one stopped talking and the other took over. "But our research team thinks that, well, that *Mad Max* is exactly the boost the brand needs. In fact, they're ready to pay big for this boost. Give the market a campaign it deserves."

I looked to Marissa, whose eyes shined like a proud mother as the shorter one with his goatee went back and forth with the taller guy with the big ears. Maybe they wanted to put Pepsi machines in the lobby or do another promotion. Whatever was going on, I heard them, but I couldn't grasp it. Not after everything. And I was tired of pretending I did. "What...what's happening?"

"Max. You. *You're* happening. We need you for this campaign, to travel, make appearances. To show up and promote other King of the Mall contests nationwide, maybe internationally. Who knows? But most of all, we'd like you to do our commercials. Real commercials."

"But with the same feel as the old ones," Short Suit added.

I shook my head. "I'm not an actor."

"Exactly," Tall Suit said with a snap and a smile.

"Right. Exactly. Max, we're here to offer you a contract with Pepsi Cola." Short Suit looked around the room, slapped his knee. "A lifesaver of a contract."

"Wait, so..." Again, I looked around, for a camera, hidden mikes, Scottie Snyder. The two guys laughed as I checked under the couch. "It's a prank, right? This is a prank."

They chuckled. Again, I thought about Carol, back there, clutching her cigarette pack, yelling at the crowd.

The shorter one leaned forward, his loafers shining on the dull floor. "Not at all, Max. You've done well for yourself. You've earned this."

Everything was upside-down. My mom always liked to say if it sounded too good to be true, it usually was. This sounded like a dream. Maybe I was still in my castle dreaming this up.

I was still waiting to wake up in a stall or car or lobby when I took a breath, fiddled with the frayed ends of my belt. "I'm just...confused, I guess. I lost the contest."

They waved it off. Short Suit took the lead. "The contest was nothing. I mean, it was great, but that was small potatoes. To be completely honest, King of the Mall never would have happened again. But the sample size is there, the way those promos took off, the scale at which it grew so quickly. Max, we're ready to move ahead with this. We've already partnered up with Radio Shack. I'm talking a major marketing campaign, with you as the focus. Or, Mad Max, I should say."

They leaned back. Tall Suit checked his pager, then slid it back to his belt. "Max, I don't want to tell you what to do, but this is one heck of an opportunity. We can fly you out to L.A. in the morning."

"What, like tomorrow?" I lowered my head, took off my hat. The suits watched on with matching grins. Finally, I looked up to Marissa. "This is nuts."

Short Suit chuckled. "Yes. But it's real. Real as it gets."

Another deep breath, and I got to my feet. "Well, it's good timing, I'll say that. My mom kicked me out of the house." I pointed to the restroom. "I slept here in the lobby the other night."

They set their chins back and laughed like it was the funniest thing they'd ever heard. I realized they thought it was part of the act so I rolled with it. And maybe it was the adrenaline, the disbelief that this could happen and what they were proposing, but I took a step toward them and it felt like I was floating away. I joined in the laughter, and they smacked my back, and we were still going on about it when Carol marched into the room.

"Oh good. I'm glad you're having a good time in here, Max, but we got cars out here." She wiped her stringy hair from her eyes. She had two new stains on her white manager shirt, and whatever moment we'd shared out in the lot had left town as she turned to the suits. "And you two, are you buying a wax or soliciting?"

The guys laughed again. Marissa stepped forward and told Carol exactly who they were and what it meant for me, what it could mean for the wash. Carol asked if Marissa actually thought she gave a damn right then.

I set my hat back on my head. "Carol, I kind of need to talk to you, in the office."

She threw her hands up. "Yeah, I'll go tell the customers to go away. Max needs to talk."

I asked the suits and Marissa if they would excuse me for a minute. They obliged, and I followed Carol back to her office where she shut the door and stood heaving before me.

35

"Commercials?" she asked impatiently. "You mean those little promos you did?"

"Yeah, they liked them. A lot."

Carol wasn't getting it. And I wasn't explaining it too well. My hands shook and my voice trembled. But it was now, in her office, as I picked at the peeling laminate on her desk, that I realized how real this was.

"The Pepsi guys, they want to fly me out tomorrow."

There was sheer mayhem out in the lot. I didn't have much time, but I also wanted to choose my words carefully. Which was weird, because I'd dreamed about quitting on Carol at least three times a day for the past year.

"What is it, Max, the raise? I'll bump you up to thirty-five cents more an hour but that's the best I can do."

I nodded.

She shook a smoke from her pack of Winston's and glanced out at the lot, frowning. "You could've mentioned the wash."

"Carol," I laughed, because we were slammed. Beyond slammed. "I think we're doing okay. But, I..." A quick glance to the door. "I'm serious, they want to fly me out tomorrow."

L.A. I couldn't even say it. Even still, half-perched on the edge of her desk, Carol lit the smoke and shook her head. "Like hell. You can't take any more time off," she exhaled. "Not when it's like this."

"No, I mean..." I removed my hat and stifled a cough. She wasn't exactly allowed to smoke in the store, but she occasionally did it anyway after hours. I tried to make things clearer. "I have to leave, Carol. They want to offer me a contract, like, this is kind of big."

She came off the desk and stood in front of me, blocking my escape. "Leave?"

"Well, yeah. They want me to do Pepsi commercials. Real commercials, to promote this King of the Mall thing."

A sponge hit the window with a splat. Carol's eyes never left me. "But you lost, Max. And I need you to stay here." Her voice broke some, wrinkles straining around her eyes. "I don't have enough people on the schedule. Tell you what, no pit duty. And the raise, we'll do fifty cents an hour." She lowered her head with her voice. "Just don't say nothing to Daryl, he'll have a conniption."

I glanced down to my worn and wet Reeboks. The desperation in Carol's voice made me squirm. It was easier when she was yelling at me. I laughed it off. "Carol, you can get anyone off the street to come in here and vacuum cars. You don't need me—"

She spun on her heels for the door, her voice back to normal. "I got too many cars in here to do this with you right now. You wanna go, go. Go clock out and have a nice life."

I got to my feet. "Carol, come on."

She nearly tore the door off the hinges as she stormed out in a huff, screaming at someone as soon as she got outside. With a breath, I exited the office and walked down to the closet where I found my timecard and clocked out for the last time.

. . .

I CAUGHT up with Marissa out front just as Tall Suit and Short Suit were driving off in a Lexus. Marissa saw me coming, and her smile fell. "You okay there, Max?"

I caught my breath and nodded. "Yeah, I, um, that was weird. Actually, I don't know."

Marissa laughed. "You don't look like a guy who just won the lottery."

One last glance back to the store. "No, I guess I'm in shock."

She laughed. "Well, get yourself together. We have work to do."

She had some papers for me to sign and asked what I needed to pack. I didn't exactly feel like the face of some new marketing campaign as I had mostly everything I owned in my backpack and explained my car situation. Oh, and I needed to let my mom know. Marissa motioned to a newer Acura that could use a wax job. I started for the passenger seat when Dre came running over to us, his sales clipboard in hand.

He removed his hat and wiped his brow. "Hey, man. Carol said you quit. Like for real?"

I realized this was it. I was really leaving the wash. Linwood. Virginia. But I hadn't thought about leaving Dre. "I think so. Crazy, right?"

"She's really going postal," Dre said with a laugh.

"She was already there."

Dre nodded. "Proud of you, man." He gave me a playful shove. "Don't forget us little people when you get all big time, okay?"

"Of course not." I took a breath. I wasn't sure how to say goodbye. I'd never left before. Then an idea hit. I glanced at Marissa. "Hey, they said something about needing an agent, right?"

Marissa nodded. "Yes. Definitely."

I looked at Dre. "Hear that? An agent. So get your portfolio together and I'll pass it along. Get you out there with me."

Across the lot, Carol cupped her hands to her mouth, barking for Dre to get back to work. He shook his head. "That sounds like a plan. All right, man, I gotta get back."

"Tell Kendra I said hey."

"I'll do that," he said with a laugh. We slapped hands.

"Thanks, Dre."

"Happy for you, man." Dre started walking off then stopped, looked back at me and smiled. "I'm for real. I'll get some shots ready."

"Do it. I'll page you."

He nodded, started back to the vacuums.

Marissa looked at me. "He's a model?"

I smiled. "He's going to be."

Marissa nodded. "I can see it. He's very handsome. Kind of looks like that Polo guy."

"Right?"

In the car, Marissa moved some scattered papers from the passenger seat into the baby seat in the back. I got the idea her life was always one of rushing all over the place, putting out fires.

I sat and rubbed my hands on my lap. "Well, this is crazy."

She turned the key, set the car in reverse, then stopped. "I'm happy for you, Max. Even if you cheated."

I stopped cold. "Cheated?"

Marissa shot me a look. The look she'd given me so many times at the contest. The one that said, 'don't try to play me.'

"Oh, you mean the selection thing?"

"Yes, the selection thing. With Creepy Scott."

"You knew about that? Why didn't you bust me?"

"Well, a few reasons." She checked the rearview and we got turned around.

I stole one last look at the wash, where Carol was untangling a vacuum hose, still having a meltdown.

Marissa pulled out and we waited at the light, in the midst of the Mad Max mayhem. "You were right for the contest. Obviously. A perfect fit."

I cocked my head. I guess it wouldn't hurt anything now to talk about it, considering I was flying to Los Angeles tomorrow. "What do you mean? *Right for the contest.*"

She shrugged. "Young, wide-eyed. Cute. Exactly what the sponsors were looking for."

Like the handsome thing with Dre, Marissa had a way of saying these things without it being weird. She considered everything from a marketing standpoint, not a personal one. She shot me a sideways look. "I mean, not much we could do with Mark Faartz. Although it would've been nice to bust Scottie's chops. The slimeball. How do you know that jerk, anyway?"

"He's my friend's dad." I almost said I'd known him most of my life, but she'd just called him a slimeball.

"Ah, that explains why he boosted you. Well, no offense, but he's a real asshole. Like, top notch. He asked me out for drinks that day, at the drawing."

"Seriously?" I knew he flirted, but the guy had been married forever. And wasn't Marissa? I didn't see a ring, but I knew she had at least one little kid.

"Yeah, he suggested the drink, then told me we could try out the castles before the contest. Gag."

"Wow."

"Yeah, wow. And gross too. I mean, as a woman in this profession, I'm used to sleaze, but he took it to a new level. And now I have to work with him at the station every day."

I told her where to turn to Mom's place.

"Anyway, enough about him. I'm happy for you, Max. Even if you were a headache. This is big, really, really big for you. You understand that, right?"

"Do I need a lawyer, for the contract?"

"Yes, we'll definitely get on that." She patted a notebook on the console. "I have a guy I trust out there. He's got some contacts as well, agent wise." She cut her eyes to me. "Was that for real or just part of the Mad Max thing, what you said about sleeping in the bathroom? You had them eating out of your hand back there."

"Oh, that. Yeah umm..."

I grabbed the handle above the window as she nearly veered off the road. "You slept there? In the lobby?"

I shrugged. "It was only for one night." No way I was telling her what happened in the lobby that one night.

She shook her head in disbelief, a laugh falling from her lips. "Wow. So you slept in a public bathroom on the night of the ceremony. Right before you become the face of a major Pepsi ad campaign." She blew a strand of hair from her face. "That's... wow. And here I thought my life was crazy."

WE PARKED and Marissa followed me toward the row of townhouses. Mrs. Clayton's yappy dog started barking and doing circles from behind the glass door, like he always did, but I hardly heard a thing. I was lost on a tightrope between reality and fantasy as we took the steps to Mom's townhouse, which I almost missed because someone had straightened the shutters and slapped on a fresh coat of yellow paint.

Then I remembered about Rob moving in. Of course.

It was strange, knocking on the door. I smiled nervously at Marissa as we stood on the porch. Inside, a spoon clanked against a pan. A few seconds later the door swung open, and Mom took one look at Marissa beside me and straightened. "Max, oh. What's going on?"

"Mom, I'm not in trouble." I laughed. "This is Marissa, with the radio station."

"Hi." Marissa said in a professional tone. "It's a pleasure."

With a strained smile, Mom did her best to be polite, but her eyes got back to me in a hurry. Clearly, she was expecting the worst. When it came to me, Mom wore suspicion like mascara.

Marissa smiled, nudging me along. I tried to think of the best way to begin. "So...I sort of have big news."

"Does it have anything to do with the contest at the mall?" Mom asked, like I'd been entering multiple contest and sweepstake giveaways lately. "I still can't believe what you did, Max."

Seemed not much had changed around here. Mom was still upset with me. I turned to Marissa for help, and she did her best with the particulars about Tall Suit and Short Suit—Frank and Kenneth, as she called them, senior this or that, analytic Big Wig or whatever they were. The whole time, Mom shook her head, occasionally glancing at me.

"But he lost the contest, right?" she asked, struggling mightily to see me as anything other than a loser.

"Yes, Mom. I lost the contest," I blurted out. "I'm only here to get some clothes. I'm flying out to L.A. in the morning."

She laughed in my face. A full on, hand to the chest snort. And this time it was her turn to look for the prank cameras. From somewhere in the townhouse, Rob asked if she wanted the peppers diced or sliced. Good old Rob, always aiming to please.

When she saw we weren't laughing, she recovered with a frown. Confused, she invited us inside, but Marissa begged off as she needed to rescue her kids from their crazy aunt or whatnot. She jotted down a quick schedule and phone numbers and handed it to me with a notebook, and I couldn't help enjoying how impressed Mom looked when Marissa tapped the notebook and reminded me about the lawyer.

Lastly, Marissa informed me that a car would be sent for me tomorrow to take me to the airport. She was all set to leave when Mom, finally sensing this was real, shook her head. "So Max has a job, with Pepsi Cola?"

Marissa smiled broadly as she patted me on the back. "Yes, you could say that. But I think it's a little bigger than a job." She turned to take me in. "You're looking at the face of a brand-new marketing campaign."

My mom blinked a few times, opened and closed her mouth in shock. "I'm sorry, *what?*"

For years I'd dreamed of this shining moment. And now, with sweet redemption staring me in the eyes, I couldn't enjoy it. I was too ashamed to be standing here, bickering with Mom, her post-cruise sunburn flaking and peeling on her nose.

Marissa continued with the praise. "Yes, it's been an overwhelming success, this castle thing. And it's clear people love this Mad Max guy. Can't get enough of him."

"Remember those promos I did?" I mumbled, trying to move things along.

Mom nodded, tilting her head some. Although now she was looking at me in a new way, like she was trying to see what everyone else was seeing but not having much luck with it.

Marissa nodded. "Well, it's been a pleasure, but I must get going. Anyhow, don't forget. Car will be here at nine, sharp. Good luck with everything, Max."

"Yeah, thanks Marissa."

She started off.

"Wait," I said, running to catch up to her, trying to escape the embarrassment of it all.

Mom was still watching as Marissa turned, and suddenly I

wasn't sure what I wanted to say, but it felt incomplete ending like this.

"I umm, I wanted to say thanks for never telling my secret. That I cheated or whatever."

Marissa shot me a smile. "I was never going to."

"Even after we snuck off?"

"Well..."

I laughed. "The movies. Karaoke? You were so upset with us. And that fight thing had you ready to kill us."

"At that point you were basically begging me to kick you off," she said, twirling her keys. She threw her shoulders up and down. "I guess we'll never know."

"Yeah."

She regarded me for a minute, then, as though reading my mind, tilted her head. "Julie gave a nice little acceptance speech. She mentioned you."

My cheeks went warm. I looked off with a smile. "I heard something about that."

"I still think she's too old for you."

"What? No. I didn't mean..."

Mom called out. "Sweetie, are you staying for dinner? Rob is making his special dish."

"Sure, Mom, thanks." I turned back to Marissa with a shrug. "I guess it beats the Clean Car lobby."

Marissa gave me a warm smile. "I'm sure your mom is proud. Give her some time to adjust. And as for Julie, you two were cute together. I'll say that. I think you made the right choice. She can start anew with her little girl now."

I nodded. "Good."

"It is. And hey, I guess it worked out for both of you. Good luck, Max."

"Thanks."

36

Walking into Mom's house should've felt like a victory march. But as I took in the same lumpy sofa, the same fragrant flowery smell, same split apart baskets of curled magazines, I had mixed feelings about all this.

Mom, who'd been shocked into silence, watched me closely, still trying to figure out what the Pepsi guys saw in me.

Rob worked the skillet. Whatever he was doing smelled great, although maybe a little oniony. "Hey there," he said, probably thinking, *didn't we give you the boot?*

Mom plopped down at the dinner table that sat in the living room right outside the tiny kitchen. "So, you're going to California, is that right?"

"Yes, tomorrow."

She raised her eyebrows. "*Tomorrow.* You're leaving for Los Angeles, California, tomorrow?"

I resisted the urge to tell her I was going to Los Angeles, Iowa. "Kind of hard to believe, isn't it?"

Mom's face went tight as Rob walked into the room, wearing an apron, like the dork he was. "You're going where now?"

Mom waved a hand over me. "Max has, well, he's..." She turned to me. "What exactly are you doing?"

Even being told I was the face of Pepsi hadn't won my mother's seal of approval. I repeated what the suits had said. "They want to film a few commercials to kick things off. Then I'll travel, make appearances at the other contests," I said, before my anger won out. "I thought you might be happy for me."

"I am happy, Max, geez. I was only asking."

Rob, deflecting all the tension in the room, nodded with a smile. "Well, that's some big news, guy." Then he frowned. "But I thought you lost the contest? Didn't you leave or quit or something?"

I gazed up at the cracked ceiling, too exhausted to go through the details. Besides, it wouldn't do any good to try to explain why I threw the contest. I needed a few minutes to myself. And my car, with all my stuff. Shoot. My car. I couldn't leave it at the mall parking lot. Who knew how long I'd be gone. Then there was Julie. I kind of wanted to see her before I ditched town.

All this was running through my head as Mom and Rob discussed how strange all this was. She was talking like an old lady again—the way she did when she wasn't happy with me. *This is all quite sudden, you know. No need to jump down my throat.*

Watching Mom, I reminded myself I was leaving in the morning. It might be a while before I saw her again, and I needed things to be right. "Mom, I didn't mean it like that, okay? It is sudden, but so what, right? We should celebrate." Then, because I couldn't help myself, "And hey, you guys wanted me out," I said with a smile. "I'm out, right?"

Mom frowned. "Well, I wanted you to get a good job or go to school. I certainly didn't mean...whatever this is."

Whatever this is. Just, wow. Out of options, I pushed my

chair back, got up, and started for the stairs. But I couldn't make it before I turned around. "This is a pretty good job, you know."

I stomped up the stairs to face the boxes in my room. My bed had been taken down, my mattress up against the wall. A desk had been set up. Okay then. That didn't take long.

Whatever clothes that weren't in my car had been left behind. I found my backups—boxers with holes in them, socks that didn't match. I went looking for my least favorite pair of jeans when I realized they were also in my castle. Wait, there was no castle anymore. Oh well, Marissa had mentioned the suits would probably get me a new wardrobe when I arrived. Still, I was going to show up looking like a guy who'd slept in his car. Whatever. For now, a clean pair of Dickies work pants would have to do.

I stuffed everything in a bookbag, turned, and saw Mom in the doorway.

"Max."

Her voice was strained, eyes watery. But I was still too mad to talk so I turned away from her, started looking through my closet. "Yeah."

She slumped against the doorjamb. "I am excited for you. You know that, right?"

"Oh yeah, Mom. You're thrilled. I can tell." Some of Rob's clothes had made their way into the closet. I shook my head, and Mom sighed, one of those heavy sighs that was so much a part of her breathing.

"I worry, okay? You might not believe it, but I worry about you."

I rolled my hand over the desk. "I see my bed's gone. Did that help with the worrying?"

She closed her eyes before she tried again. "We can lay the mattress down, Max. Would you look at me?"

I dropped the bag and glared at my mom, saw the deep lines

around her eyes, her lips tight and nearly shriveled. She stepped in the room, took me by the shoulders. "I'm proud of you."

She dabbed her eyes. Her chin quivered, and as angry as I was, as badly as I wanted to keep dishing things out at her, blaming her, telling her off, it was no use. I let out a gust of a breath and brought her in for a hug. "Thank you."

Her shoulders shuddered and she started sobbing. Like, a deep, shirt-drenching, hiccupping sob. The kind of crying you didn't want to see from your parents, no matter what age. She mumbled into my chest, about failing me, about life in general, and I stroked her rough, too-many-times dyed, straw-like hair.

"Mom, it's fine. Hey, maybe I can help you now. Pay you some back rent."

She sniffled.

I rubbed her back, shaken from her burst of emotions. I was so used to her agitation, her predictable anger, that I wasn't sure how to react. I set my hands on her shoulders and held her out some. "You and Rob can fly out. You can shop on Rodeo Drive like you've always wanted to do, okay?"

It didn't seem real, these words, these places, talking like this with my mom. Still, she smiled through her tears. Man, she was a complete mess. And sure, she talked like an old lady, but when had she started *looking* so old? Time for some humor. "Mom, come on. You're going to have Rob's apron in a tangle."

With a chuckle, she wiped her face and sniffled. "I'm really happy for you, sweetheart."

I bit my tongue. All this pride and happiness for me. I couldn't help wondering where it had been for the last few years. But this was a time for happy goodbyes, not revenge or spite. Not that it was easy. Not after she'd basically called me a loser for the past four years, to the point I'd started thinking she was right. Nope, I hugged her and told her it was all good. And maybe one day, with some miles and years between us, I'd start to believe it myself.

After dinner, Rob drove me out to the mall to try to get my car home. If I could get it running, I planned to park it in the back lot near the tennis courts and hoped the property manager wouldn't have it towed. I told Rob I might as well sell it, and he launched into one of his motivational speeches about opportunities and various celebrities who'd come from humble beginnings and gone on to do great things. Good old Rob. All I could do was stare out the window and wonder when I'd be back again.

It was cool that he was excited for me, although I could tell he was excited for himself too. This was a win-win in Rob's book. He got Mom all alone and didn't have to boot me out to do it. Looking at it from his perspective, I guess I'd be drumming on the steering wheel too, jabbering about hard work and perseverance. He did everything but tussle my hair. I would've drawn the line there.

We jumpstarted the Volkswagen, and I was good to go. As it idled, my foot occasionally pumping the gas pedal to keep it from dying, Rob was gearing up for a moment. I revved the engine and thanked him. Told him I'd be home later.

"Alrighty then," he said, in his best Ace Ventura voice.

You had to love the guy for trying.

37

After Rob got on his way, I rolled all the windows down to let some air in the car. I was feeling sentimental, hopeful, even a little sad as I gassed the engine and studied the scenery like it was the last time I'd ever see it.

Setting the car in gear, I started down the hill for the light. Across the street, the bay door to the wash was down as Clean Car had done another record-breaking day. I thought about Dre and how we'd left it, hopeful about flying him out to L.A. so he could work his charms on the west coast.

I was in that sort of daze when two honks of a horn broke me from my thoughts. A shiny, black sports car pulled in—a new Ford Probe. It slowed in passing, and Julie leaned her head out and gave me a wave.

Her hair was all over the place, but it was the huge smile on her face that had my attention. My heart clanged in my chest. How? What?

She stopped beside me in the other lane and motioned for me to turn around. I managed to get my head around, but she rolled her eyes and laughed, then stretched her head farther out the window and pointed toward the mall. "Turn the car around, dork."

"Oh, right." I nodded, then did a U-turn at the intersection and putted back up to the mall parking lot.

I pulled up a few spaces from her and climbed out of the car. Julie leaped out and ran over to me like we hadn't seen each other in years, crashing into me with a hug.

She stepped back and threw her arms out. "Whatdya think?"

I didn't know what to think. How was she here? What was she doing?

"The car, Max. Oh, and yeah, Marissa called me a little bit ago and said you'd be around to get your ride, so I've been cruising around, kind of stalking you," she said, nudging me with her shoulder. She smelled like flowers and it made me a little dizzy.

She was talking so fast, I realized I hadn't said a word. "It's nice. I like it. I thought you won a truck?"

"I did, but I managed to talk them into this." She smiled at me for a few seconds, the spray of freckles on her nose seemingly moving with her breaths. Then she nodded. "I thought it would be better for driving Haley around and all."

I was staring at her when she waved a hand at my car, which looked a bit dingy in comparison to her sleek new Probe. "And this is the world-famous Rabbit?" she said with a smile.

We turned to my car. I laughed. "It is. This is my trusty ride." I looked at Julie. It was so weird to see her outside. The contest seemed like years ago. "So, you just…"

"Why did you let me win?"

Her words came out in a gust. I looked away, to the mall, as she'd caught me by surprise. Her new car, her smile, the way she was almost bursting at the seams with happiness. It was obvious why. Not that she wanted to hear that. I smirked. "Who says I did?"

She watched me for a second. A car honked in the distance, and she blinked. "Haley is with my mom. I moved out. I'm officially starting over. Night school and everything."

"Wow. Really? That's...Julie that's awesome."

She nodded. "I'm going to do it, Max. And you helped talk me into it. I'm going to be a teacher." Her eyes flashed, then she looked to her feet. "Which, I mean, isn't as glamorous as moving to L.A., I mean, wow, but you know."

My cheeks went warm. "No, it is. It totally is. So you heard about that?"

Her smile doubled. "Heck yeah, I heard." She leaned closer. "Max. It's amazing, and well deserved. I can't wait to see your face on a billboard and be like, 'I know him!'"

"Billboard?"

She took my chin in her hand. "Oh yes, this mug needs to be *Maximized*." She cocked her head. "See what I did there?"

Her hand was still on my face. And maybe it was because I was leaving, or how I couldn't believe she'd come to see me, but standing in front of me was the most beautiful girl I'd ever seen, inside and out. And so I stepped in, closed the distance, and went for it.

She kissed me back, perfectly, and soon my hands were around her waist. She pressed against me as her tongue touched mine, and we sort of got into it for a minute, to the point I thought maybe going out to L.A. was not the best idea.

And then she pulled away.

"Okay," she said, a little out of breath. "I guess that happened."

"Yeah," I said, dazed. I still had a hand on her hip. She leaned away, and I took my hand back.

Julie looked off, a slight smile on her lips. She set the back of her hand on her forehead and took another step back. "Well, I just... I was only coming to see you off. I guess I did."

"Yeah. Hey, maybe we could talk, I mean, when I get back?"

She closed her eyes. "Max."

I came forward. "You could come visit me. I mean, I'm sure we could..."

"Max. No. Look. This isn't..." She turned away and shook her head furiously, like she was trying to outrun a bad idea. "I didn't come here to kiss you. Although it was a nice kiss. I wanted to say thanks, and goodbye, and...well, I don't know what else but that was just extra."

"Extra." I repeated with a smile. We stood in the vast, empty parking lot, the sky brimming behind us.

Her smile fell and she looked me in the eyes. "I have Haley, and that's enough for me. But I fully expect you to do big, big things, okay?"

I followed her gaze to the sunset. Big things. Tomorrow. The salty taste of her lips still lingered on mine. Thinking about all those dreams she had, I hoped she planned on chasing them. Kindergarten would never be the same.

She took me in and hugged me, tight and quick, before she pulled away and started walking backward, to her car. "Now go," she said. "Go wow them, Mad Max."

I smiled, half heartbroken and half floating. Julie nodded, climbed into the Probe, wiped her eyes, and pulled off. I watched the car drive away, and with one last wave she was gone, down the hill and out of sight. I looked out to the horizon, thinking what could have been and what would be.

Then I got in the Rabbit and turned the key. Nothing.

The battery was dead.

ACKNOWLEDGMENTS

Okay, I've done it. I think I've written my favorite book yet. At times, while working on this, I almost felt like I'd found a time machine back to the mid-nineties, when I was no longer a kid but hardly an adult. I remember feeling as though I'd been lied to, like there was some big secret no one had bothered to share with me. I was overwhelmed by all the adulthood out in front of me, struggling to find my place. Luckily, I made my way through, and I have so many people in my life to thank for it, but for now let's stick to the book!

Thanks to Katherine Kenzora, host of *The History of the Nineties* podcast. What a great way to procrastinate, I mean, uh, research. To Staci Olsen, Holli Anderson, Jason King, and the rest of the staff over at Immortal Works. You guys have made this dream possible.

Thanks to Diane Fanning for being my mentor. To Wayne Fanning (who actually *did* live in a mall for a week). To Sue Fanning, for putting up with me during all that struggling. To Dean Wilson for the early reads and encouragement. To Anne Fanning, who faithfully listens to whatever mess I've created long before it ever sees a word document. To countless others, whose kind words and encouragement keep me going. Thanks!

Pete Fanning is the author of *Justice in a Bottle* and *Runaway Blues*. He lives in Virginia with his wife, son, baby girl, and two very spoiled dogs. He can be found at www.petefanning.com, where he's posted over 200 flash fiction stories.

This has been an
Immortal Production

www.ingramcontent.com/pod-product-compliance
Lightning Source LLC
Chambersburg PA
CBHW061650190726
48289CB00006B/1816